CN00865198

1 MONTH OF
FREE
READING

at

www.ForgottenBooks.com

By purchasing this book you are eligible for one month membership to ForgottenBooks.com, giving you unlimited access to our entire collection of over 1,000,000 titles via our web site and mobile apps.

To claim your free month visit:
www.forgottenbooks.com/free792959

ISBN 978-0-483-63002-4
PIBN 10792959

Microreproductions / Institut canadien de microreproductions historique

199

tes / Notes techniques et bibliographiques

L'Institut a microfilmé le meilleur exemplaire qu'il lui a été possible de se procurer. Les détails de cet exemplaire qui sont peut-être uniques du point de vue bibliographique, qui peuvent modifier une image reproduite, ou qui peuvent exiger une modification dans la méthode normale de filmage sont indiqués ci-dessous.

☐ Coloured pages / Pages de couleur

☐ Pages damaged / Pages endommagées

☐ Pages restored and/or laminated /
Pages restaurées et/ou pelliculées

☑ Pages discoloured, stained or foxed /
Pages décolorées, tachetées ou piquées

☐ Pages detached / Pages détachées

☑ Showthrough / Transparence

☐ Quality of print varies /
Qualité inégale de l'impression

☐ Includes supplementary material /
Comprend du matériel supplémentaire

☐ Pages wholly or partially obscured by errata slips,
tissues, etc., have been refilmed to ensure the best
possible image / Les pages totalement ou
partiellement obscurcies par un feuillet d'errata, une
pelure, etc., ont été filmées à nouveau de façon à
obtenir la meilleure image possible.

☐ Opposing pages with varying colouration or
discolourations are filmed twice to ensure the best
possible image / Les pages s'opposant ayant des
colorations variables ou des décolorations sont
filmées deux fois afin d'obtenir la meilleure image
possible.

3

1

2

MICROCOPY RESOLUTION TEST CHART

(ANSI and ISO TEST CHART No. 2)

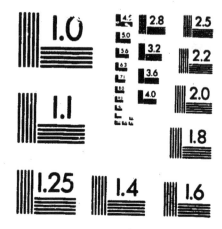

APPLIED IMAGE Inc

1653 East Main Street
Rochester, New York   14609   USA
(716) 482 - 0300 - Phone
(716) 288 - 5989 - Fax

Aunt Libbie
Sept. 13
Marion

UNCONVENTIONAL MOLLY

UNCONVENTIONAL MOLLY

BY

JOSEPH ADAMS

AUTHOR OF "TEN THOUSAND MILES THROUGH CANADA"

TORONTO
BELL & COCKBURN

PR6001
D28
U63
1900z
c.2

TO

THE FAIRIES

THE "GOOD PEOPLE," REAL AND IMAGINARY,
WHO WATCH OVER THE DESTINY
OF NATIONS AND INDIVIDUALS

UNCONVENTIONAL MOLLY

CHAPTER I

ON the outskirts of a western Irish town a crowd of peasants was rapidly gathering. The elements of strong emotion showed themselves in tear-stained faces, unrestrained sobs and indiscriminate jostling to reach the door that led to the railway platform. It wanted the best part of an hour before the train would start, but the sense of time was lost in the intensity of excitement. Periodically there was the loud "keen," expressive of a grief too intense to last and often cresting into the froth of a joke, followed by a ripple of laughter.

The station was closed and the clamour for admission showed that feelings found a new outlet in anger and took a harsher key at each repetition of the demand, "Open the door there, will ye? Open the door."

The crowd was the advance guard that accompanied a number of emigrants to the train. The dusty clothes and dishevelled appearance bore witness in many cases to the strain and fatigue of a long journey. The common adversities of the distressful country in which emigration took a foremost place served at least to intensify the spirit of clanship. Each batch of young manhood and womanhood that sailed from the Irish shores was the occasion of the gathering of the clans, and a send-off in an outburst of sympathy in which prayers and curses. laughter and tears jostled each other in inextricable confusion. From early morning they had been massing, some from island homes off the coast, others from outlying districts, villages and hamlets until the number swelled into proportions that thronged the road and formed a long, irregular procession. Those coming from the more distant parts were on horseback, others rode mules or donkeys with suggawns—that is straw saddles—or bare-backed, according to the circumstances of the rider. But the great majority of those who took to the road that morning had no other mode of transit than Shanks's pony, and tramped on foot the many miles that lay between them and the distant town. These comprised the younger generation of the Irish race, the bhoys and colleens in which the warm Celtic blood asserted itself in the easy swing of lithe and erect bodies, the ready flow of wit, the innocent fun and the complaints of Ireland's woes rung out in voices loud enough for the mountains to hear, and in tones sufficiently pathetic for them to weep over.

It was the first contingent outstripping the rest that now reached the railway station and, finding the platform barred against them, gave vent to feelings of indignation in no mean terms. Louder and louder rose the cry, " Open the door! "

A voice from the other side, answering in a tone more in protest than explanation, increased the tumult and fanned the flame of anger. The crowd jeered and thundered in return. At length a big fellow called out for room to get at the offending obstacle and a passage was made. His broad shoulder was placed against the door whilst the others closed up and formed a living battering-ram of regular but increasing pressure. The woodwork, constructed on a scale not intended to bear such a strain, after a groan like a thing in pain, was torn up the centre in a loud rending noise that culminated in something like a pistol-shot. The bolts had given way and the door fell in, carrying the leader of the assault and half a dozen more in a sprawling heap on to the platform, a spectacle which added greatly to the hilarity of the bystanders.

The people poured in through the forced passage like a pent-up flood that had burst its barriers, until every available space was filled. The train standing by the platform consisted of half a dozen carriages, with seats constructed on the knifeboard principle which ran up the middle. Another seat on either side afforded further accommodation for passengers. The woodwork in which the windows were fixed gave hospitality as a lean-to. The windows themselves were made to fully open or shut, any compromise between these two positions being evidently regarded as superfluous. With heavy rain the closely-packed passengers had to choose between drenching and suffocating as cheerfully as circumstances permitted. In the centre of the train there was a single compartment; its comfortably-upholstered interior practically dispensed with the necessity of the large letters on the door which described it as First Class. In front and behind it there were two other compartments of similar design, but less pretentious, of the Second Class order. All the carriages were locked and a guard stood in front of the select compartments. He wore an official cap and coat and a brown and very unofficial pair of trousers. Some of the emigrants singled him out as a consenting party to the conspiracy to exclude them from the platform.

" In throth it's aisy to see he's been a gaoler—look at his cap," one of them observed, elbowing his way towards the guard.   " Sure, that goold band is the kind they all wear at the county gaol.   He's an owld hand at barrin' doors."

" Arrah, ye're mistaken, Micky; it was in we wanted to go an' not out. Them gaolers are free enough at opening doors, sorra a many times ye have to knock to gain admission. It's something else he must be."

" Maybe he's a gombeen man and mistook us for the brokers; there's a yellow meal look about him."

" Arrah, howld yer whisht, he's on the list for promotion; he's only gained his cap and coat—he hasn't earned his breeches yet."

Whilst these bantering amenities proceeded the engine, that had been growing noisier every moment, gave a loud whistle. The throng that had segregated into groups, talking, jesting and crying, coagulated once more into a unity of deep feeling and sentiment. The doors of the carriages were thrown open and the emigrants crowded in. Their departure from the platform was signalized by a weird cry. It began at one end, but was caught up and spread until there was scarcely a voice, young or old, male or female, that did not become contributory. The crowd grouped round the doors and engaged in their farewells to the accompaniment of many touching demonstrations of grief. "Good-bye, Pat " . . . " God be with you, Mary " . . . " Cheer up, Ned avic. It's soon we'll b after ye ourselves, bedad; the green sod won't have many feet to press it presently."

Near one carriage stood an old man with the arm

of a young girl entwined round his neck like a clinging rose to a tottering stake.

" Don't say that, father dear. Please God, I'll come back to you. I'll be able to keep ye from the hunger while I'm out there. There wasn't the work for me; the boys could do it all. . . . There will be one less mouth to feed or it's meself wouldn't be leavin' ye."

" No, alannah, God be good to ye," replied a voice that struggled hard with hopelessness. The face was pinched and drawn with a grief that left it tearless. The look of yearning in it was the only animation that survived.

" Stand back there, stand back," came a shout, followed by a shrill whistle from the engine. But the cry of grief that burst from the bystanders drowned it— a cry that could be heard in the stillness of the evening a mile away. The crowd swerved as the train rumbled out of the station, its carriages in front and rear crammed with struggling, screaming, sobbing humanity. Its middle compartments disclosed a space of cushioned emptiness—true type of the country—its worst spaces congested, its best untenanted.

Again the cry came, but this time from the by-standers, " Stand back . . . air—let him have air ! " . . . Only a poor old man that occasioned it—torn from his daughter's embrace whilst the train was still in motion. He had fainted.

Amongst the crowd stood a young man, simply but tastefully dressed. His bronzed face indexed recent residence in a tropical climate. His languid air and thin cheeks, despite the tan, singled him out as in the convalescent stage of an illness. The bones, wherever prominent, would have been judged by the medical eye as presumptive evidence of a large frame that lacked nothing but flesh upholstering to form a virile type of humanity. A head of copious chestnut hair, a delicately carved nose and mobile mouth indicated that the physique was not deficient in either handsome or kindly qualities, whilst the frank look in a pair of fine brown eyes was expressive of a mind incisive and critical.

He had arrived from London a few days before and was on his way to a distant part of the West, where he had taken a shooting-lodge. He was sauntering aimlessly through the streets of the town, where he awaited a boat to convey him to his destination. It was quite by accident that he had stumbled on the emigrant procession and followed it to the railway station. He was curious to see something of this panacea for the ills of Ireland that he had often heard advocated on platforms and discussed in drawing-rooms and London clubs. It was by this method the congested districts would be relieved of the pressure that checked the life-blood of the people and perpetuated an anæmic race. Thus many hungry mouths would be filled and the troubles of the peasantry cease. How far thi. would prove to be the case he had yet to learn. The scene he had witnessed at least disclosed the nature of the remedy. If it were as efficient as drastic the cure ought to be complete. As he studied the faces of those who filed out of the station and resumed their march homewards, he read hatred there as well as grief—the remedy cut so deep as to leave behind a scar.

Amongst the crowd the stranger noticed a young man who in appearance and demeanour differed from the rest. He was dressed in a tweed suit, superior in cut and material to the rough homespun worn by the humbler classes. Although deeply moved in common with the crowd at the pathetic spectacle, he exercised studied restraint on his emotions and held in check feelings which on the part of his companions were freely expressed. It was not difficult to read in his face a deep sympathy with all that had just taken place.

As the people withdrew from the station the stranger came into contact with him at the tail of the procession. He bade him " good-evening," but received a scant acknowledgment of the salutation. Nothing daunted however, he proceeded to allude to the scene they had both witnessed and asked:

" Were there any of your friends amongst the emigrants? "

" They were all my friends," came the answer in a tone that did not encourage conversation.

The stranger accepted the rebuff so good-humouredly that the Irishman's prejudice was disarmed and his answer amended:

" There were none of my relatives amongst them," he said.

" I am afraid the times make you suspicious," said the visitor, encouraging the friendlier mood. " The fact is I have come on a visit to your country and am waiting for a boat to take me to my destination. I am—"

" Oh, I beg pardon, sir," interrupted the Irishman, his tone and manner transformed in a moment. " I did not know who I was speaking to. You are Mr Warren, and I have brought the boat. She's at the quay, but I did not expect you to-night. I hope you'll excuse me; the tim·   bad and every stranger is a suspect. Faix, I   ou for a detective that was shadowing me," he added with a laugh, breaking into

Irish vernacular, " but it's mighty glad I am to meet you and welcome you to the country."

" Oh, come now, I'm lucky to stumble on you in this way; you are Mr Doonas," said Warren, on his side equally surprised. " Mr Pinkerton, the agent, said you would give me a sail down the bay—let me thank you in advance," extending his hand, which the Irishman grasped cordially.

" When do you purpose to sail? "

" I am ready, at your convenience; the tide will suit any morning."

At that moment a woman approach. ˙ the two men, and touching Doonas on the arm said, " I want to speak to you for a moment, Mr Martin."

He asked to be excused and walked back a few steps.

" Here's a note for you from Dinnis," she said, handing him a scrap of paper.

" I thought so," he said, after reading it. " All right, Mary, I'll attend to it," and hastened forward to join the Englishman.

" I am sorry, sir, that I won't be able to go with you in the morning; my plans are knocked on the head."

" Indeed, if it is inconvenient postpone it for a day or two; I am in no hurry," Warren hastened to suggest.

" I fear that would make it no better; the fact is I believe there is a warrant out for my arrest; the police, I am informed, are watching the yacht."

" A warrant for your arrest? What for, may I ask? "

" A charge of interfering with the process of law at an eviction. It is not uncommon to have to answer such a charge in this country."

The stranger was about to question him further but Doonas excused himself.

" I must get out of the way for to-night, anyhow.
There is the chance that I may give them the slip for
a day or two. In any case I'll let them have a hunt
for me. You are stopping at the hotel; tell the
manager last thing at night that you want to be driven
to the quay at six o'clock in the morning. The yacht,
the *Witch of the Wave*, is at the slip. If I am not there
my men will be and you can trust them to take you
down the bay in safety. It's likely you may pick me up
somewhere off Inishlyre. It's rude I am to leave you
in this way, but you must excuse me."

The next moment Doonas cleared a stone wall on
the roadside and cut across the fields. Warren watched
him until he disappeared in the distance. There was
enough light left to pick out a mill-stream in the meadows
skirting a wood deep in shadov in the direction which
the fugitive took.

CHAPTER II

EARLY next morning Charles Warren became sensible of a loud commotion at his bedroom door. It was the second application of the boots's knuckles on the panels, and the third call of " Get up, sir, if ye plaze." The traveller, who had been in a sound sleep, slowly emerged into wakefulness.

" What is it? " Warren asked sleepily.

" It's mornin', sir, if ye plaze, an' I've brought your water."

" Oh, all right. Come in."

In obedience to this invitation the servant threw open the door and entered, carrying a large can in one hand and two pairs of boots—or, to be quite correct, a pair of boots and a pair of shoes in the other.

" Mornin', sir," from a head emerging from a large green baize apron.

" Good-morning. What kind of a day is it ? "

" Oh, grand, yer honour; a fine mackerel sky, that means more heat very likely. Is it the high lows ye'll wear, sir? " holding up the shoes—" or the others? "

" The boots, I think," Warren answered, doing his best to hide a smile at this novel description of a pair of shoes.

" All right, sir, I'll pack these. Breakfast will be ready immediately."

Warren looked at his watch and dressed hastily. On reaching the breakfast-room he found the same attendant, napkin in hand, waiting at table.

" Mornin', sir," the waiter said as if the new rôle demanded a fresh salutation.

" Still a mackerel sky? " Warren asked as he responded to the greeting.

" It's blue now, sir; changes in this country are rapid."

" So I see," Warren observed, looking meaningly at the black coat of shabby-genteel reputation which had taken the place of the green baize apron.

" Indeed then the same is convanient where a good deal is expected of ye. What would ye like for breakfast, sir? "

" Well, I suppose it's what I can get at this early hour."

" Ham an' eggs? " the waiter asked, as if that were one of a score of rare dishes ready to hand.

" Yes, that will do."

The attendant left the room and returned in a moment with the viands in question.

" Is the car ready? " Warren asked.

" I'll send for the driver, sir; he'll be here immediately."

" Well, there's no time to be lost; I'm a little behind already."

" All right, sir. The car will be at the door when ye've finished yer breakfast."

Warren did not linger long over his meal, and when he had slipped on a light overcoat he found the driver at the door with the whip under his arm, dressed in a close-fitting pilot coat.

Warren looked round the hall for the waiter.

" The things are all in the well, sir." Boots, *alias* waiter, had undergone a further transformation in the person of the driver. Warren laughed outright at the discovery.

"Sure, we have to be masther of all trades here, sir; cook an' bottle-washer used to be enough wanst, now ye need a more liberal education."

"Well, but I want to pay my bill."

"Ah, never mind, sir; when ye come round ag'in will do."

"Oh, but I don't know that I am likely to come round again."

"An' what of that? But sure, if ye like ye can pay me when we get to the quay. I am book-keeper an' clerk as well."

"All right," Warren answered, and mounted the car.

The road to the quay lay through a park with fine stately trees and grass-grown roads, by the side of which a stream coursed. Rabbits scuttled across open spaces, and rooks answered each other in loud caws from the tops of beech and elm.

"There's grand trout in that, sir," said the driver, noticing that Warren looked at the picturesque water with a special interest. "That's where himself lives," pointing to a large house amongst the trees, "when he's at home, an' that's not very often, and the place is gone to rack and ruin."

"Who is he?" Warren asked.

"Oh, the Squire, sir. An' there's a sight of the lake an' a taste of the bay. Isn't the view grand? Go on, out of that"—this to the horse, which was moving very leisurely.

"Yes, it's a fine view, but I wish you would drive a little faster; I shall be behind time. Why is the horse going so slowly?"

"Oh, he always goes slow here; on the old road

now, where there's nothing to see, he gallops like mad; it's holdin' him in I am all the time."

" Well, why does he make an exception of this route? "

" Well, indeed, I don't know, sir, except it may be he likes to give ye time to see the scenery."

The humour of the joke was intensified as Warren looked at the broken-down beast with which it was difficult to reconcile such æsthetic sentiments.

They left the park and drove along a road that approached an almost deserted quay. A row of warehouses, many-storied and commodious, indicated a once-flourishing mercantile industry. Closed windows, from which fragments of wire lattice hung, broken doors of worm-eaten timber and patches of moon daisies growing between the posts, showed that the industry was a thing of the past. Decay rapidly spreading further intimated that the hope of revival of the once-flourishing trade was distantly remote. If further corroboration were needed the quay itself supplied it. The dock, extending a distance of a quarter of a mile, with room for one hundred ships, did not anchor more than half a dozen. A coaling steamer which plied to and from Glasgow, a barque with a load of timber, a schooner laden with Indian corn, a couple of fishing-smacks and the yacht which was to bring the Englishman to his destination, constituted the flotilla of vessels by the quayside.

As the car drove along, the light breeze that swept across the bay charged with ozone struck pleasantly on the senses of the traveller. The full tide which lifted the hulls of the vessels above the level of the road gave a pungency to the atmosphere which acted like an invigorating drug on his system. The tide of health

which for many months had been at a low ebb seemed
to be gathering strength, and stirred within him
rhythmic waves in sympathy with the ocean. His
anxiety for the man who had come to the town on his
behalf for the moment was forgotten. The thought
of the warrant had been troubling him. All the way
from the hotel he had been hoping that the fear of arrest
would prove groundless. The appearance of a couple
of constables stepping from the yacht to the quay
showed that Doonas's suspicions were only too well-
founded. The members of the Royal Irish Constabulary
eyed the stranger as he stepped on board. One of
them whispered to the other, who responded with a
shake of the head. They had searched the boat but
failed to discover their man.

Warren was struck by the sullen faces of the two
boatmen. One was sitting on a coil of rope in the bows
with a small black clay pipe in his mouth; the other
was consuming tobacco by the more direct method of
chewing. A cabin-boy, with surprise depicted on his
face, was passing a straw from one side of his mouth to
the other, the best substitute for a pipe that the restraining presence of his seniors permitted.

None of them spoke or noticed the stranger.

" Has Mr Doònas come? " Warren asked.

A gleam of kindling anger lit up the man's face. It
flashed out in an oath.

" Ye can search the boat and spare me breath.
Ye're as likely to believe me as the other pair. Do ye
think yer plain clothes is going to deceive me? Bedad,
it's good trade for the carmen anyway, eh, Jimmy? "
winking at the driver.

" Faix, early risin' doesn't suit yer eyesight, Dinnis,"
the driver answered. " Ye cannot see the differ between

a detective an' a jintleman goin' down the bay to shoot curlew. Here, put these in the cabin," drawing a gun-case and a bundle of fishing-rods from the well—" an' stop yer blatherin'."

The man, astonished into sudden action, disappeared down the cabin stairs, followed by the traveller.

" I ax yer pardon, sir," he stammered. " Sure, I didn't know who ye were; we were expectin' himself wid ye. We've been annoyed with the police all last night and since daybreak this mornin'. Arrah, what has the master done that they should be doggin' his footsteps. Isn't he comin' at all, at all? "

" No, we must get off as soon as you can and pick him up off Inishlyre."

" Troth thin it's the bad times we're livin' in, when a quiet man like himself is hunted like a hare across the mountains. Arrah, he's one of the greatest pace-makers in Connacht. Bad men will have a hard time of it when good ones are treated that way. But let us be gettin' away in the name of God; the tide is turned and there's a slant of north wind. Get up that main-sheet, Shawn, and e that shore cable, Shamus." And with these and other orders the yacht in a few moments pushed off and moved away with the tide.

The creaking of the pulleys and the clattering of the men on deck attracted the attention of the con-stables, who still waited about the quay. The departure of the boat ended their vigil.

" They are off now, and with nothing for their pains but an appetite for skilly," one of the sailors exclaimed.

" The divil go wid them," said Dennis, " although it would please me better if they stayed where they are; it's no good they're up to, I'm thinkin'."

The yacht quickened her pace and soon cleared the harbour. Wooden posts rose out of the water on both sides of the channel, marking the spots where dangerous rocks lay submerged. The number of these perches, as they were locally called, showed that the danger was an oft-recurrent one. Spring tides allowed sufficient sea-room, but at neap or half ebb only small crafts or rowing boats could face the treacherous passage.

Dennis, who had taken charge of the tiller, looked at the swift-flowing tide and said, " They must start soon if they are to clear the corrigeen. Loose the jib and fores'l," he called aloud to his companions.

The sails shot into the wind, fluttered loosely, then drew taut. The boat leaped forward with new energy, amidst thickening surf at her bows, as she cut deeper into the sea.

" Bejabers, we'll show them a clean pair of heels if they follow us," Dennis observed, putting his head on one side and eyeing his craft with evident satisfaction.

" Follow us—you don't expect that, do you? " Warren asked.

" I don't think they will, sir; it's down to the coastguard station they'll drive, if they have any suspicion of the truth, but it's glad meself will be to sight Inishlyre headland."

" How far is that? "

" Three or four hours' hard sailin' if the wind keeps good. Sit down here, sir, and ye'll be more comfortable," motioning the visitor to his side.

Warren, accepting the seat, was in a position to take more careful note of the boatman who acted as skipper. Dennis Fahy, to give him his full name, presented the appearance of a well-proportioned man of about five-and-thirty, his head small and bullet-shaped, was surmounted by thick hair, the greater part of which was pressed beneath a peak cap well tilted back. The free fringe overflowing his forehead and extending down his neck was jet black with a natural inclination to curl. His face had the particular deep tinge of tan that is the effect of an out-of-door life and constant exposure to sea air. His collarless blue shirt was carelessly unbuttoned and left a slit that opened and closed to the quick movements of the head as it dodged from side to side and dipped underneath the sail in quest of bearings. Dennis's deep-set eyes were as black as his hair, so were the bristles of a moustache and beard a couple of days old. The right hand that grasped the tiller was capable in shape rather than large, and matched his face in colour. In short, such a pronounced appearance did the skipper present that he was generally alluded to by his companions as "Black Dennis," a convenient sobriquet, which distinguished him from the other members of the Fahy family, a very extensive one in that part of Connemara.

As the traveller took in these salient features a freshening of the breeze led to a further discovery. The left arm was suddenly stretched out for the purpose of shortening the mainsail, and instead of a hand the forejoint closed on the rope, and Dennis, ducking his head forward, caught it in a flash of white teeth and drew in the sail by a vigorous tug. A stump covered by a knitted worsted bandage showed the place where the left hand had been severed through a gun accident.

Warren, for a moment shocked at the discovery, turned his face away and directed his attention to the skipper's companion. Shawn, whose surname was O'Grady, was a lank, high cheek-boned fellow, with arms and legs that looked as if they had outgrown his jacket and trousers. The truth was that no one among Shawn's benefactors throughout the country could match him in bone, and being dependent upon their personal supply, clothes generally fell short of benevolence. O'Grady, being in the habit of remedying these sartorial defects by letting down the hems, presented a fringed look about the arms and legs which gained for him the name of " Scalloped Shawn." Whilst he had no fixed calling he possessed many accomplishments, which were pursued on both land and water. He could pole a fishing cot, trim a hooker, cut turf or kill a pig with such efficiency that he was seldom out of employment. He was a specialist in the art of poaching, and as this appealed to his own tastes, more than all the rest of his natural gifts, he frequently played that rôle. Whenever he was missed from the town it was assumed that he was away on the mountain or by the river, and the larders of a good many homes were repleted at a trifling cost as the result of these expeditions.

Shawn played another part held in high esteem in the town and throughout the countryside, and which often atoned for delinquencies in other particulars. He was regarded as an authority on those matters, occult and superstitious, which bulk so largely in the imagination of the Irish peasants. O'Grady was judged to be deeply skilled in fairy lore and so *en rapport* with the ways and doings of the " good people " as to hold the enviable post of high priest of the faculty. Indeed, he was regarded as a dweller in the shadowland betwixt the real and phenomenal, and his sudden disappearance from the haunts of men was commonly regarded as a migration to the fairies, with whom he was held to be a *persona grata.* His talent as a story-teller of their ways and customs supplied a basis for this; Shawn's skill in that respect was exceptional. His own belief in what he described was so real that he rarely failed in convincing others. Possessing a marvellous fluency of speech, with which many Irish peasants are gifted, and a rich vocabulary, the flow of Shawn's oratory became irresistible. Indeed, only to the credulous would he consent to be a reciter. In the presence of unbelief his lips were sealed, and if a sceptic happened to be among the fireside circle O'Grady remained doggedly silent, which is only another way of saying that folk-lore was regarded by him with the reverence due to religion.

Such were the leading characteristics of the two men that were piloting Warren. The yacht held on her way, making rapid pace with the aid of the tide and north wind. The face of the tourist tingled with a sense of kindling interest in the surroundings. As the boat rounded a headland that almost landlocked the bay and opened up a full view of water which rivalled Naples, he exclaimed involuntarily, " By George, how stunning! "

" Ye haven't been in these parts before, sir? " Dennis asked.

" No. What is that mountain? "

" That's Croagh Patrick, where the saint banished all the serpents and snakes. On the side beyant there's a small little lake into which he drove them. Troth, ye'd say it was small to hould them all; that's the story anyhow, but some people think it wants the craner's note."

The words elicited a singular guttural exclamation from Shawn, who was sitting on a coil of rope and had scarcely spoken, except in monosyllabic answers to questions about the sails under his management. The glance of anger he cast at Dennis showed that the skipper's remarks met with his disapproval.

The stranger looked from one to the other for an explanation, whereupon Dennis observed, in an apologetic tone:

" Shawn knows more about these things than I do, sir; he has the knowledge, faix, and can tell ye."

Shawn rose from his seat, and approaching the two sails under his charge unhitched the ropes and threw them indignantly from him. The freed canvas flapped for a moment, swayed idly, and then grew still.

" What are ye doin'? " Dennis cried angrily.

" Doin'? Nothin'. Don't ye see the wind is gone; the divil's cure to ye."

Almost at the same moment the mainsail swung round under a sudden slacking of the breeze.

One of those rapid changes common on the western coast becalmed the yacht. The alternation between storm and calm supervenes unexpectedly and is by no means unattended with danger. A light breeze changes into a calm or a squall in a moment, in the latter case at times tragic in its consequences.

Shawn's action in loosening the ropes seemed to Warren and the skipper somewhat premature, as the boat was still under way, and there was no sign of the calm that suddenly intervened. It is possible that the boatman saw the becalmed sea to which his companion's back was turned and used the knowledge with theatrical effect. It looked as if he had literally shaken the breeze out of the sails.

Be that as it may, the boat lay like a log on the water. The air of " I told you so " on Shawn's face left no doubt in his companion's mind that the result was referable to the scepticism in regard to the miraculous power of St Patrick.

Shawn took off his cap and crossed himself; Dennis discharged the by-product of a plug of tobacco and swore.

The tide was still with them, and by the aid of an oar the boat drifted in mid-channel. The sharp peak of Croagh Patrick, or the Reek as it is called, rose clear above the range of blue mountains, every feature of which showed distinctly in the brilliant light of the morning sun. The backbone of the range formed a sky-line of curves and gaps, rising and falling irregularly. It swept up on one side and described a pyramid. Further west the line ended in an abrupt headland. Below the summit bare rock glistened, more distant parts shaded into blue. The foreground presented a picturesque, mottled effect, owing to the granite boulders sprinkled through the heather. The sea washed the mountain's base and the bay was studded with islands. Like a mirror the water lay, unruffled but for the slight scintillation of the vast ebbing tide, like passing thoughts on a peaceful brow. In its becalmed depth the whole range of granite and heather-clad peaks and islands were reflected in perfect inversion.

Warren, deeply impressed with the beauty of the scene, watched it for some time in silence. It was of little account to him that the boat should be becalmed. He had no rôle on hand for the moment but that of a time-killer, and was ready to prolong the process indefinitely under circumstances of such entrancing interest. At one moment its charm held him captive, at another its mystery overwhelmed him. The scene and the one he had witnessed the day before were flung together in mental antithesis. That emigration procession with its social misery, its unmeasured hate, its passionate emotion and bitter cry against real or imaginary wrongs, and here, the strength, the repose, the great things of Nature silently, exultingly triumphant.

Yet little did he know that this, like the emigrant scene, was only a mood. Not half a dozen days in a year would mountain and bay be set in such tranquillity. The hills were more frequently cloud-swept, and bluff and crag were grudgingly revealed at rare intervals. At times the veil was so thick as to wipe out the entire landscape, and blinding rain churned the blue sea into grey.

Perhaps the day would come when, like Nature, Ireland's storm-swept children would disclose another side, the counterpart of what lay before him.

Whilst Warren was occupied with the beauty of the surroundings a pair of eyes stealthily watched him from behind the idly-flapping mainsail. The Londoner's feelings were reflected in his looks. Admiration shone in his eyes, and his thoughtful moods found quick interpreters in a sensitive face. It was easy to see from Shawn's attitude that he was intent on fathoming the stranger's musings. The fierce look cast on Dennis half an hour before had given place to one of sympathetic interest, and although suspicious of all strangers, Warren's rapt expression was not lost on the inquisitor. On turning round he noticed Shawn's face. The passage-of-arms between the two sailors and Dennis's allusion to the peculiarity of his comrade led the visitor to cultivate his acquaintance.

" This is beautiful," he said, approaching him. " I have travelled a great deal and have not seen its equal. What is the name of that queer-looking island?"

"The Scotchman's Bonnet, sir; there's two of them, the near one for Sunday, the far one for every-day."

"There . material for a great many bonnets, judging from the number of islands I see. Why, there must be a hundred."

"Three hundred and sixty-five in all, sir."

"One for each day in the year," Warren commented.

"That was the contract St Patrick bound the divil to, God betune us and harm, to make one every day for a year."

"And he succeeded?"

"Oh, bedad, he did."

"The devil is a big property-owner in these parts it would seem."

"He is, yer honour, but he's one of the absentee landlords."

Warren's eye twinkled in appreciation of the joke.

The island in question, a couple of roods in extent, stood high above the water, its banks like perpendicular walls. The constant washing of the sea had made inroads all round, and the long, stony beach spreading away showed that at one time the "Bonnet" must have been considerably larger. The surface was covered with short grass of the beautiful green tint so characteristic of the Emerald Isle. In shape it corresponded with its name, its sides rounding off at one end and curving to a point at the other, which established without question its similarity to Donald's headgear.

Looking westward the number of islets that could

be seen justified the estimate of the devil's output of labour. There were hundreds of these green gems lying close to each other.

Shawn, who saw the look of admiration on the stranger's face, came close to his side and whispered, " They dance there in the moonlight."

" Who? " Warren asked, " the islanders? "

" Arrah, no, sir, the good people, the fairies; look how smooth the top of the bonnet is. . I often row out at night to watch them, and it's grand to see their small feet trippin' on the green."

There was something so naïve in the statement, and it was expressed in such evident sincerity, that despite the draft it made on credulity Warren became interested, and Shawn found in him an attentive listener. In the middle of a graphic description of the fairies' doings the narrator suddenly stopped, looked round, and exclaimed in a loud voice, " The wind is comin'."

Dennis, for whose benefit this declaration was intended, was lounging in the stern, smoking his pipe in silent dudgeon at the disappointment of the journey and concerned for his master, who was depending on the boat to outwit his pursuers. The sails were still as empty as a sack and there was no visible sign of any change. Shawn repeated his assurance, " The wind is comin'."

" Keep yer mouth shut or you'll swallow some of it," Dennis replied irritably.

But Shawn took his place in the bows and busied himself with the ropes under his charge. The forecast, strange to say, proved correct, and for the second time that morning Shawn showed himself an unerring prophet. Almost before Dennis could seize the tiller the mainsail shot out, and the boat leant over and made rapid strides to the accompaniment of soft, lapping waves.

" Bejabers, that fellow can see the wind as well as the fairies," Dennis whispered to Warren, who took his place again by his side.

" You look the wrong way, Dinnis, for the wind," Shawn exclaimed in a bantering tone. " When you know the mountains as well as I do you'll turn to the right place for the breeze. It's up there," he said, waving his arm towards the Reek, " that they brew the storm, an' thim's the boys who know how to let it loose when they have a mind. Well done, my hearties," he exclaimed as an extra gust of wind dipped the boat over and strained upon the ropes to a point of groaning tension. " Well done, bedad, there's another hand at the bellus; it's myself knows yer ways, good luck to ye."

The mountains undoubtedly were the explanation of calm sea and sudden wind alike. The breeze was brewed in its heights and swept down unexpectedly with dangerous force, but how Shawn was able to fore- tell its advent with such accuracy was a matter not so easily explained. The aspect of the mountain to ordinary eyes did not differ from what it was when the sea was calm. But Shawn was a child of the wild, and like all persons in close communion with Nature under- stood her ways and wrested from her her secrets.

CHAPTER III

THE breeze held good, and in an hour Inishlyre was sighted. The island, lying westward, derived its name from its harp-like appearance. The coast assumed the shape of the instrument associated with Irish minstrelsy. Like a discarded toy hurled by some petulant giant hand it lay on the surface of the water, the wild waves resounding among the rocks, and the soft notes of the golden plover were the only music heard along its lonely shores.

As the boat drew nearer, the sea became chameleon in refracted tints, emerald in places and clear as a spring well, in others dark and murky. This phenomenon was due to the changing condition of the ocean bed over which the boat was sailing. Stretches of silver sand, long trailing flora and the dark surface of deep-set rocks, each left its own peculiar effect on the surface. As a bed of weeds was crossed Shawn busied himself in catching handfuls and drawing them into the boat and examining each bunch before throwing it back. At length he gave an exclamation of satisfaction, and disentangling a couple of oysters from the weeds presented them to Warren.

" We are crossing an oyster-bed," Dennis said. " If Shawn were seen at that work we'd have two summonses to dodge instead of one."

" It's a private one, I suppose," Warren observed, sniffing the shell-fish and enjoying the sea odour.

" Oh, bedad, it is, and we are not allowed to sneeze

at it. Oysters multiply like the sand, and for that reason, I suppose, are a monopoly. We are allowed to dredge for them in certain places, but the expense is more than the profit. We have to wait on our betters and be content with cockles and winkles. We must hold off here a bit; there's the mainland"—pointing to the north shore—" an' look out for himself; lower the jib there, Shawn, as a signal."

The sail in question was dropped and the boat brought round so that anyone on the lookout might see it more readily. Shawn, who was shading his eyes with one hand and looking towards the low-lying coast, made out the form of a rowing boat. To Warren the object could not be distinguished from one of the many rocks that lay along the shore, half stripped at low water. But the practised eye of the boatman discovered details.

" He's not alone either, someone's rowin' him; 'oth, I believe it's the colleen herself."

' Bedad, it's as likely as any," Dennis said; " she's never far off where there's throuble. Raise the jib again an' let us reach them as soon as we can; it's tired waitin' they are, I'm thinkin'."

The distance between the two boats soon closed in and Warren recognized Doonas. He was sitting in the stern steering; a young girl was bending gracefully in time with the action of a pair of oars.

" Faix, himself must be worn out when he's not rowin'," Dennis commented.

"Arrah, what else could he be? Sure he's been on foot all night an' as tired as a coursed hare," Shawn observed.

When the yacht shook the wind out of her sails and the occupants of the small boat came on board Doonas presented all the appearance of a fugitive. His clothes were dust-stained and his eyes bloodshot and heavy for want of sleep. As he attempted to walk, his trembling legs failed him, and he would have fallen but for the steadying hand of one of the men.

"It's kilt entirely ye are, sir," Dennis exclaimed sympathetically, "and indeed it's glad we are to see ye safe and sound. Sit down there, sir; bad luck to the calm that delayed us so long."

"All right, Dennis. And how are you, sir?" turning to Warren; "but let me introduce Miss Molly MacDaire, the aider and abetter of my crimes."

The girl so introduced stretched out her hand and cordially took Warren's.

"You are welcome to our country," she said in a soft musical voice, "although it's a poor opinion you'll have of it to find yourself so soon amongst the criminal classes."

Warren took in at a glance the striking personality of the girl and replied, with easy gallantry:

"Thank you, but crime clearly doesn't lack elements of interest, since you allow yourself to be included."

"Ah, now indeed, that's the way Martin shows his gratitude. He tries to make out that everyone is as bad as himself."

"Now, Miss Molly, what about the way you tricked Sergeant Nolan this morning? Sure I'd be nabbed if it hadn't been for you."

"Do be quiet, Martin. I didn't protect you for the purpose of incriminating myself. I am told, Mr Warren, that in England the women get the men into trouble; here most of us spend our time in getting them out of it. Bring me a hand-line, Shawn, I see the mackerel breaking the water. Indeed, Martin, if you studied my want as well as my crime you would know that I have tasted nothing since six o'clock this morning. I have an appetite if I haven't a conscience."

Doonas, challenged in this way, hastened to apologize. " A thousand pardons, Miss Molly," his bantering mood at once giving way to solicitude for the girl. " I am a criminal now in earnest to forget about that. What have you got, Dennis? "

" There's some mate, sir, an' it won't take us long to boil some praties."

Shawn meanwhile brought forward a couple of fishing-lines.

" I've no bait, miss.   Mebbe the masther has a new clay."

" Who will sacrifice a clay pipe? " Molly asked, looking round.

" A clay? " Warren repeated.   " I have a briar."

Molly laughed aloud, a hearty ring in a soulful voice, dangerously infectious. " Curious enough," she said, keeping up the joke, " mackerel, like the peasants, smoke nothing but clays."

" Catch," Martin cried, whirling a pipe through the air.

Molly caught it and broke off an inch from the stem and threaded it on a piece of strong gut, with a hook on one end.   With this attached to a weight she seated herself in the stern, and uncoiling the line from its wooden frame commenced fishing.

" This is interesting," Warren remarked with delightful ambiguity.   An impartial judge would have difficulty in deciding whether he meant the fisher or the gentle art.   To him, at least, both presented features of novelty.   Familiar as he was with the devices of the tackle-shop, its phantoms and spinners, a piece of pipe-shank as a bait was new.   But the girl, as she leant over the gunwale in an attitude that showed much grace and charm, presented a still more fascinating study. In age Molly had not long emerged from her teens, carrying with her all the freshness that belongs to that interesting period of girlhood. Physically the lines and spaces suggestive of womanhood had passed from the prophetic to the actual stage, giving complete beauty of form. Her extended arm, as she held the mackerel line, was bare to the dimpled elbow. Her beauty was of the fair type, the eyes blue-grey, the common characteristic of her race, lending themselves to the mirth that twinkled there, and with a depth befitting more thoughtful moods. Her mouth was large and sensitive, every line of which bespoke good-humour. Molly's head was intellectually attractive and firmly poised on a shapely neck. One of her most striking features was a crown of thick hair, which, in the sunlight, sparkled as if it were sprinkled with gold dust.

As Warren took in these details in a rapid rather than intrusive glance Molly began to chat with the easy grace which is the charm of a simple, unspoiled girl. She motioned him to a seat near her, where he might watch the fishing-line, which trailed away at the end of the boat.

" As soon as we catch a fish for bait you can have a line," she said, " but there's too much way on the boat at present. Ah, now, Dennis," she exclaimed, " it's in a great hurry you are. I wish that mood had been on you when we were shivering on the mainland; slow her down a little . . . there's the shoal again right in front of us. Shawn, lower that foresail or we'll be through them before they have time for a snap."

Both men quickly responded to these imperious command · with alacrity, as those who had been accustomed to obey, and the boat assumed an easy gait, more suitable for fishing.

" There now, I knew we'd get one," Molly cried, her arms busily engaged in recovering the line, which was rapidly jerking. In a few moments an electric blue blur appeared in the clear depths, that grew more marked as the captive came nearer.

" What beautiful iridescent hues," Warren said, as the fish was landed on deck.

" Yes, it looks as if it had been drawn through a rainbow. . . . Now, Shawn, cut off a couple of baits. Mackerel," Molly added in explanation, " not only affect the civilized method of clay pipes, but the ancient habits of barbarism; they are cannibals."

With the improved bait the mackere' bit freely, and Warren and his companion soon strew: l the deck with the spoil. Amongst the mottled tints the red of a gurnard strongly contrasted here and there, and even the nondescript colour of a fat coalfish, which had vied with the mackerel in seizing the lure. The simple sport continued at intervals, wherever the boat struck a shoal, and as fast as the line was let out and recovered a mackerel was attached.

Warren saw the economic side and put the question: " Is mackerel-fishing one of the industries here? "

" Only for home consumption. The islanders catch and salt them for winter food," his companion answered.

" They ship them to England surely? "

" No, but to America."

" America? " Warren exclaimed in surprise.

" Yes, it pays them to send them to New York, but

not to Liverpool. Higher up the coast there is a curing station in Blacksod Bay, from which they are shipped in barrels. That is one of the little anomalies of which you are likely to find a good many examples here," Molly added, with a perky toss of her head and a merry twinkle in the blue eyes.

" How comes it that it pays to ship them to America and not to England? "

" Ah, now, you are getting beyond me. Martin can tell you more about that when he's had his sleep. Poor boy, he's worn out. If you ask Dennis there, and he doesn't know, he'll say the Government; that is the one answer to all the unanswerables."

" You don't consider that fair, surely, Miss Mac-Daire? "

" Well, indeed, the Government is like a fishing-rod a gentleman brought here last year; it had a great many different tops but they all fitted the same butt; the Government is the butt for all kinds of grievances. Fair! ah, no, but you see the moral of it. Give a dog a bad name—" and there was another mischievous twinkle.

Warren smiled as he listened. " I have heard that every Irishman is a politician; is it possible that ladies are included? "

" Ah, indeed, they come to me with all their griev-auces and one quickly learns local economics. When I see the mackerel breaking in the bay, and the nets lying idle, I tell them that they are negligent and lazy, and I get nothing for my trouble but a lecture on freightage. It is the cost of that that prevents the harvest of the sea as well as the land from paying. ' Arrah, what's the good of ketchin' mackerel, Miss Molly,' they say, ' when you can't sell them; sure,

Irish hens have stopped layin' since they heard that it's cheaper to send eggs from Denmark to London than from Galway.' "

" Then you can't get them to catch these fish? "

" Oh, I shame them into it, but work under such conditions, they think, demands an apology. ' Ah, now it's yerself, Miss Molly, would like a taste of fresh mackerel; throth, an' it's meself wouldn't be disappointin' ye; run home for the lines, Miles agra, an' we'll ketch a few; they'll make a bit to ate for the childer anyhow.' That's how I'm put off."

" Are they naturally thrifty? "

" Thrift means a balance on the right side; the Irishman's idea of economy is to save a sovereign but drink a shilling."

" Is that an Irish bull? " Warren asked.

" Oh, no, an Irish bull has a dash of philosophy in it; any that lack that you can reject as spurious. Here, Martin, is a ready pupil for you," the girl said as Doonas, refreshed from sleep, came forward. " Mr Warren wants to know something about your revolutionary notions."

" Well, there won't be much left for me to teach after he's passed through your hands, Miss Molly. I warn you, sir, that Miss MacDaire is the high priestess of revolution in Connacht, but I'm afraid I'm too late. I see the look of triumph in her face," scrutinizing the girl good-humouredly; " bedad, she has only to wave her hand and all the West is at her heels."

" Ah, now, Martin, be quiet, I tell you. Your sleep has been too refreshing; fitter for you to keep your wits for navigation. Do you know the time, and how are we to reach home to-night? "

" Bejabers, I forgot that I'd been asleep. We won't make more than Inisheeny at this rate."

" Inisheeny! " cried the girl, " and another night of it."

" Well, it will be bad if it is not a better one for me, sleeping in a damp cave, every bone in my body still aching. But here's Shawn with the mackerel."

A cloth was spread on the deck and they all sat round. Warren, who had little appetite for the food the larder provided, soon began to exclaim in praise of the fish. Making due allowance for the gustatory effects of fine sea air, there is nothing more delicious than broiled mackerel fresh from the ocean.

" How good," said Warren. " I fear, Miss MacDaire, that even improved transit will not preserve this flavour."

" No, indeed, everything seems to lose flavour in crossing the Channel—even the Irish reputation."

" Come now, that's too severe."

" Oh, it's the ice takes away the flavour, and we have scarcely any in these islands nearer than the top of Croagh Patrick, which things are a parable."

The wind had again fallen away as evening advanced and the sails creaked as they lazily swung to and fro.

" Put out the oars, boys," Martin ordered, " the night will be upon us before we reach the island." Soon the regular plash of rowing beat softly on the water, and a silent mood stole over the party. Warren approached the prow of the boat and watched the changing light that played on the sea. The sun was hidden by a bank of clouds low down on the horizon. It streamed its rays through a break in the piled-up mass like a great lantern, picking out the far-off green islets in clear relief and burnishing the rocks on their margins. Subtle pencils of light touched the western sky, sprinkling gold along a sapphire pathway. Croagh Patrick, which flanked the bay on the south, was growing dim in the distance, and a mystic violet tinge haunted its peal·s.

Warren mar:ed all the changes; far off a heron slowly flapped its wings as it drew nearer to the island, where it roosted. Its loud cry could be heard far across the bay. A cormorant on a perch, like a black sentinel, waited until the boat was within a score of yards before it lowered its long neck and threw itself off in flight, to the accompaniment of swift beating pinions. . . . The gold dust faded in the sky . . . the gloaming lingered for a while, then all things grew indistinct.

It was night when the dim coast of Inisheeny Island came in sight, and the boat was rowed round to a rough landing-stage. Shawn jumped on shore and made her fast. The small cabin of the yacht afforded ample accommodation for the men. Doonas and his lady and gentleman friends made their way towards a farmhouse that nestled on the sheltered side of the island.

As the party approached the house there was nothing to indicate that it was inhabited. No light gleamed in its small windows, three of which did duty for an equal number of rooms. The front door in the centre of the building furnished means of access to the principal apartment, and approaching this Doonas knocked vigorously with his knuckles. After a few moments' interval the door was opened by a woman, whose approach was silent, for the simple reason that she was barefooted.

" God save all here," Doonas said in customary greeting.

" God save you kindly, sir," came the friendly response. Then, after a pause, " Arrah, is it yerself that's in it, Mr Martin . . . and Miss Molly? Come in, sir. Come in, miss; it's welcome ye are. Arrah, Tom, get a light there; pull a coal out of the greeshogue."

" Faix, I thought you were all in bed or on the mainland when I saw no light."

" Small blame to ye indeed, Mr Martin; what else could ye think when we'd raked the fire? "

" And it's so early too."

" Indeed you may say that, but bed is the best place in the dark, and bad luck to the pig for aitin' the candles, and the divil a bit fatter he'll be for them, I'm thinkin'."

" Oh, it will make him all the brighter, Mrs Ryan," Molly interposed with a laugh.

" Throth, then, there's no need for that, miss, it's bright enough he was already. He saw the candles in me hand when I came from the fair yesterday, and he never pretended a thing until he got me back turned, the skamer, and grabbed them. Arrah, Tom, be quick now and light a piece of bogdale. It's a fine messenger ye'd make for death; bedad it's yerself would take yer time over it."

Tom, the head of the Ryan house, was meanwhile struggling with a piece of turf in which some sparks of life still lingered. The ember was held in a pair of tongs close to his face, which grew redder as he blew it, to aid the process of ignition At length the bogdeal was lit and became the nucleus of a peat fire that soon beamed so brightly as to bring all the objects in the room into view.

" We're expectin' the boy and girls in every minute,"
Ryan said after the welcome was duly repeated on his
part and with equal heartiness to the visitors. " It's
becalmed the yacht was; ah, well, it will go hard with
us if we can't find a corner for ye all, although it's poor
accommodation we have to offer a gentleman from
London   Mr Martin and Miss Molly are used to our
ways

"   very kind of you to allow us to take you unawares," Warren hastily interposed. " I don't think
London hospitality would stand such a strain as that."

" Ah, now, Tom, you need not be making apologies,"
Molly said. " What you lack in stock you will make up
in welcome. Mr Warren has been in foreign parts
and is now visiting us; it's the country and the people
he wants to see, and you know how to give him an Irish
welcome. But when are the girls coming back? "
she hurried on. " Martin will be wanting to have a
dance with Rose, and who knows but Mr Warren would
like to have a turn too? "

" Arrah, aisy now; maybe the gentleman would like
a turn with Miss Molly herself," slyly interposed the
simple hostess.

Miss MacDaire joined in the laugh at her own expense, and Warren cordially acquiesced.

" Ah, now, Mary, I see you are getting to know the
ways of the Englishman—honey from every flower.
Well, you have a choice rose anyway."

And when the girl came on the scene an hour later
she fully bore out Molly's description. Her coarse
dress draped a figure of strength and charm; a simple
shawl was carelessly thrown across a pair of finely-
moulded shoulders, her complexion was like the tint
of the flower whose name she bore. Rose's eyes

gathered into themselves the blue of the sea that surrounded her island home, so deep and liquid were they.
Later on, when divested of her shawl and led out by
Warren to dance, she presented a striking figure of
native bashfulness. The dance, the simple schottische,
to the accompaniment of a violin cleverly played by
the young brother, revealed phases of movement un-
familiar to the Englishman. To him Rose displayed a
lithesomeness distinctly rare. The girl's feet scarcely
seemed to touch the ground. The secret of her fine
dancing was disclosed when Martin and she took the
floor for a reel, the dance in which Irish peasants are so
proficient. The demi-semiquavers of the music tumbled
over each other in the rapidity of execution, and nimble
feet materialized every note, for that, indeed, is the
true technique of dancing. The mechanical side of the
art passes into poetry where grace of movement supple-
ments it. Without the latter the achievements of
terpsichore could be as well and more correctly per-
formed on the drum. On the other hand, body and
limb movement apart from the mechanical becomes
sensual.

The youth and maiden stood *vis-à-vis*, their feet
speeding like lightning, their bodies answering in bend
and curve. Their whole being quivered with the intensity of emulation. They were not united in partnership as in a waltz, it was art in challenge, vying with
each other; enthusiasm had taken the floor and physical
endurance would determine the issue. Martin shouted
aloud in his zeal, Rose answered back in quickness of
step, that doubled each bar of music; gallantry decided
the reel in the lady's favour, and abruptly stopping,
the youth bowed to his partner, and extending his hand
like a courtier led her to a seat.

The round of applause that greeted the close showed how deeply the spectacle had moved the observers. Warren understood the secret of the island girl's step.

" I am half afraid to ask you to waltz with me," he whispered to Molly, " after that exhibition of native skill.   Dare I? "

" You will have to dare many things in Ireland and take bigger risks than that," Molly answered easily, taking his arm.

In a moment Warren felt the grace of his partner. " Ah," he said, " another graduate in the same school." But he was at home in the waltz, and Molly knew it, and responded in simple abandonment of delight. Round they glided in perfect unity, both accomplished dancers; movement became automatic, leaving room for thoughts and emotions to contribute their pleasant counterpart.   Warren felt the thrill of life all the more keenly after a long sojourn on the borderland where death's shadow had overspread the dial and threatened to wipe out the final figure.   Life had returned with the full sweep of a rising tide, and flowing inland, called into being emotions which had lain listless, like stranded flora beyond high-water mark.   The simple country folk he had met, the delightful restfulness of the mountain-girt bay, and now the grace and charm of a beautiful girl of wit and vivacity—these were rich treasure-trove from life's wreckage, and involuntarily his arm tightened in a firmer grasp, as if to assure himself of the reality of his newly-recovered possessions.

And Molly? The manners of the Englishman deeply impressed the Irish nature.   Aloofness and reserve, the antitheses of the Celtic temperament, fascinates.   They stand out in contrast to the emotionalism of the race and attract, as a counterpart always does.

It is the missing part in oneself that is most coveted. Molly, mixed up in the disputes and quarrels, hatred and jealousies, at times deep to the point of tragedy, and at others trivial and intangible as froth, lived habitually in the region of emotion. The quiet strength of the man by her side made its bid and not in vain. Pleasure is the blend of qualities. Warren found his needs in the girl's emotionalism; Molly's emotionalism found repose in her partner's strength.

Neither of them spoke. Warren caught the golden glint of the beautiful hair against his shoulder; it came and went in the firelight flash in alternate gyrations, momentarily and elusive as a sprite. Now and again a pair of deep blue eyes would speak their rapture.

But the eyes were doomed to make an alarming discovery; the calm, strong face of the Englishman suddenly blanched and a spasm of pain contorted it. Warren stumbled and would have fallen had not Molly steadied him.

" You are ill, Mr Warren," she said. " A chair, Martin, quick. . . ."

" It's all right, Miss MacDaire. . . . . I'm awfully sorry, it's so stupid of me . . . a little water, please."

The door was opened, and in the refreshing air Warren revived, but a sharp pang in his side warned him that a wound ripped by a Boer bullet proved unequal to the dancing exercise. He pressed his hand against the place and struggled for breath.

Quiet consternation pervaded the room, and sympathetic whispers were exchanged by the members of the good-natured household. A muttered curse on the Boer War and this new fruit of its iniquity came from one quarter. The hostess, who had suddenly vanished, returned with a large stone jar in her hand.

" Here's the best cure for faintness in all Ireland,"
she said in triumph, drawing a huge cork with her teeth,
the left hand holding a tumbler.

" What is it, Mary? " Molly asked, looking suspiciously—" poteen? "

" An' what else would it be, an' what could be
better?   Sure, it cured the cow of the colic."

" Ah, no, Mary agra, the gentleman isn't used to it;
the hot room has been too much for him, let him rest
a little."

Warren, catching the look of disappointment on his
hostess's face, said, " Thank you, Mrs Ryan, it's really
nothing.   It would make me ill indeed to spoil the
evening's pleasure.   I want to see you and your husband dance—that will be the best remedy."

" Faix, it's meself would dance all over the island
to cure ye, an it's the brave boy ye are God bless ye,
pretendin' in that way whilst ye're racked with the
pain."

And Tom and Mary, Martin and Rose did take the
floor, " just to plase the gintleman."   And the elder
couple, alert and active, stepped it merrily.   Just as
the dance drew to a close a ripple of laughter came
from Molly. The company looked towards her,
questioningly.

" Mr Warren wants to know what the greeshogue is,
Mary."

They all laughed, and Mary replied, " In throth, thin,
I think he ought to know, for it's himself, poor boy,
that has just passed through the hot ashes, and the
sooner he gets to the blankets the better."

Warren was not sorry to take the hint, and the party
soon afterwards broke up.   He and Martin shared the
best room.

" I am so sorry to have upset things," Warren said when they were alone. " These people are most kind, but are we not putting them to a great deal of inconvenience? "

" Oh, hospitality is a plant that grows freely in Irish soil. The Ryans feel that you are paying them a compliment."

" But where do they all put up? "

" There's another room like this, a loft overhead, and a collagh in the kitchen."

" A what? "

Doonas enjoyed his companion's embarrassment and was glad to notice a smile on his face. " You saw where a dark curtain was hanging against the wall? That space is used for a bed; they call it a collagh."

" My education has been neglected. I shall return to town with an enriched vocabulary. They reach the loft by a ladder, of course. Is it furnished as a room? " Warren asked.

" Oh, dear, no. Young Tom will sleep sound enough on a scraw-buggaun."

Warren put his hand to his side or the effects might have been disastrous.

" O..e wants to be in perfect health to stand this kind of thing."

" Oh, it simply means a shakedown."

" Well, it's awfully kind of these people to put themselves about. I have no claim upon them. If I might hazard a guess, your case is different," and Warren looked meaningly at Doonas, who blushed self-consciously. " I envied you that last dance; she is a beautiful girl, such grace and charm are rare. She would create a sensation in London if she were presented at Court."

" Oh, life is very uneventful in these lonely islands, and the people are only too glad of the opportunity of accommodating us," Doonas answered, evading the delicate point and feeling a wave of pleasure. " An Englishman's visit is a great event."

" Despite the hatred of the Saxon? " Warren queried.

" Ah, that's the system; we know how to distinguish."

" It's a case of hate the sin and love the sinner, eh? "

" There's something in that, but our people are always courteous. But you need rest," he said.

" Oh, a night will set me up. I'll turn in."

CHAPTER IV

THE following day Warren was on his way to the shooting-lodge. A short drive along a main road brought him to a boreen. Tall bracken gave a softening effect to the broken-down stone wall on either side. The grass springing up among the debris indicated that the breaches were not of recent date; and they occurred at such frequent intervals along the narrow lane that it looked as if it were everybody's business to pull down the walls and no one's to rebuild them. A dip on an incline made the car rock from side to side to such a degree that Warren, unaccustomed to the Irish patent, had to grip the back rail to keep his seat. A corresponding uphill climb followed.

At the top a field of gorse disclosed all the wealth of its golden bloom, and the stranger found himself drinking in the delightful perfume. The time was May, when the gorse and plantaginet were in full bloom, and the nesting season made vocal bush and briar with snatches of song. At length the car turned in at a gateway and drove between tall hedges of red flowering fuchsias that led to the lodge.

The door stood open and framed the person of a portly woman. This was to be Warren's housekeeper. Deeply curtsying, and with one hand nervously twisting in her black apron, she approached him.

" It's welcome yer honour is. I hope ye had a pleasant journey."

" Yes, thank you. You're Mrs Maloney," said

Warren, prepossessed by her good-humoured, honest face.

" The very same, yer honour. Mind what yer doing, Pat, with the gintleman's things," addressing the boy, who was pulling a gun-case out of the well. " My name is Bridget, sir, although I am called Biddy for short, and they have lengthened my son's there to Paudeen, although he was christened Pat to make up for it; faix, it's the way round here, what ye lose in one way ye gain in another. I hope he drove ye comfortable, sir? "

" Yes, Pat is a capital driver."

" That's right; but come in, sir, and welcome. I put a bit of fire in the grate, the evenings get cowld, but the dinner will be ready immadiately."

The lodge commanded a view of undulating hills, at the foot of which it stood. They sloped away on the left from the lowland, and grew sparser in vegetation until little but bare rockland caught the eye. On the right similar features presented themselves in the disposition of the landscape, but instead of the bare rock running up to the sky-line, shades of green and brown could be seen like a patchwork quilt, as if it had been the fantastic output of some gigantic loom, in which colour was the object aimed at, regardless of design. Warren's eye wandered down the valley again; a distant ribbon of a river caught it, and the softening effect of woodland on the heather slopes; then a lake flashed into sight, and further on the blue of an inlet of the sea.

Under Biddy's culinary supervision Warren soon began to thrive, but the effects of the dance warned him that he would have to observe the rule of *festina lente*. The mountains daily beckoned him for a climb, but he had to be content with short rambles through the scented heather and by the river-side, rod in hand, to try his luck amongst the salmon and trout.

Mrs Maloney deplored the fact that the chickens would not fatten. " Look at that one now," she said, as she served up dinner. " Sure, it has a breast-bone like a razor "—setting her head on one side and glancing contemptuously at it—" there is not a dinner in a clutch of them, and it's good meal too I fed them on. It's meself has been misfortunate with the whole brood. The scaldcrow stole two, and three of them died of the pip. Mebbe yer honour never heard of that complaint," she observed, catching a puzzled look on her listener's face.

Warren had heard of it, and although it was pretty bad at times he confessed he had not known it to have quite such serious consequences.

" See that now, and they die of it in this country regular. But I'm reckoning on the young ducks to be good later on," Biddy added more cheerfully; " they thrive on anything, even the clauber."

" The clauber—what is that? "

In Biddy's explanation of this form of diet Warren diagnosed a judicious mixture of road mud.

" Oh, it's grand to see them after a shower of rain shovellin' it into their yellow beaks."

But although the chickens were thin and the young ducks not yet in season, a weighing-machine would have given a better account of the visitor. There was an elasticity in his tread, and the blood tingled as he strode across the heather. He was soon able to face the hills, and one day made his way to the patchwork quilt far up the slope. As he came nearer, the fertility of the patch puzzled him. It seemed as if the rock suddenly ended and fertile soil yielded to the industry of farming.

He got near enough to see a crop of oats and a potato plot. A beaten path led up the hillside, and he followed it. A boy in front was driving a donkey, laden with soil, followed by an old man who had an additional creel on his back. The laboured pace, owing to the heavy loads, enabled Warren to overtake them.

" It's hard work uphill," Warren remarked.

" It is, yer honour," the man replied, putting down his load to rest.

" What are you carrying? "

" Clay, yer honour."

Warren looked at the three panniers and noticed their similar contents.

" What do you use it for? " he asked.

" To make the land."

" Do you mean to fertilize it? "

" No, in throth, but to make it. We spread it out on the rock; the divil a ha'p'orth would grow there without it."

" But there are crops there already," Warren observed, pointing to the green husbandry on the hill; " the land has not been made in the same way, surely," the real facts of the case beginning to dawn upon him.

" It has, and no other."

" You have carried the soil from the bog to make these patches? "

" I have, me and me father before me."

" Good heavens, what a labour! "

" Hunger is not an aisy masther, yer honour; sure we must get the bit an' a sup somehow." And content with that philosophic view of life the man ordered his donkey to " go on out of that," and re-shouldering his creel the toilsome hillside journey was renewed.

Land-making being a new industry to Warren, he

volunteered to accompany them and see how it was done.

"Yer honour is welcome indeed, although it is simple enough in everything but the carrying. Meself and the ass are gettin' owld, an' we cannot draw as many loads as we used to; the gossoon is soft yet for anything but a skibful or the like."

The spot was at length reached where the panniers were emptied and the soil spread out on the bare rock, thus literally snatching from the hard limestone an economic victory. Necessity is truly the mother of invention, and here was a remarkable witness to the truth. But necessity is also a tyrant, and the invention itself was the severest comment on its despotism. There are triumphs in life self-condemnatory. Was there any defence of this one? Warren looked round to see.

"Is the land so scarce that you are compelled to make it?" he said, bluntly, giving expression to his thought.

"It is, sir, for the likes of us. We have the bog and the hillside. The soil in the bog is too wet to grow much except a few potatoes, and they are soft and wathery enough; they do better on the rock, because the moisture is soon dried out of the soil. Throth, a perch up here is worth an acre below."

"What is that stretch of land yonder?" the higher position bringing into view a vast track unseen from the lodge side of the hills.

"Oh, that belongs to the big cattle-dalers; sure, we have not the stock or the money to rent it."

"And what kind of land is it?"

"Well, some parts are good, others bad, and there's a good deal mixed middlin' like belly bacon. All along the valley there is not better land in all Ireland, and in throth it's the same pasture that's causin' a great deal of bad blood."

" In what way? "

" Well, ye see, some of the boys won't go to the trouble of carrying up the bog soil, and it's younger and stronger than meself they are. Ye see the hillside beyant? Well, that's close to the best grazin' land, and there's one Gallagher there who says that the baists are aitin' up the men, and it's themselves and the childer that have a right to the good land. An' indeed it's hard to gainsay that same. God Almighty scarcely meant cattle to thrive in one field and human cratures to starve in another. Yesterday," he continued, " Mr Doonas was arrested."

" Doonas arrested! What, on a charge of cattle-driving? "

" Oh, no, sir, it was not that, and meself does not rightly know what the offence was," the peasant added, with characteristic Irish caution; " but indeed he's a lauby man, and a good neighbour, and when he gets into trouble it's generally on somebody else's account."

" Who is your landlord? " Warren asked.

" Lord Ballyshameon; but indeed he has not much to do with it. He lives in London and does not bother his head as long as he gets the rint."

" An absentee landlord? " The question was given in a tone as if to elicit an opinion.

" Indeed then he is, and the boys are down on him for that same; the curse of the country is that it's overrun with absentee landlords."

Warren recalled Molly's definition of a bull. Here was current coin, with a dash of philosophy in it—the true hall-mark.

" You think the landlord should live on his estate and take a personal interest in things—is that it? "

" Well, they say he's afraid "—skilfully avoiding a direct answer—" although, indeed his lordship has no reason. We're paceable and quiet round here, and sure, if shootin' was the remedy isn't there the middle-man who comes and goes, and the divil a hair of his head is injured."

" The middleman is unpopular then? "

" Oh, in throth it's him that does the harm. He pays the landlord an equivalent for the land, and charges his own price after. That's how the rent is raised. The landlord has the first pull out of it and the middleman the second; throth, betune the one and the other the tenant has a bad time of it."

" But Ballyshameon has his own agent; does not he collect the rents direct? "

" Oh, indeed then, he does, and it's no complaints we make about him. He is a civil man in throth, and it often goes against his nature to collect the rents when it's a bad harvest. It would be better if every-thing was left in his hands. . . . There's nothing about here for the middleman," the peasant observed in an afterthought; " it's in the islands the trouble is. There's Inishlyre that used to belong to the Bally-shameon estate and now it's rackrented up to the teeth. Throth, there will be trouble there some day."

Warren recognized the name immediately and vividly recalled the evening spent on the island. A troubled look overspread his face, which the peasant quickly noticed.

" Faix, it's blatherin' I've been and botherin' yer honour with me talk. I'm told ye've come over for the sport. Throth, then, there's good fishin' in the river and there will be a run of salmon after the first flood. The water is too low presently, but indeed it's not long ye'll have to wait; there's a shower comin' up, by all appearance," he said, pointing to the west.

Warren looked in that direction and noticed a lowering in the sky. At the same time the wind, which had been rising, swept down the hill in a gust so sharp that he had to steady himself against a rock.

" The rain will be upon us immediately. Drive the ass home, Barney, there won't be any more clay-drawin' to-day. It's unaisy I am about yer honour; ye'll be wet through in them thin things before ye get to the lodge. Ye must take shelter in the cabin I'm thinkin', until the shower's over."

Warren's first impulse was to face the storm, but the sight of the hut, from which blue smoke was whirling in gusts, interested him, and thanking the man for the proffered shelter he accompanied him.

On nearing the dwelling, which was probably neither better nor worse than scores in the district its economic adaptation to the position on the hillside was striking. One gable, consisting of solid rock, was utilized as a part of the building; the opposite and side walls were constructed of rough stones not even set in mortar. Beams ran lengthwise and across, which formed a basis for a thatch of rushes and straw. Coming straight on the cabin from the hill, little could be seen but the top of the hut, which, placed as it was, gave it the appearance of a roof stripped from the walls and laid out on a heather slope. The original thatch had evidently been straw, but rents worn in the fabric were mended with rushes, and in some cases stuffed with heather when better material was scarce or unavailable. There was no chimney, but a hole in the roof invited egress to the smoke which rose from the hearth. The entrance to the dwelling served as another outlet, and on the occasion in question the wind, blowing directly on the roof, impeded the smoke from rising, and drove it through the door on the lee side.

When Warren entered the cabin the turf had fully ignited, leaving a fire that glowed with a clear flame. But beneath the roof the baffled smoke hung in thick folds. It struck the visitor in the face as if it would have him understand how men and women fashioned in the divine image may be marred and blinded. At first he could see nothing clearly. But as his smarting eyes became accustomed to the place, objects in the kitchen began to emerge like timid creatures from a hiding-place. There was a dresser with a few plates and dishes, a recess containing a bed, a corner with a tethered calf, blackened walls and rafters shining with a thick coating of carbon, the crystallization of habitual smoke. This constituted the visitor's mental inventory.

A woman came forward carrying a chair, which she wiped with the tail of her petticoat, and bade him welcome.

" Throth, I knew there was a shower comin'," she said, seeing Warren applying his handkerchief to his eyes, " the way the room smoked. It's been like this all mornin'," as if to excuse conduct quite exceptional on the part of the fire. The visitor, accustomed to a better order of things, and seeing how the present might be improved, said:

" I wonder you have not a chimney."

" That's thrue, indeed," the woman replied, " but we had the growin' family when the house was built, and there was no room for the chimney."

" What's become of them? "

" Some's married, others in America, and three died; the Lord have mercy on their sowls! "

" How many had you? " Warren asked, turning to the husband, who so far had left the conversation to his wife.

" Ten, yer honour. It's a powerful counthry for the childer, bedad, the soil is great for them."

" Arrah, whisht now, Michael Molloy, why don't ye tell the gintleman that ye've been married twice? " as if some apology were needed.

" Well, an' what of that? Sure, that does not make the number less but more," with a knowing wink at Warren.

" Ah, in throth I wish yer duty was as good as your arithmetic," said the woman. " Faix, if yer eyes were in the smoke all day like mine it is not much winkin' ye would do with them."

" Arrah, howld yer whist, Sally; you have the smoke and sore eyes and I have the hill and sore bones; the divil a much there is to choose between us."

There was a hole in the thatch through which large drops of rain were falling. Warren, noticing it, said:

" Well, you might mend that hole in the roof and keep the rain out, Michael." This remark, coupled with the criticism on the chimney, was a little too much for the peasant, who immediately marshalled his humour in defence.

" Sure, ye would not want me to go out and mend it while it's rainin'," Michael said deprecatingly.

" No, but you might mend it when it's fine," Warren said.

" Arrah, sir, sure when it's fine the rain doesn't come in."

The peasant beamed with good-humour on hearing his visitor's hearty laugh.

Sally's concerned face cleared in noticing how the pleasantry was accepted.

"Michael likes his bit o' fun, sir. He'd rather have that than tell ye the truth. It was the hens scratched a hole in the thatch this very mornin'."

"We have to make shift as best we can, sir, in these parts," the husband explained, "and put one thing against the other; and as for the chimney, sure, if ye gave Sally the choice of an iligant one or another baist it's meself knows which she'd be choosin'. But indeed, when all's said and done, it's them that gets the rent that ought to put a good thatch between us and the storm, an' the chimney too. But we can have the bit o' fun when we can't have either. Sure, that costs nothin'."

Warren listened to all this, half-pained, half-amused. It was certain that the Irish peasant's lot was a hard one. It was equally clear that it was accepted cheerfully.

"It's well you can joke about these things," he said. "They would see it in a different light in my country."

"Oh, indeed, we can do the grumblin' when it suits our convenience and when anything is to be gained by it. If it was the landlord we had here, or his agent, bedad we would put the same song to another tune, an' the divil a much fun he'd find in it. But why should we be makin' a poor mouth before yer honour that has just taken shelter from the rain."

"Oh, well, I'm grateful to you for the kindness, and I hope there will be better times in store for you," Warren said, rising to go.

" Well, long life to yer honour, and I hope when the storm clears that ye'll ketch a salmon."

He was glad to breathe the pure air of the mountain again after emerging from the miserable hovel, the recollections of which were not so easily dissipated.

CHAPTER V

THE next day was fine. Light clouds drifted in the sky, and large blue spaces showed that the rain had practically exhausted itself. Paudeen brought the intelligence that there was a big flood in the river, and Biddy confirmed it by informing Warren that a poacher had offered a salmon for sale that morning.

" And it was not meself that would be encouragin' the likes of them, seein' that yer honour has come for that same purpose "—with a delightful confusion between an art legitimately and illegally pursued.

" The poachers have not been on my part of the river? " Warren asked, the sense of proprietary rights asserting itself.

" Ah, no, sir, it's back in the mountains where they are not watched they snatch them. Faix, no one will touch your water whilst ye are here. But if it wasn't that it wasn't yerself they'd be at it fast enough. Sure, one of them sold a fish to Mrs Pinkerton, the agent's wife, one day, that was gaffed the same morning out of the salmon trap in his own water. It was when salmon was very scarce, and the sorra a one the agent would let his wife have, although the longin' was on her at the time, poor crature. It's meself that will be expectin' ye to bring one home this day, for ye are tired of chickens and ducks, I'm thinkin'."

So Warren went forth to try his luck amongst the big game. The river, which rose and fell rapidly, owing to its swiftness, had reached the condition which an experienced angler welcomes. The rapids, where the stream rushed at high speed, were foam-streaked with many an eddying current, and the water had sufficiently recovered from its turgid condition to suit the fly.

Warren was not skilled in fly-fishing. He had angled in Scotch rivers, but any success attained was due to trolling from a boat. Here he found himself on a rough bank, armed with a rod difficult to wield, and the first hour was spent chiefly in releasing the fly from the thick undergrowth of grass and briars and the branches of overhanging trees. These seemed to be placed there for the explicit purpose of embarrassing his efforts. He began to repent that he had not procured the services of a gillie. But he preferred to be alone and to wander by the bank of the beautiful stream, detachment and meditation being more to his mind that morning than the obtrusiveness and garrulity of an Irish attendant.

On the tail of a likely-looking pool a salmon broke the water. The flash of a broad silver side was no lost on the angler. It appealed to the sporting instinct and stimulated him to renewed effort. It seemed a long cast to the spot where the fish rose, and at the first attempt the fly fell short by a dozen yards. He drew off more line and tried again, but, intent on the quarry, other things were left unheeded, particularly a clump of furze behind his back. In this the fly caught, and as the rod was switched forward the line was arrested and there was a sharp snap; three feet of a broken top joint dangled in the air. An exclamation, monosyllabic but emphatic, leaped from the lips of the angler. What it was will be readily surmised by most fishermen. What is more to the point was the effect of the exclamation. It was immediately followed by a peal of laughter so sudden and startling that Warren turned round in the utmost surprise. There was far too much music in it to make it referable to those malign embodiments of the spirit world which make sport of human misfortune, and of whom Warren had heard and read so much in Irish folk-lore. Had he any doubt on the subject the appearance of a young lady in *persona propria* with a face radiant with laughter would have settled the matter. There was the origin of the mirth in the person of his recently-made acquaintance, Miss Molly MacDaire.

" I'm so sorry, Mr Warren," she exclaimed, coming towards him; " it's very unkind of me to laugh at your misfortune."

" Oh, please don't say so. It is my place to apologize. I did not know there were ladies present. I ought to have brought a gillie. I find I'm a fool at this kind of thing," beginning to walk towards the offending obstacle.

" I'll free your line from the whins," and Molly tripped back to the furze bush, and a moment afterwards, holding up the released fly, called to him to wind up.

Despite the ill-luck of the angling there was a good-humoured smile on Warren's face as he approached the girl; the afterglow of amusement still lingered on hers.

" How long have you been watching me? " he said in a tone of consternation.

" Oh, not long. In the distance I thought you were a poacher, but when I saw you casting—I mean when I got nearer," she hurriedly corrected—" I—"

" It's not a poacher's form, is it? " he said, coming

to her relief with a hearty laugh. " Well, my angling is over for to-day. I must put myself in a poacher's hands to acquire the art."

" Haven't you a spare top? " she asked.

" I believe there is one in the case," nodding listlessly towards it, " but I'm rather sick of the whole business."

" And a soldier too," Molly said, deprecatingly, shaking her head, " the hero of a hundred battles, of moving accidents by flood and field, of hairbreadth 'scapes, and a broken top renders him *hors de combat*. I'd splice it sooner than give in on a day like this. Ah, look now, there's a fish rising on Crookawn."

" I've seen that fellow before; it was in trying to reach him I broke my rod." And the effect of the banter, with the reappearance of the fish, sent Warren hurrying along the bank for the spare top.

" What a fool I was not to bring a gillie," he re-iterated.

" Ah, don't mind, maybe we'll find one—this fly is too large for the water," Molly said, eyeing it critically. " Where's your book? "

The Englishman produced it from the fishing-creel, and in a few moments two heads in close proximity were exploring the contents.

" A thunder and lightning, that's good for rising water, this is falling; we'll try a golden olive. Show me that one," and Molly's nimble finger and thumb pounced on a pattern that took her fancy. With equally facile hands the large fly was taken off the gut cast and the new one substituted.

" Why, you know all about it," commented Warren with amused surprise, running the line through the last eyelet and handing it to his companion to fasten to the gut loop.

" The proper thing is to spit on it for luck," said she, " but we can omit that part of the ceremony on the present occasion; now cover that fish."

" But that's the very thing that lies beyond my capacity. I shall break another top," he said.

" Ah, don't let your fly drop so far behind your back," his companion cried, assuming the rôle of instructor, and seeing that there was a danger of fulfilling the fateful prophecy.

" I am heavily in your debt already, Miss MacDaire. Show me how to do it. A young lady that can whip on a fly as you have done knows the rest of the subject— please—" and Warren handed over the rod to the new-found gillie.

The girl smilingly took it, and raking from the reel a dozen yards of line sent the fly swish through the air, causing it to drop on the edge of the far-off pool.

" Good gracious! " said Warren, looking at the result and recalling his own performance, " and you have actually allowed me to go on bungling in your presence; come now, that's not fair."

" Ah, indeed, it only needs a little practice. You have not been brought up on a river's bank like me."

She had thrown off a light coat when she took the rod, and raising her arms the finely-moulded figure was brought into play. With an easy grace the rod was swung and with no perceptible effort it answered to her behests.

Far off the line fell lightly upon the stream. There was no indication that what Warren's strong, muscular arms found hard work was any labour to the girl. It had no effect other than a deepening of the tint in her fair cheeks and a little parting of the lips in earnest pursuit of the sport in which from childhood she delighted.

As Warren docilely walked by her side the sense of a beautiful girl charmed him, and with each movement of the rod, dropping the fly close to a jagged rock or deftly clearing some fastening which threatened entanglement, he admired the skill displayed in the mastery of a high and complex art.

" Really, Miss MacDaire, you are a perfect genius with the rod; I envy you." The words were spoken in frank and sincere admiration.

" Indeed, I am not accustomed to this rod. I can't cast a good line with it. That fish does not want the fly, I am afraid. I think I must have covered him. . . . Oh, there he is! " There was a heavy break in the water, the rod gracefully curved, and Molly stepped back, deftly recovering some of the slack line and getting a firm hold of the fish, now plunging vigorously.

" Here, take the rod."

" No, no, you must play him," Warren objected.

" Take the rod, quick, quick, before he makes a rush," and the curving, trembling weapon was pushed into the hands of the Englishman, despite his protests. Molly's despotism was irresistible.

" I'll lose him for a certainty; tell me what to do. I—"

" Hold him firmly and leave the reel free when he makes off . . . keep the top of your rod up stream, not down . . . that's it. Oh, you are an apt pupil; he is a capital fish indeed. . . . Let him have the reel; ah, don't touch the line while he's running. He is off up stream."

The fish, which had been swaying to and fro in the current, seeming to realize the situation, made a swift rush, causing the line to cut the water with a hiss.

"After him," and Molly set the example by running along the bank, eager and panting with excitement.

"If he jumps, lower the top of the rod . . . ah, mind that rock! Wind in, he's coming this way. The line is getting slack—quicker! quicker!" and Warren, despite the characteristic English calmness, felt his hands trembling as he obediently responded to the admonitions of the Irish girl.

The fish, by this time, had reached the top of the pool and steadied himself in its deepest part after the sharp run.

"Take it aisy an' it will do ye good, darlin'," said Molly, playfully apostrophizing the fish in a rich brogue.

"I beg your pardon—"

"Oh, indeed, it's the fish I'm talking to," with a merry laugh at Warren's appropriation of such endearment. "The gaff is in here, is it not?" and she dived into the basket on Warren's shoulder and pulled out the latest telescopic patent. "Oh, what a beauty!" drawing it out and looking at the shining brass implement. "But he is not likely to give us a chance for some time. . . . There! he's on the move again; let him go." For the tyro, feeling he was called upon to do something in this new juncture, began to wind in the line. Like a flash the salmon was across the pool again, ending the dash by a clear spring from the water. There was a terrific strain put upon the line as the leap was a forward one, and the reel screamed in an agony of recoil.

"Oh . . . you must lower the top of the rod when he does that; my heart is in my mouth, I thought he was gone. He's a springer and bright as a shilling."

" How soon will he be ready, do you think? "

" No signs of exhaustion yet . . . ah, don't let him go down stream or we'll lose him."

The fish had turned and made a run with the current. Despite all the rod's pressure Warren could not stop him. In a few moments he was back again in he place where he was hooked.

" Do take the rod," Warren pleaded; " he's getting out of hand."

" Not for a thousand pounds; oh, oh, he's off down stream."

And the Englishman knew it. With a terrific rush the fish took another slant, the reel running hopelessly. Warren found himself traversing the bank with long strides, the rod high in air and a kite line trailing far off on the water.

The girl had ceased to instruct, for counsel was impossible. The fish had got into a swift rapid and, too exhausted to battle against it, was swept away willy-nilly.

" What on earth am I to do now? " came a shout.

" Run as hard as you can and try to get in some slack."

The hundred yards traversed seemed to Warren like a mile, but the fish now showed unmistakable signs of exhaustion, turning over in the water and flashing golden signals of distress.

" There's a chance yet," Molly hopefully exclaimed, " but he must be stopped before the falls. I'll run on with the gaff," and Warren had a glimpse of a pair of smart heels kicking up the embroidery of a white skirt in front of him.

Left to himself he put into practice all the points of the lesson learned. He kept the rod well up, put on firm pressure and quickened his pace almost to a run. The roar of a cataract broke on his senses in alarm, and the flash of its white-foamed water came in sight. He was almost abreast of the quarry now, which had become the plaything of the rapids and was floundering helplessly. The position gave a new sense of power, and applying it he brought the fish closer in.

Below Warren, Molly stood on a jut of the bank, not a score of yards above the fatal waterfall. She beckoned with the gaff to guide the fish towards her. A moment or two would decide the issue. A perilous strain brought the prize towards the girl. It was drifting slower now in the slacker water and in a few seconds would have been within her reach. But there are final and fatal kicks in a salmon, however played out it may be; it might have been the flash of the bronzed weapon, or a last unconscious effort, but the kick came and carried the fish a couple of yards beyond the reach of the gaff. Warren was about to exclaim, but the next moment he was horror-struck on seeing his faithful gillie more than knee-deep in the water.

" Molly, Miss—"

But the deed was done, with a dexterous stroke, a huge salmon was impaled on the gaff, and with shouts of hilarious triumph Molly waded out of the water.

" Oh, what a splendid fish! But you are wet through."

" And what else would you expect from your gillie? "

Warren reverently raised his hat and held out his hand to the blushing girl. " 'Pon my honour, you're a brick—pardon the familiarity, nothing else expresses it so well; but your dress—"

" Oh. the wetting is nothing. We are used to it in this country. Better to wet the grass with my skirt," shaking the dripping garment, " than with my tears, which I would be doing if I missed him, and your first salmon, too. But it's luncheon-time and our house is quite near. My uncle will be glad to see you and I can change my dress."

" Well, I'll see you home, but I ought not to trouble your people in such an unceremonious way. But what a weight," Warren said. slinging the capacious creel on his shoulder, freighted with the doubled-up fish.

CHAPTER VI

THEY followed the river upstream, which coursed sinuously through the valley, and turning in by a boreen, or narrow lane, Squire Fitz Martin's house came into view.

" The Big House," as it was styled by the peasants—in deference to its magnitude compared with small farm dwellings—was a building innocent of all architectural pretensions and had little to commend it apart from its size. There was nothing to relieve the severity of its rugged exterior, not even a tree or climbing vine. Its massive walls resembled the granite rock which lay behind it. In the distance it seemed to be a part of the mountain itself, and it would be hard to distinguish it from Arranmore or Clough-na-Currel.

Here for many generations lived the Fitz Martins, an old Irish family, who owned an extensive estate adjoining Lord Ballyshameon's. The last survivor of the old Celtic stock was Bryan, who had never married. Catherine Fitz Martin, his sister, married a naval officer, Philip MacDaire, of broad sympathies and Bohemian habits. He had been round the world, and being an admirable talker gave graphic descriptions to his countrymen of other lands where he had travelled, and of the social and economic conditions that prevailed there. His enthusiasm frequently exceeded his discretion. He became suspect and was ultimately cast into prison. The close confinement in contrast with his seafaring life soon told upon him and his health rapidly failed.   He was subsequently released, but an operation for blood-poisoning supervened and he died.

Catherine did not long survive her husband, and Molly, their only child, who had lived almost as much with her uncle as at home, became Bryan's entire charge.

The other inmates of " The Big House " were the wife and son of the Squire's deceased brother, Peter— " wild Peter " he was called—a rollicking, hunting, drinking type of Irishman—a brand by no means rare— who died prematurely, leaving to his good-natured brother a widow, a son and considerable debts, all of which Bryan shouldered without demur.

" You are welcome, sir," the Squire said, bowing courteously as Warren was introduced by his niece. " You have had sport too, I see, by the strain on the creel strap.   Well, there is not much more than fishing and shooting in this part of the country to offer to visitors—and a good fish too!" peering into the basket, as Warren raised the lid.   "But come in, come in; now that you have killed your first fish we'll drink its health. What did you get him with? "

" A golden olive, on Miss MacDaire's recommendation," Warren answered.

" Oh, it's a great killer after a flood, especially with a bit of jungle cock in the cheek.   I have given up fishing of late years and have delegated that office to my niece."

" Miss MacDaire is a splendid angler," Warren said enthusiastically.   " If it had not been for her I should have had an empty creel.   I only hope she won't get a chill," and Warren narrated the gaffing episode.

" Oh, that won't hurt her; Molly is amphibious. You must not be shocked at her harum-scarum ways.

You see, there is little social life in this out-of-the-way place. Molly can play a fish, shoot a snipe, break in a horse or take a stone wall with any man in the county. It's not that I mind," continued the Squire, noticing the visitor smile at this list of accomplishments. " She may take as many stone walls as she likes, if she would only not take all the troubles and squabbles of the people from Knockbeg to Bannaslaney along with them.   It's there she's likely to come a cropper. If she were a man she'd be in gaol; begad, I have threatened as a magistrate to commit her myself."

" Yes, and then get up a petition for my release," Molly exclaimed, bounding into the room, radiant after her morning's exercise. " That's Uncle Bryan's way, Mr Warren. He gave Tim Sweeny a month and privately paid the fine to get him out of gaol," and her voice reverberated in the oak panelling.

They sat down at the luncheon-table, and Molly, turning to the guest, continued the conversation.

" The fact is, we Irish are a bundle of contradictions; you must reconcile yourself to that fact to begin with, Mr Warren."

" It seems to me you have so much good-nature that the stock is not always under control and takes the line of least resistance."

" Now, uncle, all your traducing of my character has only called forth a well-turned compliment. This is the first instalment for gaffing the salmon."

" Well, if you accept such currency as that in settlement, you do not assess your services high enough, Miss MacDaire."

" Begad, you have had your answer there, Molly," said the Squire.

" Oh, indeed, uncle, I had not been long in Mr

Warren's company before I found that he came to the West via Blarney."

But Warren protested quite seriously, and, to do him justice, he was never more in earnest.

" No, indeed, I have been genuinely impressed with Irish good-nature. The way those people on the island received us and put themselves to inconvenience at a moment's notice; Doonas dodging the police all night for the sake of accompanying me down the bay, and the manner in which someone else set convention at naught "—with a sly look at Molly—" these things are appraised too highly to be disposed of with the small change of mere compliment."

Whilst Warren spoke the face of the old Squire passed from a look of amusement to seriousness and then quivered with emotion.

" Indeed you are right, sir, and would to God more of the English people put themselves in the way of making the discovery. Half the crimes of Ireland are the effect of uncontrolled good-nature. As you say, the people are ready to take shares in each other's follies, as in each other's pleasures. They would as readily go to prison for each other as attend a dance or a funeral. There is a freemasonry in all things, including crime."

" As a virtue that is admirable, but the defect of it is somewhat serious," Warren commented.

" It seems so, but unfortunately things that the law makes crime are often morally defensible. Every magistrate on the bench knows that. The conditions are so hard as to justify outlawry in the opinion of the people. Here is Ballyshameon living in London, drawing his rental to the uttermost farthing, and disposing of other portions of the estate to rack-renters. If one of them were shot to-morrow the assassin would lose no caste with the bulk of the people."

" Still, there are very few cases of crime on the part of the tenants themselves. I think you ought to point that out, uncle."

" Oh, indeed, they are all lambs and saints in your sight, Molly, and will never lack a champion whilst you live."

" Nor lie on a plank bed whilst my dear old Uncle Bryan sits on the bench; but it is the secret societies do the mischief, and the peasants have no connection with them."

" Well, as far as proof goes, I am with you, Molly; the people, on the whole, are inoffensive."

" Are Ballyshameon's rents excessive? " Warren asked the Squire.

" It is a question as to whether there ought to be any rent at all in places. Rent is supposed to be an exchange for value received. The cases where troubles arise are where there is rent and no land, and the people have to pay for rocks and stones almost bereft of soil. Pinkerton sent down a man to collect arrears at Corrigmore last year and he returned empty-handed. As he put it, ' Bedad, when I spoke about the rent they nearly threw the whole estate at me.' It is not long since eight thousand acres were offered to be let at sixpence an acre."

" Sixpence? " Warren repeated.

" Yes, and dear at that."

" Really. Well, what about the good land? "

" There is little trouble as far as that is concerned. The people who hold it are on good terms with the agent. The mischief is that there are so few tenants who enjoy its benefits. It is used for ranching, and there is bitter jealousy that men should starve on rocks and stones whilst cattle thrive on the fat of the land."

" Am I right in assuming that there are no complaints where the land is good? "

" As a rule, yes, although they hang together, as I say. There is the case of Doonas, who has just been arrested. He has a good farm and is well-to-do, yet always in hot water, on account of other people."

" The vicarious martyr seems to be a good deal in evidence," Warren commented with some asperity.

" Well, that proves that fine feeling is not extinct in the race yet," said Molly, bristling. " The soil grows martyrs if it grows nothing else. When you see the effects of the struggle, Mr Warren, you will understand it."

The blue eyes deepened and a colour like a blush rose suffused the girl's face as she spoke; a challenge still lingered in the pause that followed. Warren was half disposed to accept it—the thought in his mind being that if men like Doonas used their influence in advice rather than in participating in disaffection a better cause would be served. But recollections of the smoking cabin on the hillside, the half-blinded woman, flashed in, and the sword remained in its scabbard.

" Oh, yes, I know, Miss MacDaire, I want to learn, but one cannot shed constitutional methods like a fretted garment—that has always been the Englishman's difficulty in regard to Ireland. However sympathetic one may be one cannot sympathize with crime."

" Begad, you are right, sir, but—"

" Prove the law to be crime itself and how does the case stand? " Molly cut in.

" Look here, Molly, we are keeping Mr Warren from his fishing. You will never convince a rebel like my niece, sir. Here's to the next salmon and the country's good," and the old Squire raised his glass.

" There's another idiosyncrasy," he cried, pointing to the glass of water in his niece's hand. " That girl has given up wine because some of the feather-brains can't stand a glass of whisky."

" Another case of vicarious martyrdom, Mr Warren," said Molly, in a tone of bewitching mischievousness.

" Well, judging by the effect on your health and spirits it would be prudent to join you," Warren observed with gallantry, turning towards the picture of fine womanhood at the foot of the table.

Molly bowed with the ease and grace of a queen.

As the Englishman passed from the room a lady, dressed in black, attracted his attention. She paused on the lowest step of the broad staircase in the hall. Her face was deadly pale and was surmounted by a plentiful crop of black hair shot with white. Large, cold grey eyes, with a frightened look in them, gave intensity to the searching glance she threw at the stranger. Warren found himself staring at this unexpected apparition, almost to the point of rudeness. Suddenly recollecting himself, he formally bowed. There was no apparent recognition of the courtesy, and a moment later the figure swept through a side door and disappeared. The incident was so sudden that the Squire, who followed his visitor, could scarcely have noticed it.

By the time Warren had re-slung the fishing-creel on his shoulder and thanked his host, Molly, who had left the room, rejoined them.

" I have secured a gillie for you," she said, " who possesses the ideal qualification of being the best poacher in Connacht. Here, Shawn," she called,

" take Mr Warren's creel. You have met before, I think, when Shawn was only second mate. In angling he is captain, and will no doubt add another fish or two to the basket."

" Thanks so much, Miss MacDaire, but I regret losing the assistance of my first instructor. I may not find her successor so patient."

" Ah, now you are at the blarney again. You English seem to think it is the only road into Irish appreciation."

" Is it not rather that you credit us with so little appreciation that you label all gratitude as traffic by that route? "

Molly's full eyes searched the speaker's face, all the banter, so habitual to her race, died out of them.

" Not always," she said in soft, liquid tones, born of deeper feeling, and stretched out her hand to the visitor.

" Remember," she cried after him, " that Shawn is in league with the fairies and leprechauns. I hope they will be liberal in their gifts."

" Perhaps the queen will give her gracious commands to that effect," came the response, and Warren raised his hat in adieu. An uplifted hand waved its acknowledgment.

Shawn, leading the way, cut across a field, skirting a bluff thickly clothed with hazel bushes. A winding burn picked its way through the uneven ground. A footpath crossed the stream at several points, taking the more direct course to the valley, where the water emptied itself into a pond a couple of acres in extent.

An old ruin stood at the lower end. The thick stone walls and their great height bespoke a building of substantiality and importance; its tumbled-down state and lichened crevices also showed that its occupancy belonged to a remote period. From its position it was evident that the outlet from the pond at one time flowed underneath the building, as a crumbling wall stood on each side of the water.

Round the edges nothing grew, not even a fringe of rushes or blade of grass. This gave the pond a hard look, and made it appear more like a huge stone cauldron chipped at the two ends where the little stream entered and left it.

" This is the owld castle, yer honour," Shawn said, noticing that Warren was interested. Then in a mysterious whisper, nodding towards the pond, " And that's Poullamore. Whisht, they might hear ye," as the Englishman was about to speak. Warren turned round, expecting to see someone within earshot.

" The merrows I mean; they don't like us to talk about them. Come away, sir, an' I'll tell ye."

Warren recalled the incident on board the yacht and prudently followed the gillie, who drew away from the place with an air of awe, as from forbidden ground.

" Once," he began, " an ancient castle stood close to Poullamore, which at that time was only a spring well that supplied the inmates. It was the sate of the ancient family from whom the Fitz Martins descended. The squire of thim days was a very different man from the one we have now — good luck to him!—a man eaten up with greed, although that bad drop in the blood is not all purged out yet I'm thinkin'. It was said he sold his soul to the divil for the sake of goold. God betune us and harm. Well, one night a ship was wrecked off the coast beyant, and everybody was lost except one man, who swam to shore with a leather bag round his neck full of jools, worth a great fortune.

He was guided by the lights in the castle window, found his way through the Windy Gap and axed for shelter. Sure he got that which is never denied to any benighted traveller, and the bit and the sup besides, and indeed it must have been too much of the drink he had for he began to boast of his riches, and pulled out some of the diamonds. With that the greed began to glisten in the eye of Fitz Martin, and to make a long story short, the stranger was murdered in the night and his body thrown into the deep well in the owld castle yard. Faix, the merrows who had charge of the well were displased. Maybe yer honour never heard of them."

Warren confessed his ignorance of that branch of the Good People family.

" Indeed yer honour has the learnin' in other ways, but the merrows is the water-sprites, and having charge of the well they were angry at the insult, and small blame to them to have a dead corpse pushed down amongst thim without be yer lave or a ha'p'orth. Thin a strange thing happened; the water broke out in another place close by, and began to rise and spread until it flowed round the base of the castle and crept up the walls. Those in the house took the warnin' and escaped with their lives, barrin' the murderer himself, who had the drink as well as the crime on him. When the noise of the shoutin' at last roused him, and he saw he must swim for it, he put the bag of diamonds round his neck and plunged into the water. But the weight on him grew heavier and heavier, until he sank out of sight, an' no one could save him.

" Strange, too, his body was never found, and when the water fell once more there wasn't a trace of the owld well left, and in its place there was the bottomless pool that's before ye.

" After that the owld castle began to crumble and fall into ruin, and when the next branch of the family came into the estate they built the new big house, where it now stands, higher up the hill, and from that day to this any interference with Poullamore causes a death."

Shawn paused as if to mark the effect of this narrative upon the listener.

" That is strange," Warren commented.

" To be sure it is, sir, nothing will alter it. Throth it's a foolish thing to take liberties with the good people, it's best to obey them at all cost. I would go through fire myself sooner than displase them."

" Where does all the water come from? That little brook can scarcely account for it."

" Of coorse, sir, it can't. Sure the burn only flows from the cascade born of the shower. In summer it often dries up, and the silver belt it makes on the side of the mountain becomes merely a black scar."

" That's singular; there must be a spring somewhere that feeds Poullamore."

" Faix, then, it's meself can tell you where the spring is," and Shawn paused, looked cautiously round, and stepping close to Warren whispered, " Poullabeg."

" And where is that? "

" In the yard of the big house."

" Squire Fitz Martin's? "

" The divil a lie in it; ye did not go in there or ye'd see it. There's a wooden lid, with a cross beam on it to raise and lower the bucket. Poullamore is the big pool, Poullabeg the little one."

" And how do you know that the little pool—as you call it—supplies the big one? "

" Bekase, like this one, it never changes its height, winter or summer, and any disturbance in Poullamore is at once felt in Poullabeg. A flood that muddies the one muddies the other. When a storm ruffles the surface of the open water, sure, isn't the water under the lid ruffled too? Throth, it's all meant for a warnin', as the silent lady could tell ye if she chose; she knows all about it."

" The silent lady! Who is she? "

" She lives in The Big House, you'll meet her some day."

With this cryptic declaration Shawn's narrative came to an end. By that time they had reached the river, and O'Grady proved an admirable gillie. His knowledge of the pools was intimate, and when he took a turn of the rod, to rest his master — for salmon fishing is hard work—the most distant holes were searched by Shawn's skilful casts.

But Warren's interest in the sport, despite such admirable gillying, seemed to flag. He could not disguise from himself the sense of a missing element. He left off before luncheon, with a feeling of the keenest interest, so that he begrudged the time spent away from the river. But who can take up the thread of the dream where awakening has snapped it? A missing element transforms the scene, the absence of a face dulls the landscape. To Warren the rippling river and the rising salmon sank to the level of ordinary prosaic life. The purple of the far-off mountains had faded into drab. Had Shawn's lugubrious story proved disenchanting? The question did not admit of a ready answer. Perhaps if the story had nothing to do with it the change of gillies had.

MICROCOPY RESOLUTION TEST CHART

(ANSI and ISO TEST CHART No 2)

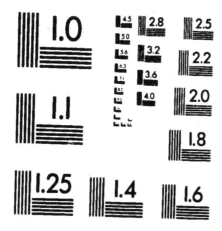

APPLIED IMAGE Inc

1653 East Main Street
Rochester, New York   14609   USA
(716) 482 – 0300 – Phone
(716) 288 – 5989 – Fax

CHAPTER VII

" PAUDEEN, come here, agra."

"Sure, I'm here already," replied Mrs Maloney's hopeful, emerging from the back door, where he was blowing a capful of birds' eggs.

" Well, don't go away again, avic."

" What do you want me for? Himself's fishin' and won't be wantin' the car."

" It isn't that, alannah, I think Bob Dorris will have a letther from Liverpool for us; he went by half an hour ago."

" Sure, he goes by every day with the post," Paudeen replied, noticing a flaw in the argument.

" Thrue for ye, asthore, but he had a great bag of letters on his back to-day; there's sure to be one for us."

Paudeen was the literary genius in the Maloney household, and through that medium the absent son Tom communicated with his mother.

Tom, the eldest, had gone to seek his fortune in the English seaport town. Like many peasants' sons he had to face the problem of straitened means and concluded that two mouths were easier to fill than three. Although only qualified for odd jobs he earned enough to keep himself and share with his mother and young brother at home. His letters came at irregular intervals, as writing was a laborious ordeal, for Tom had not enjoyed the privileges of the more liberal educational system inaugurated at a later date.

One of two things generally prompted the despatch

of these epistles, namely, the periodical allowance of money to keep the pot boiling, or advice in regard to the management of the patch of land held by the widow, live stock and kindred subjects, on which the eldest son was an authority.

No sooner was a letter received and read than the mother began to count the days before the next would be due. After a couple of weeks had elapsed a sharp eye had to be kept upon Paudeen lest he should be out of the way when the letter arrived, and various expedients were devised to ensure his presence. On one occasion his nether garments were said to be retained three days by his mother on the plea of needing patching, against which the owner loudly protested, but in vain. On another Biddy was suddenly seized with an acute attack of lumbago, a malady quite new to her, and, ensconced in her chair, the boy had to be handy and fetch the flour for the breadmaking, and the tea from the locked-up cupboard, or face the alternative of a prolonged fast, which in the healthy state of his appetite led to capitulation on the enemy's terms.

These devices were only necessary as a rule when letters were expected without remittances. Once, in an impulsive moment, the widow held out the bribe of a halfpenny, which had the disastrous effect on her intractable progeny of making him an out-and-out blackmailer.

Paudeen's remark, " There won't be money in this letter, mother," showed the workings of a diplomatic mind.

" Arrah, bads grant to ye, why would there be? Is not the poor boy skinnin' himself to the bone to send it so often? Was not there five shillings in the last one a month ago? "

" Why would he be writin' thin? Sure, he said all about the oats and the manurin' o' the potato patch in the last letter, and that Pat Sweeny was handier at ringin' a pig than Micky Joyce."

" Arrah now, hould yer whisht; sure, he said nothin' about cuttin' the turf, or the best place for the pshatie hole, or what to expect on fair day for the litter of bourmous."

" All right, mother, I'll be handy."

" Throth, thin, it's as good for ye, for although ye have the readin' and writin' knowledge more than Tom you don't know the farmin' like him, and ye will be wanting a new pair of corduroys next winter, I'm thinkin', and—"

" Here's Mr Warren, mother. Shawn O'Grady is with him, and in throth he has a salmon."

" Bedad, maybe he has, but go round and pull the bush out of the gap. I put it there to keep out Cassidy's ass that's been prowlin' round. Where's my black apron? "

These preliminaries effected, Biddy met the fishermen at the door.

" Faix, then, it's welcome ye are, and ye've had the sport in earnest. Bedad, Shawn is the boy that brings the luck anyhow."

" Have ye the pot boilin', Biddy? " the gillie asked.

" Boilin', is it? sure, it's tired boilin', it is. . . . Oh, another! that's grand and no mistake," seeing Shawn extract a second fish from the creel; " it's yer honour knows how to ketch them."

" Give me a wisp of straw, Paudeen. It's this one ye'll send away, sir? " O'Grady asked, holding up the fish that was first caught.

" No, not that one, the other," Warren answered emphatically.

So Molly's fish was kept and its companion despatched to London.

That evening Warren sat enjoying a post-prandial cigar. The events of the day flashed in retrospective interest. The angling had been excellent, and the glow in his restfully-tired limbs told of a distinct physical contribution to the asset side of his account. When had he tasted such a salmon?—a viand which never reached the hands of the most skilful *chef* of a Piccadilly club except through the medium of ice, which robbed it of half its flavour. And the boiled chickens, which Biddy feared were suffering the fate of a too intimate familiarity, what had London to compare with them? Even the spring cabbage and garden rhubarb, entities in the limited menu of the simple life, Warren praised without stint, to the delight of the fresh-cheeked, smiling Biddy.

" Troth, thin, it's the good air an' not me ye have to thank for it, an' the tramp by river and bog. Sure, I had a gentleman here from London before an' my brain was racked in thryin' to plaze and coax him to ate a bit. An' what could ye expect? He was so run down that he had not the strength to drag a herrin' off the tongs."

This graphic test of a depleted human frame Warren seriously tried to imagine, and the tax it imposed shunted him off the track of Biddy's narrative. She hitched him on again in expatiating on the mountain air and the virtue of the salt water off Port Maginnis Head.

" Throth, after that," she added, " he used to take a crust in his pocket, for the weakness of strength came upon him, as if he had the fair-gurthagh." *

* Grass hunger.

6

" Well, I hope I won't get to that, Biddy," Warren replied, assuming an air of familiarity with the particular form of robustness which victimized his predecessor.

" Throth, thin, if ye do, sir, we'll try to cure ye, but I'm thinkin' ye're a long way from that at present, for it's the shock yerself has given me."

" A shock! Why, what have I done? "

" Ye never touched yer lunch; I found it in the creel after Shawn went. Faix, I was afraid to come in an' clear away the first course for fear you would not have touched that either. Sure, I thought ye liked a piece of fresh lobster, an' it was a slice of Limerick ham I gave ye too. Tim Shaughnessy swore that tne foot of the pig that owned it never touched Connacht soil, an'—"

" Oh, Biddy, you good creature, I had lunch at Squire Fitz Martin's," and Warren laughed heartily at the subtle defence of the discarded viands.

" There now, Paudeen was right, bedad, in saying that no one would lave a meal like that except for a better one. Oh, then, it's the Squire is the lochie man, and signs upon him; it's in high regard he is held, long life to him."

" He is indeed a fine type of an Irish gintleman."

" Gintleman, is it? faix, there's more of the gintle-man in his cast-off clothes than in the body and soul of them with more pretensions. Sure, while some people are always gettin' poor cratures into trouble it's himself that's always thryin' to get them out of it."

" He is a lenient magistrate then? "

" Lenient? No, in throth, but severe. What can he do but administer the law, as he says himself. He's there for that purpose.

" ' If you don't pay yer rent, Pat Casey, sure ye

must be evicted; that's the law an' there's no gain-sayin' it.'   That's the way he ups and talks to them.''

" Well, there was not much consolation for Casey in that,'' Warren said.

" No, indeed, nor much for the rack-renter either, for he gave him a sly rap.

" ' The law is on yer side, sir,' says he, ' in the eviction of this tinant.   It doesn't put the money to which ye are entitled into yer pocket, but it gives ye the satis-faction, when ye lie down on yer comfortable bed at night, to think that the defendant, his wife an' child are shelterin' behind a stone wall or among the whin bushes on the roadside.   To be sure, this is not money, but ye are entitled to all the benefit it gives ye; so far ye are recouped.   Next case.' ''

" Did the rack-renter go on with the eviction? ' Warren eagerly asked.

" No, indeed; he slunk out of the court, like a whipped dog, with his tail between his legs, an' it drove him out of the counthry afther.   They put a tune to words an' the ballad-singers sang it outside his house every day for a month.   Indeed, it was a bad thing for thim anyhow that he left, for the crowd that gathered was surprisin', an' everyone bought a ballad.   Martin Hathen the blacksmith said that they offered to pay the rent to thry to keep him if he stopped.''

" Whose estate was that on? ''

" Lord Ballyshameon's, sir.''

" And was there no appeal made to him? ''

" Ah, he lives in London somewhere, an' there's no gettin' at him.   If he lived in the counthry it would be better for everybody, instead of givin' us the back hand.   Then we'd have the castle and the hunt and the trade, as it used to be in owld times.''

" That's your remedy is it, Biddy?   What about Home Rule? "

" Oh, indeed, Home Rule is the cure for the tooth-ache, if ye believe some people.   It's great powders it makes for the clockin' o' hens; it may be a good thing, or it may not, but to hear some of them talk ye'd think it was goin' to make grass grow on the rock an' turn sloes into peaches.   I'll take a penn'orth an' tary it, when it's on sale, tho' it isn't much better Biddy Maloney will be for the prescription.   Home Rule, faix, they don't talk so much to me about it.   There's Squire Fitz Martin now, he's failin', God betune him an' harm, an' his nephew, the lineal descendant of old Peter Fitz Martin, who drank himself to death, rest his soul, an' like father like son.   It's fine ducks and drakes he'd be makin' of the estate if it fell to him, what with his bettin' and gamblin' and drinkin'.   Throth, they may talk to me about independence as much as they like. I'll listen to them when they don't have their noses stuck in a pewter pint.   Ye should hear Miss Molly talkin' to them."

" Miss MacDaire gives them advice, does she? "

" The best of it, an' it's good hazel wasted on bad cattle.   Faix, she fights their battles the same as if her own flesh an' blood suffered, an' it's the broad back that's needed to shoulder all the load.   In throth, she'll be at the court-house to-morrow when Martin Doonas is brought up; he's another that's always burnin' his fingers in thryin' to pull other people's praties out of the greeshogue."

So Biddy garrulously wandered on until a stifled yawn from Warren checked her.

" It's tired ye are listenin' to all my blatherin'," she said, and with that abrupt apology left him to reflect on the day's adventures and her views on social and political economics.

Next morning Biddy paid an early visit to Paudeen. The lad was in a sound sleep when she entered. She held in her hand a letter which she had been perusing. Although she could not read, each word was scanned as if she knew its meaning. This practice of the widow had for its object the mastering of certain chance marks that might assist her later on in directing Paudeen in its reperusal. To this end a blot of ink, an erased word or a flaw in the paper was a godsend, and if nothing of a striking nature happened to be there the widow took care in the course of the day to supply her own land-marks, so that she could, in a moment, literally put her finger on the text.

After many ineffectual calls and vigorous shakings Paud. . . . . . . d his eyes and put the question, probably asked . . . . . . y child of Adam assailed in the same fashic . ., . . t's the matter? "

" S. . . , agra here's the letter. I tould ye it would come."

" Ye said it would come yesterday."

" Arrah, how could it come yesterday when it was intended to come to-day. Stop rubbin' yer eyes, asthore, an' read it."

" Sure, I must rub the sleep out of them. . . . .

" ' DEAR MOTHER AND BROTHER PAT,' " the boy began—" ' I hope ye are quite well, as this leaves me at pre (yawn) sent.' "

" Arrah now, Paudeen, how can I hear the word when ye yawn in the middle an' stifle the manin'? Would ye like a drop of warm milk, agra? "

" Wid pepper in it, like the last? " Paudeen exclaimed. " Divil a word I'll read if ye do that again. . . .

" ' The work has been bad on a/c of the strike,
but there's strike pay and we're all sha (yawn) rin'
alike.' "

" All shavin' alike! Arrah, what are ye readin' at
all, at all? "

" Ah, no, m ther, all shavin'—sharin', I mean.
Sure, it's yersel puts the wrong word in me mouth. Be
quiet an' I'll go on."

This deliberate misunderstanding on the part of the
widow was one of the devices to rouse Paudeen into full
wakefulness. The peppered-milk policy could not be
repeated and bribery was reserved for a second reading.
After the alteration the reading of the letter proceeded
without interruption, the greater part of which consisted of details relating to the farm. During this
time the mother followed the boy's eyes, and as he
stopped here and there to decipher a badly-written
word, or go back on a line to get the sense, she mentally
marked the spot, so that as he was about to turn over a
fresh page she interrupted him:

" I don't think ye got the sinse of Tom's remark
about the wether sheep; go back to the splash there,
where the pen dug a hole in the paper."

A first revision Paudeen rarely objected to; it was
later on, when a second and third were demanded, that
diplomatic resources came into play.

Paudeen re-read the paragraph.

" An' there was something near the crooked line at
the top about—what was it about? " the mother asked.

The boy re-read a word here and there.

" Arrah, how can I tell it from ' the ass's spanchel '?

Sure, that might be used for anything—the pig or the cow," Biddy protested.

The whole paragraph was re-read in a screaming voice.

" It isn't that, an' thank ye for shoutin'. It must be on the other page. I know that it was at the top; it's there at that small little crooked line—not the long one."

Meanwhile Paudeen had turned over, and something catching his eye he exclaimed:

" Arrah, what's this? "

" How can I tell what it is until ye read it? "

" ' And now, mother, it's strange news I'll be tellin' ye, and sure ye can't have heard it or Pat would have wrote. Lord Ballyshameon is dead and a new heir is coming into the estate.' "

" Oh, the Lord save us! that's great news an' no mistake," Biddy ejaculated.

" ' I saw it in a halfpenny paper,' " the letter continued, " ' an' in truth it's small compliments it wasted on the old lord. It said, " This noble earl held the questionable distinction of being one of the biggest landowners in Ireland and drawing the largest revenue from the most rack-rented estate in the whole country. His son, the succeeding earl, is travelling abroad at present, but our readers will remember we called attention, not long ago, to his career at Cambridge. He carried off the highest distinctions of the University and became President of the Union." ' "

" Faix, then, we don't think any great shakes of that post in these parts," the mother commented.

" Whisht, mother, will ye? " Paudeen pleaded, and continued to read.

" · '" His speeches at the Union showed a leaning towards Liberalism, and it is said some differences with his father on that question led to his going abroad." ' "

" Then it's bad they must be if they were worse than the differences they have at the Union here," Biddy commented.

" At present his whereabouts is unknown, and there is great reluctance on the part of the family to give information on the subject.   This reserve has not, unnaturally, led to much speculation, and even to the canvassing of the opinion that the young earl is dead.' " "

" Dead?   If he's dead too, mother, sure we'd be all landlords, wouldn't we? " said Paudeen, looking up from the letter.

" Well, well, this is strange news indeed," Biddy crooned, rocking herself to and fro, " the owld lord dead and the new lord lost.   Providence guide us, in whose hands will we be at all, at all?   I wonder if Mr Pinkerton knows of it?   Faix, he took the rent anyway, as if it was goin' into the owld lord's pockets; och, wirra stru, what with the death of ⌐ ⌐r Fitz Martin, an' Sergeant Doyle, an' now Lord ɒallyshameon, bedad, there's people dyin' this year that never died before."

Biddy hovered round Warren's breakfast-room that morning with an air of great mystery and importance. The possession of news which the whole town, nay more, the entire county, was ignorant of, was a matter of no little moment.   The inhabitant that was instrumental in floating off any straw that ruffled the even tenor of the stream of gossip enjoyed not riety as long as the ripple lasted, but to convey the s' rtling news of the demise of the best-hated man in the county was to launch a dreadnought, with cataclysmal effect, which would agitate every skiff along the entire Western coast.

Biddy felt encumbered with the sense of so great a secret; how to unburden herself in a manner befitting the occasion was the question. Were it a betrothal, a marriage, or a birth, or a death of an ordinary character she would have found no difficulty in negotiating it into the small coin of gossip currency. At first she thought of Bob Dorris, the postman. He knew who the letter was from that had been delivered that morning, and a word to him would mean the circulation of the news at every door. But the matter was too big for such piecemeal handling. It must be presented with all the importance of a valuable draft, with the name of the payee duly endorsed on the back.

So engrossed was Biddy that she laid the table without including the plates, and when Warren called attention to the omission it afforded her the opportunity of making him the first recipient of the news.

" There, now," she exclaimed in apology, " my mind is gone to smithereens this mornin'; faix, ye'll have to keep an eye on me to-day, for I won't be accountable for my actions! " with a shake of her head and a mysterious air that invited questioning.

" Why, what is the matter, Biddy? " Warren asked, looking up from a coil of line that he was winding on a salmon reel. " Are you not well this morning? "

" Well! In throth I wish other people was as well as I am. It's good to have the health for our own sake, but indeed we can't have it for other people."

" Is Paudeen ill, then?   I thought I heard you in his room early this morning."

" Paudeen ill!   Indeed, you might draw him through the river an' it would not hurt him any more than an otter.   The boy is well, thank God; it's me other son that upset me—asking yer pardon for forgetting the plates.   They say bad news travels fast, but it's slow enough this has been, so that the poor man's cowld in his grave before we knew anything of it.   Me boy Tom—" said Biddy, pausing under evident emotion. Warren looked up apprehensively, fearing that the bad news referred to her son.

" Throth, thin, it's often I get the good news an' the good advice, so that I'm countin' the days until the next letter comes, but this one has the bad news of death; pages 4 and 5 and a separate half-sheet is taken up with it."

The lugubrious tone in which all this was said led Warren to think that the bereavement was a family one.   Feeling his way carefully he said:

" Oh, I am so sorry; what was the illness? "

" That's what I don't know, indeed, nor Tom himself, it seems; leastways, he doesn't say."

A half-puzzled, half-amused look stole into Warren's face at the deceased's reticence upon the nature of his own demise.   Evidently relieved, he added:

" It's not your son that has—is ill, then? "

" Tom dead! " Biddy exclaimed, not putting too fine a point on it.   " Why should it be me boy? "

" Who is it then? " Warren asked bluntly.

" Lord Ballyshameon, sir, and no other."

The abrupt communication had a startling effect on the listener.

" God bless my soul! " he exclaimed.   Then, after
a pause, " I happen to know his son."

" Faix, thin, didn't the news come on meself like a
thunderclap without be yer lave or a word of warnin'."

" His Lordship must have been an old man? " the
other asked, recovering his composure.

" Throth, thin, owld age scarcely kilt him, for it isn't
long since the eldest son came of age himself," and Biddy
ran off all the particulars in the extract from the Liverpool evening paper.

Warren was an attentive listener to all this, and
questioned Biddy as to the likely effect of the intelligence
upon the tenants.

" It's that same that's botherin' me; sure, they
don't know a thing about it, an' when the news gets on
its legs it will be over the counthry whilst ye'd be sayin'
thrapsticks.   Sure, the Squire himself doesn't know
or he'd have towld ye."

" He made no allusion to it, certainly."

" Then it's meself would like him to know, an'
maybe you'll be seeing him or Miss Molly," she added,
deeply sensible of her own importance in being the
indirect medium of such a communication.

Warren's enthusiasm as an agent of the tidings did
not commend itself to his informant, and Biddy withdrew to devise a policy of her own.   The question put
to her by Warren on leaving the room as to the time
Doonas's trial would take place that day materially
assisted her plans.

CHAPTER VIII

THE court-house to which Martin Doonas was brought for trial was a square, white-washed building, as grim in appearance as the purposes for which as an institution it existed. There the petty cases of drunkenness and larceny amongst the civil community were heard, the debts which made defaulters, and the assaults, the outcome of exuberance of feeling, leading to broken heads or torn garments at the close of market and fair days.

The latter episodes incidental to all civic conviviality are accentuated in the case of the Celt, whose temperament lends itself to acts of petty violence, which are repented of as quickly as they are committed. The great majority of cases never find their way into court, the parties concerned settling their differences by expressions of mutual regret and vows of friendship, frequently with no basis of fact apart from reactionary feeling. When they become the subject of litigation the object of the plaintiff is as a rule not vindictive. He is more concerned with demonstrating to his neighbours that he is as good a man as his assailant, or a great deal better, although he may happen to get the worst of it on occasion, and the sole object of the trial is to reinstate himself in their eyes. If it can be shown that the broken head or blackened eye is not the effect of inferior pugilistic qualities the complainant is content, and a judicial fine of half a crown is accepted as a *quod erat demonstrandum.*

The court is usually well attended when cases of assault are heard, the parties concerned taking care to advertise them liberally. A bandage worn on the head on market-day preceding the trial is in itself all that is needed to elicit questions. Put directly to the sufferer, he pooh-poohs the matter as of infinite insignificance, a mere scratch, and a little difference between himself and Paddy Casey on the way home after the fair. . . .

" Oh, indeed, nothing worth talkin' about; the vet. put a piece of plaister on it just to keep the frost out."

This modest disclaimer would be immediately supplemented by a friend, who accompanied the injured one and judiciously dropping behind would supply particulars of the real state of affairs.

" In throth, it's light in the head he is with the loss of blood, an' it's himself does not know rightly what has happened."

" I don't mean that," in answer to some demur on the part of the sympathetic inquirer. " Bedad, then, I do mean it. Wasn't I an eye-witness? Sure, Paddy used a lump of rock when he was gettin' the worst of the fray. Throth, it might have been a case of murder out an' out. . . . Micky ought to be in his bed; I promised Mary to keep an eye on him,—weak as he is. Paddy had better keep out of his way, summons or no summons! "

Meanwhile the opponent, at the other end of the town, would be telling his version of the story to his admirers. " Throth, thin, it's ashamed I am meself of the same fight. Sure, if I thought he was such a wake crature I wouldn't have raised a finger to him; arrah, a puff of wind would knock him down. . . . An' to hear him talk ye'd wonder where he'd find room to bury his dead. I'd feel better plazed meself if it had been his grandfather that stood before me. It's little credit to be top dog when Micky's underneath."

When it comes to a matter of trial such modesty is set aside, an' the strongest case of incrimination is advanced on the one hand and defended on the other.

When assault and battery become the dingy background to a *cas célèbre*, such as moonlighting, cattle-driving or eviction, the disputants take care to employ the smartest solicitors in their respective interests.   On such occasions the court is crowded to its utmost capacity, and as the minor cases are disposed of the victor in the suit prides himself on his notoriety.

When Warren entered the court one of the officials in attendance, a member of the Royal Irish Constabulary, beckoned him to a seat at the solicitors' table, a courtesy invariably shown to strangers who evince an interest in these judicial proceedings.   The same functionary called in a loud voice for silence the moment the magistrate took his seat on the bench.   In the hush that followed the tramping of a man in heavy boots attracted the constable's attention.

" Didn't ye hear me call for silence, Tim Flaherty? Then be quiet; ye are putting too much ground under ye."

Tim, so pointedly admonished, stood still, and the first case was called.   It was that already advertised in the market.

" The plaintiff, your worship," the solicitor said, in opening, " is the victim of one Paddy Casey, a man of notorious habits, who is known from Tubbercurry to Ballyglass for his violence.   This assault is the climax of a series of threats which have kept the plaintiff in such a state of nervous apprehension as to make him incapable of defending himself.   In fact, if it hadn't been for the unfair method of attack, the case before your worship would be probably reversed, and the plaintiff would have to be answering the charge instead of pleading it. Your worship knows that a bit of a fight on the roadside is no unusual occurrence in this county. As long as human nature is human nature we must not expect perfection. But this ; a case where one man threatens another regularly, systematically, and with *malice prepense*, until the plaintiff's courage melts from him like water. When the critical moment arrives he is paralysed and incapable of making the defensive stand which prevents these cases from coming into court.

" It is one thing, your worship, for a man to stand up against another and settle a quarrel, the effect of an extra glass or an outburst of excitable feeling; it is another thing to stand up against a man that has threatened your life and has a dagger or a loaded stick up his sleeve. No one can fight a hedgehog without gloves on, and the plaintiff had no weapon to match the defendant. The short and the long of it is that this same Paddy Casey is a danger to the whole country-side. Such a man doesn't deserve to be at large, and Micky Dugan will have conferred a benefit on the whole community by coming here to-day as a victim of such villainy, for how he has been maltreated a glance plainly shows."

The plaintiff stepped on to the green table and the clerk handed him a copy of the New Testament to be sworn. The magistrate pulled down his glasses from his forehead and on to his nose and looked hard, dwelling particularly on the dimensions of the bandage. The clerk repeated the usual form, " To tell the truth and nothing but the truth," ordering the plaintiff to kiss the book. Micky took the Testament between his finger and thumb, raised it to his lips and kissed his own hand.

"You haven't kissed the book," the magistrate exclaimed sharply.

Micky protested it was the very thing he was after doing.

"Then kiss it again, sir, in the regular form."

Micky repeated the performance, bringing his lips nearer the book, but skilfully avoiding the volume.

"Stop, stop!" the magistrate said, intervening again as the Testament was handed back to the clerk. "Kiss that book, sir, or it will be the worse for you; you may deceive the Almighty with your tricks but you cannot deceive me."

Micky accepted this estimate of the magistrate's perspicacity, and with a loud smack on the back of the greasy volume complied with the requirements of the law.

The examination-in-chief followed the outline of the solicitor's opening speech. Then the cross-examination began. At this point the spectators commenced to nudge each other, and knowing winks were exchanged, a system of wireless telegraphy in vogue long before Marconi's.

Paddy Casey's solicitor commenced in dulcet and insinuating tones. For the first ten minutes the sympathetic form of the questions was so marked that it seemed as if the plaintiff had enlisted the service of both solicitors. "You complain," he proceeded, "that the defendant has shamefully threatened your life and like an honourable man you scorn to strike back with loaded weapons."

"I do."

" Am I wrong in surmising that he has injured you in other ways? "

" Bedad, he has. "

" He sold you a pig some time ago, I believe? "

" He did."

" What became of it? "

" It died of the swine faiver."

" See that now, and you say nothing on that head; you only complain of your own head "—casting a sympathetic glance at the bandage. " This is a court of justice, Micky, and its object is that full justice should be done to the likes of you. Now, without pressing you unduly—you don't want to be too hard on a neighbour—is there any other way the defendant has wronged you? "

" There is "—followed by a pause.

" I must remind you that you are on your oath; you promised to tell the whole truth, and even if it hits your neighbour the court ought to hear it. We are not ere to bolster up villains as the defendant has been described. What was the other wrong? "

" He sowld me seed potatoes—Protestant Peelers for Early Dewdrops."

Here a ripple of laughter rang through the court, followed by a loud cry of " Silence " and an indignant comment from the cross-examiner. " Your worship, I protest against this unseemly interruption; these are serious charges we are investigating."

" Go on, Mr Whee"e," the magistrate said deferentially.

" You are a teetotaller, I think? " was the next question, but the hilarity of the court put Micky on his guard.

" I am," he replied," in the same sense that yersel' is."

This was such a palpable hit that Micky turned the laugh against his cross-examiner.

"Oh, you like an occasional glass, do you? You had one or two the night of the assault?"

"I don't deny it."

"How many?"

"I didn't count."

"You had them on the way home?"

"I did."

"At what point did you stop counting?"

"I said I didn't count."

"You don't know how many you had then?"

"I do."

"But how, if you didn't count the glasses?"

"Oh, me throat holds a glass to a dhrop."

"Well, that's a convenient way of reckoning; and how many times did you fill it?"

"Until the drooth stopped."

"A very liberal method of measuring. It was a hot day, I think?"

"Oh, bedad it was."

"It was beyond Farrell's public-house the assault was made on you?"

"It was."

"And you dropped in and had a throat-filler just before?"

"I did not; I had only a thimbleful."

"Was it a tailor's thimble? You mentioned about the pig that died of the fever at Farrell's—"

A pause. "I might have—"

"Did you say anything about half the money being returned by the defendant?"

"I don't remember."

"Nor the threat you made against Casey?"

" No."

" What, sir! I have witnesses to call. Do you remember falling down after leaving Farrell's and being carried into the public-house again? "

" I do not."

" You were too drunk to remember."

" I can't carry as much as some people that I could name."

" It was after that you met the defendant."

" After I left the public-house to go home peaceably."

" And it was then the assault was made. Very well. There's a deep cut on your head, judging by the size of the bandage. Who attended you? Doctor Mahon? "

" No, the vet.," followed by laughter.

" The veterinary surgeon that attends pigs and cows and asses generally? Begad, your case was quite in his line. Take off that bandage and let the Bench see the gaping wound."

" In throth I won't, beggin' yer pardon, the—"

" Take off that bandage at once. Your worship," addressing the magistrate, " has an important agrarian case. The course I propose will save time and there will be no need to call witnesses."

There was a demur on the part of plaintiff's solicitor on the ground that the Bench was not there for the purpose of considering surgery but law, but the magistrate overruled it, and a constable was called, who began to unroll the bandage. It consisted of several yards of calico, and when the folds began to lengthen inordinately there was a titter that swelled into a loud laugh when nothing more than a slight scratch proved to be the occasion of such elaborate surgery.

The magistrate dismissed the case with a few words of caustic comment, and the defendant's solicitor had a parting shot.

" If," said Le, in applying for costs, " the plaintiff gained nothing by the case he would, to use the words of his learned friend, be conferring a benefit on the community at large by treating them to the sight of a new shirt, made out of the bandages, which, in the exigencies of the case," looking hard at the plaintiff, " seems highly desirable."

The case of the Crown versus Doonas was next called, and a perceptible change passed over the court, a change possible under all circumstances where public interests are at stake, but more remarkable where the volatile Celtic nature is concerned. The faces set in anticipation of amusement a moment before—every hard line relaxed, mobile mouths half-way on the road to laughter, liquid eyes expectantly twinkling—gave place to countenances rigidly prejudiced against the law and its administrators. The spectators suddenly became an unpanelled jury, that without hearing a word had already mentally pronounced the sentence of " Not guilty."

Let it be said, in explanation of this temper, which, like a subtle spirit, filled the court, and was immediately felt by the Bench, that every man and woman there knew the circumstances of the case more intimately than the magistrates, after witnesses had been called. It was the oft-repeated agrarian drama of landlord versus people, a set piece in which the acts were rehearsed *ad nauseam*—the man behind in his rent, notice to quit given, and the curtain falling on the last sordid scene — eviction. This tragedy, with changing *dramatis personæ*, was so frequently per-

formed that it was known by heart, and the consequences bit so deeply into human sensibility that the
law which defended it was deemed a monster.   Doonas
nad been an active sympathizer and was summoned
for a technical breach of the peace.

The constable who attended to give protection to
the landlords' " Crowbar Brigade," as the evictors were
nicknamed, alleged that Doonas had endeavoured to
prevent the tenants' removal and forcibly restrained
the police in the discharge of their duty; that he incited
other persons to combine in the same unlawful action,
and conspired with them for that purpose.

The defendant conducted his own case and cross-
examined the witness.

" Who are the persons I attempted to protect? "

" A man and woman."

" Was there an infant in arms? "

" There was a child."

" Was it in its mother's arms? "

" It was clinging to its mother."

" So that if the mother was injured, accidentally or
otherwise, the child might be hurt? "

" Possibly."

" At what age would you put the child? "

" I don't know."

" Was it old enough to walk? "

" I can't say."

" Come now, I want your opinion.   You are a father
yourself."

" More pity for his wife," a voice exclaimed from
the court, and approving murmurs, which   d a
loud cry of " Silence," followed with a thre   clear
the court.

" I put it to you," Doonas continued, " as a man

of experience, whether you think the child could walk? "

" I 'an't say."

" You can read—read that," and the defendant held out a document, but the magistrate interposed.

" You are not entitled to pass any written com-
..iunication to the witness; any document bearing on the case must be submitted to the court. What is that? "

" Only a certificate of birth, your worship," Doonas answered, handing up the paper. " It shows that the child is seven months old."

" Silence, sir. You must not make statements; you can only question the witness."

But the statement had its effect and thrilled the court. It is characteristic of the Celtic temperament that the legal point of view, as compared with the humane, is negligible. It was the juxtaposition of the two upon which the spectators fastened. Every person in the court, the magistrate excepted, knew that Jimmy Sweeny's child was an infant in arms. The disclosure of the fact, despite the ruling, caused a wave of emotion that made a hero of the accused.

The continuation of the cross-examination only vivified this point of view.

" You allege that I interposed to defeat the process of law; in what way? "

" By trying to prevent the eviction of the woman."

" She refused to leave the cabin? "

" She did."

" Whereon you used force?

" We did."

" And one o. the levellers took her by the arms and began to drag her towards the door. Is that so? "

No answer. Again a low murmur of indignation—the sign of a rising storm, not destined to be kept long within bounds. The magistrate felt it and looked round to estimate the strength of constabulary present. Not satisfied with the scrutiny the order to clear the court was not given.

" It was at that point I interfered? " defendant asked.

" It was."

" To protect a woman and child from violence? "

" I don't question your motive."

But here the magistrate interposed. " Are you going to call rebutting evidence on that point? " It was evident that the court was getting out of hand.

" I am not, your worship," Doonas replied emphatically.

" You admit interference? "

" In the interest of humanity I do."

An approving movement swayed the people. The magistrate commanded the witness to stand down, and without further preliminaries gave judgment.

" This," he said, " is the case of a person known conspiring with other persons unknown to keep possession of lands and tenements unknown, thereby causing a breach of the peace, and inciting divers other persons unknown to do likewise."

Then followed a glorification of the law, which provided redress against wrongs, the punishment of evildoers and ill-disposed persons. As to the accused, whilst giving him full credit for humane motives, he was ill-advised in attempting to prevent the process of law by consorting with other unlawfully-disposed persons, thereby setting them an example in lawlessness. He (the magistrate) was willing, out of his clemency, to be content to accept bail for good behaviour. At this point in the finding a new sense of commotion animated the spectators. It followed on the entrance of a woman, who hurriedly whispered some intelligence that passed round the court like wildfire.

The magistrate looked up angrily. " If anyone interrupts me in the administration of the law I shall commit him for contempt."

" Are you prepared to find bail? " he asked, addressing Doonas.

" I decline to do so."

"Then three months' imprisonment and—" But the rest of the sentence was lost in a loud shout of " Bail or gaol," followed by a cry of " Ballyshameon is dead," which was taken up by a score of voices and hurled defiantly at the Bench. " Dead, and the divil die along with him," from another voice, in a tone of bitter vindictiveness.

"Arrest that man," cried the magistrate, pointing to the interrupter, who was waving his stick and shouting excitedly. Two policemen moved forward, but there was a rush from behind in defence of the offender. The situation became critical. Half a dozen sticks were flourished, and the constables, armed with bayonets, laid their hands on the hilts. The magistrate rose, and vainly endeavouring to command attention abruptly declared the court closed and left the bench. In another moment the surging throng would have swept down on the small knot of policemen. It was checked by the intervention of a young woman who sprang on to a seat and held up restraining hands. The rush stopped and the clamorous voices grew silent.

" It's the colleen herself," came the whisper from different quarters.

Warren, seated at the solicitors' table, had risen with the rest, apprehensive of the serious turn events had taken. He felt a shock of pained surprise on seeing Miss MacDaire interposing in such a brawl. In the momentary pause there was no time to divine motives, but Molly's first words explained themselves.

" Men, men! " she exclaimed, and there was a tremor in her voice, the effect of deep feeling, " is this the way to serve your cause? I am ashamed of you. Martin Doonas is going to prison without a murmur."

" We'll release him this minuit if ye'll only say the word," a voice shouted.

" Oh, indeed," Molly retorted. " When I want a champion I'll send for you, Gallagher," a light touch that brought smiles to the scowling faces. " Fools! " she exclaimed in a tone of fine scorn. " Don't you know that Martin is charged with inciting to a breach of the peace? Your conduct is the only proof that the charge is true. Where is your sense, where is your tact? What has Martin Doonas done that you should turn witnesses for the prosecution? "

" Sure, the sentence is passed anyhow; it can't make a difference now."

" Then is this the last of the evictions? " Molly astutely retorted. " Are there no other infants in arms beside Bridget Sweeny's that want protecting? " followed by assenting murmurs of " Oh, ah, bedad, the colleen is right."

" There is not a man in Ireland who stands charged with the same offence that will not suffer if this is a sample of your policy. Where is your common-sense?" she asked, the deep blue eyes scanning the countenances and challenging an answer. Sullen faces turned away from hers, sobered and ashamed.

"If you want to break heads go outside and then bandage them like Micky Dugan's."

The reference evoked a burst of laughter; the audience was glad of the diversion, and in a moment not a serious face was left.

"Oh, it will do you more good than Micky; thick heads need cracking to let in a little light," Molly added, floating off a home truth on a humorous wave.

"But it's no joking matter. I'm ashamed of you. Martin Doonas has broken the law in a humane cause, and has accepted his sentence in dignified silence. Law or no law we're proud of our fellow-townsman."

A loud cheer went up, repeated again and again.

But, despite Molly's good offices in averting a breach of the peace, which might have had serious consequences, there were faces which never lost their scowl and silently resented her interference. Her quick eyes discovered them. From a secluded part of the room she had been watching the spectators throughout the trial; she knew that the court was charged with inflammable material, and that the injudicious use of a match would cause a conflagration. The man Gallagher, upon whom she rounded, was a firebrand, and there were others of a similar temper. Irish people are easily led, and as Molly was the good angel, others like demons, seized on excitable moments to side-track them down a steep place.

When she felt sure that she had them in her hands she tactfully led up to that.

"Are you going to take my advice now," she

asked, when the cheers subsided, "and go quietly to your homes?"

"We are, colleen," came the response generally.

"Ah," she exclaimed, "your answer is ready enough now, but before you are round the corner some of you will be equally agreeable to a different proposal; like the church weathercock, any breeze turns it. When some of the wind-bags that emptied themselves last night are filled again the policy of shillelaghs will be adopted. But the heads that advise it take care to keep in the background; there is not much fear of them getting broken. When will you have the sense to see that oysters cannot be opened with black-thorns?"

The crowd became plastic in the girl's hands as she addressed them. Her face was flushed, her voice rose and fell in tones of persuasive emotion. She knew every man in the room, and by sharp glances directed to different parts singled out the firebrands in such a way that the point of the reference could not be mistaken.

"Go back to the Jimmy Sweenys, the certificated seven-months'-old babies, stand by them as Martin Doonas did, and take your trial like men."

The allusion to the evictions and suffering children went home to the hearts of the listeners, and the crowd, with a sob, followed by a loud cheer, swayed towards Molly, and hands were stretched out to grasp hers. They would have carried her from the place had she permitted it, and with a "God bless ye," and "Long life to ye, miss," a sobered, orderly people filed out of the court and quietly dispersed their several ways.

Warren witnessed the scene amidst conflicting feelings. His sense of decorum was sorely hurt at the first evidence of disturbance. Such an exhibition was intolerable, and he was in full sympathy with the magistrate who had threatened to clear the court. As to the trial, the evidence of the constable seemed too slender to base a conviction on. Doonas's cross-examination severely shook it. The magistrate, fastening on the accused's admission that he had interfered in the interests of humanity, and pronouncing summary judgment, seemed a miscarriage of justice. The law of the matter seemed strangely muddled. To require bail for good behaviour from a man who, on the magistrate's own showing, was to be credited with humane motives, seemed to Warren to be out of keeping with all legal usage. In short, his sympathies were with Doonas.

Then came the cry of " Bail or gaol," and again the sense of the fitness of things was rudely disturbed; but when it was followed by an exhibition of bad taste, and the name of the dead nobleman was hurled defiantly at the Bench, Warren was shocked and deep feelings of resentment stirred within him.

" This is scandalous," he exclaimed, loud enough to be heard by those near him.

Then came the interposition of Molly. Warren had an innate dislike to the interference of women in public affairs. He was an opponent of female suffrage in the learned professions and in politics, and had won distinction in a debate on the subject at his University. He described women's ambitions to enter the lists with men as hybrid mascularity. The arguments, marshalled academically, were convincing enough, but here was a practical demonstration of a woman's power, and all the fine-spun dialectics against sex disqualification were shattered before it. No " mere man " could have grasped the situation more tactfully and handled it with greater skill, and Warren's admiration, as he listened to the girl, flamed up and consumed his prejudices. It was impossible, also, to disguise from himself the interesting personality of the speaker. Molly's face showed in profile from where he sat, and the beautifully-moulded cheek and white throat quivering with eagerness, the swift glance that seemed to flash fuller meaning into words, gave persuasiveness to argument, the imperiousness of beauty that coupled with reason and good sense never makes its bid in vain.

CHAPTER IX

THAT evening a group of men met in a blacksmith's forge. They were eagerly engaged in discussing the events of the day: Martin Doonas's trial, the demise of Lord Ballyshameon, and the intervention of the colleen in the fracas betveen the people and police.

The forge was on the outskirts of the town and stood well back from the road. A turf-fire ring, used for heating tyres before clamping them on the cart-wheel, was still smouldering after recent use. Near by there was a wooden trough of water for cooling. A scrap-iron heap was on one side of the forge and a stack of turf on the other. Immediately behind spread the undulating moor, the heather so close that its bells could be seen swinging in the wind. The music in them could only be heard by the fairies who, when the moon rose, danced to the strains. To poets they were censers that swung out aromatic perfume, with which the evening air was laden. Beyond the moor there was black bogland, and in the far distance mountains.

Inside the forge the earthen floor was blackened with waste-iron dust, once thrown off in brilliant meteoric sparks—born of a sledge stroke—which fell in radiating showers and died in a moment. Heaps of coarse filings caught the spasmodic light from the fire and responded in dull reflection.

Jack Bolan, the smith, a fine type of the modern Vulcan, was the recipient of what might be described as " court news." He was one of the few absentees from the day's proceedings.

" I was drawin' on me coat to join the fun," he explained, feeling that an apology was due, " when Mr Pinkerton called with his horse, which had dropped a shoe as he was goin' rent-collectin' on the Rathskeemin estate."

" Then ye missed a treat. Micky Dugan's bandage was not bad for a start, but it would have warmed the cockles of yer heart to hear the colleen."

The speaker was squatted on the hub of a wheel on one side of the forge, the blue shirt opened at the neck, the prominent " Adam's apple " rising and falling in his throat as he spoke, and the stockinged stump of the left wrist easily proclaimed the identity of Dennis Fahy.

In the pause the smith tucked the long handle of the bellows beneath his left arm and blew to the creaking accompaniment of the leather sides.

" Bejabers, before she jumped on the form the boys were ready to strike their ould grandmother if she came in the way, and in two minuits they were as quiet as lambs. The way she talked took all the edge off the fun, and ye began to feel as if ye were goin' to commit murder."

" She saved the bobby's head anyhow, which would have been nately combed after his evidence against Martin."

The comment came from Ned M'Guire, who sat cross-legged on an old anvil and formed the apex of a triangle, of which the smith and Dennis constituted the base.

Between the creakings of the bellows the smith jerked out his words.

" Blackthorns are useful enough of a fair day (creak, crake) but they are no match for bayonets (creak, crake); at close quarters you stand no chance" (creak, creak, crake), came the closing spasms of the bellows in two shorts and a long.

When the sharp rings on the horse-shoe ended and the vibrations of the hammer ceased—after knocking the nonsense out of the hot iron—the point raised by the smith was discussed in all its bearings.

" Arrah, they cannot do much with them bayonets in a crowd—it's like swinging a flail in a pigsty. They daren't stab ye, an' can only lay about them with the flat; ye could wring them out of their hands."

" Howld yer whisht, Ned," the blacksmith said, sending a shower of sparks helter-skelter with an extra vigorous blow. " The sorra much ye would ever do with the hand that touched the bobby's bayonet" (whack, whack! klink! klink! klink! klink!)

" Why not? "

" Because there's a jagged edge half-way up the back like that rasp"—pointing to a tool on the bench— " only as sharp as needles; one drive and the hand that held the weapon would be scarified to the bone."

" Of course it would," Dennis corroborated.

" Yes, an' what's more," the blacksmith added, ready to point a moral, " crackin' heads and sawin' hands won't cure the pshata rot."

" No, nor women's chat either," came from a distant corner of the forge. The only evidence of the speaker's presence up to that moment consisted of the flickering light that came from the pipe in his mouth and the extra smacks to draw it into life. This was of frequent occurrence in the course of conversation, and during the smith's description of the bayonet the vital spark ebbed so low that the efforts were followed by loud gurglings in the bowl.

"Faix, yer head, like yer pipe, needs clearing, Tim," Dennis replied, warmly taking up the challenge. "Women's chat, as ye call it, was more than ye could answer in the court this mornin'."

This sally raised a laugh against Gallagher, who, by keeping in the background of the court and egging the others on to a conflict with the police, championed a policy which on more than one occasion got others into trouble. He was one of a small class that always hung on the outskirts of agitation and was ready with unconstitutional methods frequently leading to outrage.

"Psha! it's not women we are fighting, nor do we want them to fight for us. The colleen is very well in her way; there's a soft place under the boys' waistcoats that she is always touching," and Gallagher came forward to the fire and applied a red-hot iron to his pipe. In the act the white glow passed into a dull red.

"Look at that," he said, holding up the rod; "the minute you stop blowing and take it out of the fire it grows cold. Women's talk is a poor bellows to keep an agitation alive, and without agitation where are ye? What has Ireland ever gained without it?"

"Throth, Tim, you are like the doctor, who writes the prescription but never takes the medicine himself. Agitation, ye say! It's all very well to direct that from the background, where there isn't much danger of head-breakin'," Dennis caustically observed, rubbing in the taunt.

"Oh, I'll take my share when the time comes, never fear."

"Oh, indeed, no one doubts that; you lit your pipe

8

with the hot iron but the sorra a hand ye gave Jack with the bellows."

" Oh, it's aisy enough to raise the wind," the smith joined in, " but ye want other things as well," and he stretched his hand towards the cooling tank and drew out a brush dripping with water. " Ye need a damper where there's too much combustion," giving the fire a dab that set it hissing. " Tim is all right at the bellows, but when I employ him, throth, I'll want the colleen with the damper."

Gallagher smarted under all this raillery and tried to divert the light from himself as soon as possible.

" It's all very well for you to give illustrations," he said, " but you can use the damper too freely and put the fire out, and that's what's happening in any case. As you find it so useful, why don't you use it in other cases? "

He paused, to give effect to the new point he was raising. The blacksmith's arm remained suspended on the bellows' handle, and the glowing fire sank, deepening the shadows in distant corners of the forge.

" Who is this friend of the colleen's that goes about fishing and shooting and ferreting out the price of land—poking his nose into every hut on the hillside— why don't you put the damper on him? "

" That's another iron to hammer," the smith laconically observed.

" An' not enough heat in it to shape it into anything useful," Dennis added. " What about him? He came in Mr Doonas's yacht and he is a friend of the colleen's, as you say. None of us is likely to hang him on the strength of that evidence."

" And he has rented the shooting-lodge from Mr

Pinkerton, Lord Ballyshameon's agent; that count must not be left out of the indictment," said Gallagher.

" The shootin' is for anyone that likes to pay for it, I suppose," Dennis replied.

" Well, but how do you know he is not a land-grabber? "

The presentation of the case in that light had its effect on the listeners, and sympathetic " ahs " and " begorras " were ejaculated.

" I don't pretend to know other people's business as well as my own," Dennis rejoined evasively.

" Are you sure he is not a land-grabber? " Gallagher pressed, following up his advantage.

" I'm sure," Dennis replied quietly.

" You're sure but not certain? "

" Oh, I leave that to other people."

" Have you asked him? " Gallagher inquired, reading sympathy in the silence.

" Asked him? I know my place, I hope."

" Yes, but do you know your duty to your country? "

" Oh, in throth I do, an' too well to go about asking impertinent questions. I have talked to Mr Warren and heard him talk, and I can tell a land-grabber when I see him."

Gallagher met this with an acrid laugh, then added:

" Ah, indeed, to hear some people talking you'd think butter would not melt in their mouths. It's short memories they have, but that's a convenience, no doubt. Do you mind the Scotchman that used to say he was just ' gangin' aboot to have a look at the crops and the baisties,' and who used to put up his hands in holy horror and say, ' Twa poond for that wee bit land,' and gave four pound for it after the tenant was evicted? Psha, you talk about ' putting on the damper.' Why don't you put it on that kind of thing?" and Gallagher jumped from where he was sitting and brought his fist down on the bench with an oath.

His violence excited the listeners in the passage-of-arms between the two countrymen. The smith laid on with the hammer to a piece of iron as if every blow fell on the head of a land-grabber; sparks of passion flew from excited eyes as well as from the red-hot iron.

Dennis himself was by no means unaffected, but he knew his man better than the others. His association with Doonas and Molly put him in possession of other views on these vexed questions. He often listened to their condemnation of methods which got innocent people into trouble and did more harm than good to the cause. He was anxious, however, to avoid an open breach with Gallagher. The latter had slipped off the grill on which he had been roasting; the wise course was to try and get him on to it again, a favourite method of procuring the best of an argument in Ireland.

" Don't let us be mentionin' names, boys," he said, n   ards the open door.

"   't care a thrawneen who hears me," the other eja   l, spitting over his shoulder.

" Ah, yes, of course, it is easy to say that here. Every cock crows loudest on his own dunghill; but why did not you attack the Scotch land-grabber at the time, when you discovered him? The sorra many questions you asked him."

" We got rid of him anyway."

" We? Who's the 'we'? Are there pigs in your belly? Ask the two boys that are in gaol this minuit, and in throth some of us need not walk far to put hands on the man who egged them on, but who took good care to keep his own head out of the halter."

Gallagher writhed under this rehearsal, and the black passion in his face could be seen in the dull light of the forge. During the final words he groped on the bench and his fingers closed on the head of a heavy hammer. The smith saw the move .nt and stepped between the disputants.

" No, Tim," he exclaimed, holding up his hands in protest, " you began the talk and cowld iron isn't fair argument."

" I can't fight him," Gallagher cried angrily, " he has only one hand."

" Bejabers, that's a fine reason," Dennis sneered, now thoroughly aroused and jumping to his feet. " He won't fight me because I've only a single hand, and wants to make things equal with the help of a hammer-head. Throth, then, the one hand is good enough for such a coward. Come on, ye sneakin' spalpeen," and Dennis leaped into the centre of the floor.

Gallagher came forward to meet him, but Paddy Murray, the fourth man, who had taken little part in the conversation—a big, strapping fellow—interposed, and taking Gallagher round the waist lifted him bodily and set him on the bench again.

" It's polite to keep the fightin' until the conversation is finished," said he, with the greatest sang-froid. " The divil a word have I been able to get in edgeways. Throth, ye keep the monopoly of the chat to yerselves, like Owney M'Kaffery with a pint o' porter. Be quiet, will ye, or I'll carry ye out an' dip ye in the tank; it's good for coolin' brass as well as iron "—this to Gallagher, who made a fresh feint of pugilistic bravery.

" I say, boys," he continued, " did any of ye hear what Shawn O'Grady did to Mrs Mulligan, the hotelkeeper? No? Oh, begorra, it was a great joke. Arrah, don't be talkin', me sides are sore laughin' at it. Ye know the old lawyer that came down from Dublin to act for the Crown in the thrial? "

" We do, to be sure," the smith replied.

" Well, ye know he stayed at the hotel. Shawn heard that nothing would plaze him but a jugged hare for dinner. Biddy Maloney happened to be in town and Mrs Mulligan asked her if she could get one.

" ' The divil won't plaze the same lawyer, Biddy,' says she.

" ' Faith, then, he must be hard to plaze,' says Biddy.

" ' What have ye to ate, Mrs Mulligan? ' says he.

" ' Chicken an' ham, sir,' says she, thinkin' that would be substantial and accommodatin'.

" ' Oh, cock and bacon agen',' says he, throwin' up his hands. ' I'm so sick of it that I'd rather hear an ass brayin' than a cock crowin'.'

" ' Oh, the disrespectful baist,' says Biddy.

" ' I suppose all the cattle round here have the foot-and-mouth disease too,' he says, lookin' hard at Mrs Mulligan. ' That's what they tell me all over the circuit.'

" In throth Mrs Mulligan took her cue from the same excuse, an' says she, knowin' that Malory Kelly had nothing that mornin' but fresh-killed mutton and beef as tough as leather, ' Well, sir, I don't know about the disase out an' out, but indeed the cattle isn't lookin' well lately.'

" ' Oh, God bless me,' says he, ' I wonder there's anything for lawyers to do down here, the people are so frank and honest. It is so thoughtful of you to keep an eye on the cattle and watch their state of health.

Is there no game to be had—grouse or hares now?'
says he.

" ' There is, sir,' says she, ' but it's hard to get them.
We used to have plenty at one time,' settin' a thrap for
him.

" ' Foot-and-mouth-disease affects the supply?'
says he, innocently.

" ' No, indeed, sir,' says she, ' but forty shillin's or a
month hard.'

" Well, he laughed a power.

" ' Indeed, sir,' says she, ' if you gentlemen
were a little more lanient the game market would
improve.'

" ' Well,' says Biddy, ' may the first bit of a hare
he ates choke him.'

" ' There's a good many clerks would say amen to
that prayer,' says the widow, ' an' if for no other raison
I'd like to get him one. You wouldn't have one in the
lodge to spare, Biddy? ' says she, ladin' up to the rale
raison for the chat.

" Biddy had a hare, but it occurred to her that she'd
rather fatten the gentleman at the lodge with it than
run the risk of cbokin' the lawyer. 'But,' says she,
' Shawn O'Grady sowld it to me, an' he might have
another. I'll ask him.'

" Well, back Biddy went to the lodge.

" ' You wouldn't have another hare to spare? ' she
axed Shawn, who was tyin' flies for the gintleman.
' The owld lawyer at Mrs Mulligan's is dyin' for a taste
of one.'

" ' Is it Mrs Mulligan that wants it? ' says Shawn.
' If I had a hundred I wouldn't let her have a scut of
one o' them and I haven't—'

" ' Oh, Shawn, don't be so hard on the widow, and

she putting in a word for the poachers too,' says Biddy.
' It might be all the better for ye when they have ye up
the next time for trespass in pursuit of game. Sure,
that owld divil could hang ye if he liked, an' the best
way to prevent what is past is to put a stop to it before
it happens. What's the leg of a hare to you if it keeps
your legs off the treadmill? '

" Well, whilst Biddy was talkin', Shawn began to
scratch his head as if he was thinkin'.

" ' It goes against me grain altogether,' says he,
' to be afther doin' anything for the same widow; she's
disrespectful,' says he.

" It was that was killin' Shawn out an' out. One
day, when he was talkin' about the fairies, she says to
him, half jokin', whole in earnest, ' The divil a
fairy there is in the counthry at all, at all, except in
your own head, an' the sorra thing else it's fit for
howldin'.'.'

" In throth I was standin' at the door meself at the
time, an' to me dyin' day I won't forget the look he
gave her. Bejabers, he could have eat her without salt
that instant minuit.

" ' Throth, thin,' says he, turning on his heel, ' ye'll
know the rights o' that some day.'

" Well, he hadn't done scratchin' his head for some
time an' at last he raked somethin' out of it.

" ' Well, I must run over to Scarrajoul for a hare,
but I'll be back agen before I've well started. How-
somedever,' says he, ' maybe I ought to drag the pelt
off your one before I go.'

" ' All right, avic,' says Biddy, bringing him the hare
to skin.

" ' Sure, it isn't the pelt yersel' will be wantin',' he
says to Biddy, lookin' at it with an admirin' eye. ' It

will do for a cap for Johnny the whip-maker; he made a new one for his reel-footed son out of the owld one he wore himself all the winter.'

" So off goes Shawn, pelt an' all.

" Well, in no time he was at the hotel with an elegant hare in his hand.   Sure, Mrs Mulligan gave him all the blessin's of the saints, an' a few more, when she saw it.

" ' Is it high enough for to-night's dinner, Shawn? ' says she.

" ' Well, ma'am,' says he, ' it would be better for hangin' a little longer,' pushin' the lids apart an' showin' a fine clear eye.

" ' The quality is good? ' says she.

" ' Oh, the best,' s.ʼ   ` ' but it's short notice ye gave me, or it might i   ʌste higher.   But keep it hangin',' says he, ' until ʓue last instant minute before skinnin' it; it will be all the better for that.'

" ' Very good,' says she, an' throth she gave him an extra shilling for the hare.

" Well, me dears, when they came to skin it, just as a fine piece of pork was boilin', the divil a thing was underneath the pelt but tow, with sheet lead to make it heavy, and didn't a pair of glass eyes drop out on the table.   'Oh, the saints preserve us!' says the cook, crossin' herself and lookin' at the two eyes rowlin' along all as one as if they were alive.

" Well, the rows an' the ructions Mrs Mulligan kicked up when she found how she'd been tricked by Shawn is beyond all tellin'.   ' A thrick? ' says Shawn, when someone told him about it as he was lavin' the court this mornin'; ' the sorra thrick in it. If people are disrespectful to the fairies they must take the consequences,' says he, with a face on him as long as a fiddle, an' sorra another word could anyone get out of him."

This story, told by Paddy Murray in his swift, rollicking style, completely changed the temper that a few moments before pervaded the forge, and was on the point of causing serious consequences. Angry faces relaxed and frowns melted into smiles. The subject was immediately taken up and discussed.

" Arrah, there isn't a man in Dublin can stuff a bird or a fox like the same Shawn O'Grady. Small wonder the widow was desaved," observed the smith.

" Indeed, there's great wisdom in him," says Gallagher, forgetting his anger in the course of the story. " The man that bought Shawn for a fool would be a long time out of his money."

" It isn't so much folly or wisdom with him as religion, Tim," said Dennis, responding to Gallagher's advance in friendliness. " He believes in the fairies, an' thinks it his duty to do anything they bid him. If he thought they wished him to drink Poullamore dry he'd attempt it."

" Is that so now? " said Gallagher, looking very grave.

" The sorra lie in it; he takes his orders from the fairies as Johnny would for horse-shoes, and he'd let nothing interfere. I don't think the word of the priest would turn him."

" It's very convanient to put the blame on the fairies; they are not subject to summary jurisdiction like the rest of us," said Paddy. " Ye mind the case of the ass, Dennis, that was found in the whinny field pit, spanchled so that it couldn't rise? "

" I do well; the one that was always trespassin' in the Poullamore field? "

" The same, in throth. Well, it was the fairies did that too by all accounts, although Shawn O'Grady was seen twistin' the soogaun that bound his legs the day before."

" Well, boys," said Paddy, " I think it's time for us to be goin' home *now*," and the emphasis on the now was accompanied by a knowing look, which passed into a broad smile when he heard good-nights exchanged between Dennis Fahy and Tim Gallagher.

Oh, Ireland, what storms sweep you, what shallows and deeps you reveal. How swift is your anger, like sudden squalls lashing peaceful water into surging tides! How subtle your humour, turning passion-strained faces into laughter, the spray of conflict into smiling April tears! Ah, beneath your impulsive wayward-ness there is a hidden depth from which these contradictions emanate—like sparks from fine-tempered metal, music from high-tensioned strings. Other eyes may read in this blots and failings; to one of your sons, dear country, these conflicting passions in your heaving breast are but the travail of a native genius which awaits the hour of its birth!

CHAPTER X

ON his return from the court Warren found an invitation to dine at Squire Fitz Martin's. He sat down to luncheon full of conflicting thoughts in regard to the scene he had witnessed. He partook of the fare in so automatic a fashion that at the end of the meal he was probably ignorant of the nature of the dishes that the kindly housekeeper had provided. His mind was preoccupied, his thoughts in a whirl.

When the table was cleared he sought relief in unburdening himself in a letter to Max Montagu, his college companion.

" I have just returned from a trial in an Irish court," he wrote, " which has supplied me with material of an extremely indigestible nature. One of ordinary police-court sordidness opened the proceedings. A mere case of assault during a drunken brawl, the details of which, under usual circumstances, one would be gladly excused. In the course of the hearing, interests clustered round it of such a nature as to give its gruesome particulars quite a poetic setting. Assault and battery in the hands of the Irish Bench become wit and comedy to such a degree that one might imagine himself in a theatre instead of a court of justice, and be pardoned for applauding the genius of an author for conceiving the play, and the actors for the manner of its performance. There was no mistaking the air of expectation with which the auditors sat down to listen to the proceedings, and none of them could complain that they had been disappointed. The way the common clay of everyday life is moulded into fancy figures bespeaks a rare genius. The solicitor that did not show an aptness for this and give it a leading place in forensic art would be intolerable. Plaintiff and defendant freely contributed to the same end. It seemed to me to be a case of *noblesse oblige*, and the man that failed in his part would be denied in the future the luxury of a broken head or the right of giving someone else the privilege of claiming damages. A bewitching air of humour filled the court, and for the time being the impersonator of justice, instead of being robed in wig and gown, might have found in cap and bells a more fitting symbol of office.

" I do not wish you to infer from this that justice in any sense of the word miscarried. If I ever doubted that humour was a valuable servant of justice, what I witnessed this morning would have convinced me; indeed, the case where justice seemed to me to miscarry was where the tragic, in its most grim and unrelieved form, had the rôle all to itself. Humour has deft hands to strip off the hypocrite's mask and insinuates itself into truth's sanctum sanctorum. These genial-faced Irish lawyers have no faith in bullying out the truth; they simply laugh witnesses into it. Then the mobile, humorous mouth closes like a trap in a merciless grip of its writhing victim.

" The scene I have been describing proved, however, to be only a curtain-raiser to the real piece, with all the setting of human tragedy. It was shorn of humour, and—I have a grave suspicion—of equity into the bargain. It was the trial of Doonas, the young farmer mentioned in my letters. The Government have fortified themselves against the miscarriage of justice by giving magistrates powers of summary jurisdiction.

Finding no jury would convict, judge and jury are embodied in the magistracy. As a matter of jurisprudence no fault can be found with such an exceptional provision. The law must be administered, and if trial by jury breaks down a substitute is necessary. Whether the provision of summary jurisdiction is the best is an open question. What strikes one forcibly is the fierce antagonism of the people to the law as an Institution; it is there one finds so much indigestible material. It would be easy to understand this if the Irish were not a law-abiding people in other respects. In civil offences, barring the fight at the fair ' for fun,' as it has been put to me, or the rare faction skirmish, the crime-sheet is practically stainless. Compared with Scotland and England in this particular Ireland is a saint.

" I can see you stop and rub that monocle of yours. Get returns on the subject, my dear Max. How to account for the prevalent opinion to the contrary in our circle it is difficult to explain. It must be defective logic, despite Stanley Jevons, that you and I are supposed to have mastered. Given the winging of a landlord or the drowning of a rack-renter, accidentally for one purpose, or any other of the agrarian crimes of which Ireland is by no means blameless, we mentally scale up all other vices to the same proportion. This strange, cross-grained, impulsive, Celtic humanity at bottom is charming. It rings true as steel; there is no limit to its generous impulses, no scales for dispensing its kindness. This is characteristic of all classes, and of none more than the peasants. Here lies the secret of its antipathy to the law. When it is a question of Lord Ballyshameon's rent, or Jim Sweeny's hardship through eviction, his lordship must take a second place. When Martin Doonas is charged with conspiracy to defeat the ends of justice, and conspiracy means the protection of the tenant from physical suffering, then justice—to use a local simile—is a small potato.

" It is this element in the Celtic nature that lay behind the demonstration that attended Doonas's trial. To the judicial mind it is unreasonable, blind, violent even, but there it is, and in any reasoned philosophy of the Irish question it has to be reckoned with.   All the humour that characterized the earlier proceedings gave place to a whirlwind of indignation at the notion that for a common act of humanity Doonas should be faced with the alternative of bail or gaol.   Talk of contempt of court! the phrase is altogether inadequate to express the contumely that was hurled defiantly at the representative of justice on the Bench.   The sacred Ark had hands laid upon it with as little compunction as if it had been a scavenger's cart.   Even the name of Lord Ballyshameon, my dear Max, was consigned to a warm climate.   I felt the scandal of it, lost my temper, and would have joined the police, who attempted the arrest of a ringleader, had not a sensational and unexpected intervention saved the situation. There is in that girl's nature an entangled web, which is beyond my power of unravelling.   Her unconventionality is *outré*; there are no canons of propriety with which it squares. Miss Molly is *sui generis*, yet, tangled as the web is, there are strands of fine gold," and Warren proceeded to describe, with painstaking accuracy, what transpired in the court.   The thing he omitted to explain was that he had accepted an invitation to dine with that very unconventional miss the same evening.

Having delivered his soul in this fashion to his

Cambridge friend Warren set out for Squire Fitz Martin's. He crossed the fields leading to the boreen. It was a fine September day, and in the hush of evening the call of sea-birds sounded all the more clearly as they flew across the Whinny Hill. The tinkle of Poulla-more stream, in its accelerated flight down steep places, was not unlike cattle bells that the traveller hears on the Alpine slopes. The limestone, which holds so much music in its composition, was plentiful in the district, and gave out soft, liquid notes in answer to the plash of the water.

Warren, sensible of the poetry of the surroundings, walked along, swinging his light felt hat in his hand, and allowing the gentle breeze to have its way amongst his thick, waving hair. The daily tramps by the river in quest of fish, and climbs across the mountain for grouse and hares had wrought a miracle of healing—bracing his unstrung nerves and tuning his pulse to a firmer beat. He felt himself for the moment to be a part of all he saw, all he heard. There was some mysterious affinity with the blackcap that swayed on the clump of foxgloves on the old stone wall. Some kinship with the linnet, whose blood-streaked breast contrasted with the golden bloom of the gorse, amongst which it flitted and poured forth fragments of raptur-ous song. What a contrast to the broken-down, list-less youth that grew too tired to show his face at the club or to hold intercourse with more than a friend or two. What a medicament was hidden in that Irish air! What a mental rest in its remoteness from clamour, bustle and society functions! And the people whose psychology puzzled him, whose problems per-plexed him? Even to them the Englishman owed more than he knew. They furnished the mental tonic, the counterpart of the physical renewal of youth, due to the mountain and riverside recreations. The sudden swing from comedy to tragedy, which he had witnessed that morning, was like the stimulus to the mind of the scientist, who gets a fleeting glimpse of so ne recondite truth and every fibre stiffens in the effort to grasp it.

And Molly, with whom he was going to spend the evening, was the embodiment of this unique phase of the Irish character. He recalled how he could have dragged her from the bench upon which she stood, forgetting, as he thought, all womanly decorum, and how he could have knelt at her feet in worshipful admiration for the way she had woven her magic spell around the passions of the people. A pleasant glow of feeling swept over him as he dwelt on that part of the scene.

The subject of his musings met him with outstretched hand and cordial greetings as he passed within the door that all day long stood hospitably open.

" My uncle will be down in a moment," she said; " he has been late to-day. Will you come in, or have a look at our old garden whilst the light lasts? "

" It is delightful out of doors," said Warren, " but perhaps you "—looking at her low-necked dress—" will find it chilly."

Molly reached down a shawl from a peg and they took their way across a well-kept lawn, separated from the garden by a hedge of wild fuchsias, the small but copious bloom giving it a warm tone.

" This is beautiful," Warren said, running his hand through the clustering blossoms. " You find the same thing in Devonshire; it shows a very mild climate."

" Oh, yes. We are close by the Gulf Stream."

" And yet it is so exhilarating. Biddy can scarcely keep pace with my appetite. I'll give you fair warn-

9

ing," he added, suddenly recollecting that he had come to dine.

"Oh, I think we can manage; the potato crop has been excellent this year," his hostess replied with a sly glance.

"That is the *pièce de résistance*, I understand, in the West?"

"And buttermilk."

"Well, some people seem to do well on it," Warren commented, returning his companion's glance with interest. The clear blue eyes and well-chiselled face, alert with smiling mischief, corroborated the opinion.

"Buttermilk is called kitchen, but the potatoes have to do double duty in its absence, the little ones making kitchen to the big ones."

Warren expressed his admiration of the novel device.

"That is an example of how imagination can be turned to domestic uses," Molly added. "It isn't all used up in the service of poetry and superstition."

"Speaking of superstition, I hear you have a remarkable well," and Warren gave Shawn as his authority.

"Yes, you mean Poullabeg. We are going that way."

They strolled to the end of the garden, pausing to notice a fine yew tree with sticky berries, a close-set holly and a row of tall poplars. A wicket-gate led into a coach-yard, on which stables abutted. Molly's voice evoked an eager whinny from one of the sheds.

"Ah, that's Cuchulain; he generally expects me at this time of day. Come and see my horse."

They passed into the straw-littered stable and paused before a beautiful sleek-coated hunter, which looked round at his young mistress and flapped his silky ears in recognition. A lump of sugar was extracted from somewhere, which the large upper lip swept from the trustful hand that held it; then whispering endearments followed, the girl leaning her cheek against the handsomely-curved neck—a charming picture, and by no means a cu   : a romantic temper had a third party in the group   ...n disposed that way.

"This is the shrine at which Shawn worships," Molly said as they stood a few moments later on the brink of the mysterious well. "It looks nothing out of the ordinary, but it is strangely in sympathy with the pond by the old castle. Any disturbance in Poullamore affects Poullabeg. A storm that ruffles one agitates the other. A beast fell into the big pond a few years ago and was drowned, and Kitty declared that the water was surging and dashing over the side here. This is the more strange as the pond is some way off. The peculiarity is an old one, according to the inscription on this stone," pointing to a weather-beaten slab, green with age and damp, on the edge of the well. "You notice the hieroglyphics; it is in Gaelic," and Molly repeated the words in the vernacular; they sounded soft and musical to Warren.

"You don't understand that," she said, smiling.

"Alas! no. What does it mean?"

"Read the face of Poullabeg to know the heart of Poullamore."

"That is interesting," Warren answered.

"Oh, it's pooky," Molly pouted. "I don't like it; Shawn has horrid things to say about it."

As Warren stood peering into the open well he was startled by a loud scream, which was immediately followed by the clang of a dinner-gong, as if the latter were intended to drown it. He thought he heard in the clamour the words, " Go back to your own country," and looking towards an open window caught a momentary glimpse of a black figure with outstretched, menacing arm, then it vanished.

Warren turned to his companion, who looked pale, but with great composure remarked, "There's the dinner-bell; it's getting chilly," at the same time drawing the shawl close round her shoulders.

" You have been seeing the lions of the place," the Squire said, extending his hand to the visitor. " That's Molly's special weakness," drawing the said weak person towards him in an affectionate salutation, which had the effect of restoring some of the lost colour to her face.

" Take the bottom of the table, dear," he added. " Your aunt has a headache and asks to be excused."

Hare soup being the first course the Squire commented on the scarcity of the game as compared with early days. " When we went out on the 12th we had to stop shooting them, to spare the keepers; you could load a cart in no time," he said.

" How do you account for the falling off? " Warren asked.

" To the Peace Preservation Act," the Squire replied with a smile.

" The Peace Preservation Act! " Warren inquired, scanning his host's face to see if he were joking.

" It certainly needs explanation, but it is simple enough. The series of Crimes Acts, so long in force, prohibited keeping a gun, you know, except on a magistrate's licence; the poachers were consequently compelled to procure game in other ways, and the art of snaring and trapping became so general and efficient that a great quantity of game was taken. When poachers kept guns there were few really good shots amongst them, and shooting attracted the keepers. Snaring and trapping make no noise, and the skill of the rascals is wonderful."

"That is certainly remarkable," said Warren. "The Crimes Acts, then, have not been an unmitigated hardship to some of the peasants."

"Oh, it's an ill wind that blows nobody good, but there's a danger connected with that kind of poaching. These fellows have a villainous method of digging a hole in the bog and covering it with heather and a sprinkling of turf mould. It is always made in a hare's track, but more than hares are exposed to the danger. I have stepped into one and found myself up to my thighs in water. Begad, there's a risk of breaking one's leg. Then the dogs are constantly getting their feet into traps and come home lame."

The Squire had a store of anecdotes about poachers that were brought before him as a magistrate, and after the salmon came roast snipe, which he scanned closely. "I thought so," he said, looking up in triumph, "two with broken legs. Do you hear that, Miss Consorter with poachers and vagabonds?" addressing his niece at the other end of the table in good-humoured banter.

"Well, and couldn't a grain of shot do that?" Molly replied with an air of cleverly-assumed innocence.

"A grain of shot does not leave a mark like that on the bird I am sending you, Miss Innocent. That is another example of the poacher's art," addressing Warren. "The fellow goes to a pool of water and makes a furrow with his bare heel round the margin, in which he places a spring trap. The snipe always runs round a furrow and finds a gin instead of a crustacean."

"Is that so, really? Prohibition proves in this case a handmaiden to art."

" You see, Mr Warren," said Molly, " that the Irish are as irrepressible as rabbits; if you stop one hole they open another. But come now, uncle," she said, with a dainty toss of her head, " you admit that snipe are plentiful; the tenants surely might be allowed to shoot them.'"

" They have permission to shoot the whole of Longford Bottom, but trapping is a far easier and cheaper method. By the way," he continued, " an amusing case was brought before me the other day. A fellow was suspected of poaching game. He had permission to shoot snipe, but he was using large-sized shot in wire cartridges for long pot shots obviously. ' Well,' said I, ' if it was snipe you were after why were you using such large-sized shot? '

" ' Ah, yer honour,' says the rascal, ' sure snipe is so small that you want something big to hit them wid.' "

" He deserved to be let off, now, didn't he, Mr Warren? " Molly said after the laugh had subsided, proud of the peasant's witty defence of himself.

" Excuses, like poaching, have become a fine art too, it would seem," Warren remarked.

" Oh, indeed, an Irishman is never hard up for an explanation," grunted the Squire.

" They are so frequently called upon to defend themselves that practice makes perfect," observed Molly.

At the close of dinner the Squire's niece withdrew to the drawing-room, while he and his guest smoked. But the light touch of nimble fingers on a harp soon attracted the visitor's attention.

" Molly has quite a passion for Irish music, but it isn't everyone likes it," the Squire said tentatively; " the prevalent tone is sad."

" I am deeply interested in it," Warren replied. " The subject of Irish minstrelsy is charming."

" Well, my niece will be at home with you in that;
it is her pet subject.   She is a good Gaelic scholar, I am
glad to say."

" May we forgo the gentleman's privilege and
join Miss MacDaire? " the other asked.

" By all means;   take your cigar, she will not
object," and the Squire led the way to the drawing-
room.

" Can we come in and smoke, Molly? " the old
gentleman courteously asked.

" Oh, indeed you can.   I'm not so fond of my own
company that I prefer it to other people's."

" Mr Warren is interested in Bardism;   I shall leave
him in your charge.   I want to speak to Owney about
Shaughraun "—Owney was the ostler, Shaughraun the
Squire's hunter.

Molly was sitting under a large shaded lamp, the
soft rays of which fell in a warm tint round her, discovering many a glint in her sparkling hair.   She wore
an Irish poplin dress of a delicate heliotrope shade,
bordered with old Irish lace, which half revealed and
half concealed shoulders that might have been the
original of the tinted Venus.   One bare arm encom-
passed the harp that rested on her knee in a fond embrace, whilst the other freely moved up and down the
strings, and with graceful fingers drew responsive
melody from them.

Warren, from a side position, looked admiringly at
the picture she presented, as of some Greek muse.

It was soon evident that in music as in everything
else Molly was wholly in earnest.   She played as if

" Soothing her love-laden soul in secret hour
With music sweet as love that overflowed her bower."

Her country was the theme and she sang sympathetically.

"That is charming," said Warren, his face beaming with honest admiration. "It is the first time I have heard the Irish harp." He threw himself into a chair close to the girl's side and began to examine the instrument.

"It is a very old harp and has had a romantic history," Molly explained. "It belonged to the last of the bards, Teige MacDaire MacBrody. He was thrown down a ravine and killed by one of Cromwell's soldiers, who accompanied the cruel act by the heartless taunt, 'Go, say your verses now, my little man.'

"A young Irish girl, who heard of it, climbed down the slope and carried the dead man and his harp to the shore and rowed to an island, where the bard was buried. His arms were extended and his hands firmly clasped on the harp when the girl found him. The instrument itself was uninjured, with the exception of one of the strings, which was broken. Tradition says that this string "—touching it—" has never since been in tune. As a matter of fact it cannot be raised to a scale higher than the relative minor to all the other strings.

"You notice," Molly said, leaning on the harp and striking two of the strings in turn, "that this one is a third lower than it ought to be. It is also remarkable that there is a prevalent sad tone in it," and Molly struck a few notes which, compared with others, died off in a wail. "The traditional inference is obvious," she added, "that this was the last string that the bard's fingers touched."

Warren listened to all this with deep interest. "It is marvellous," he said, when the girl had finished, "how the fine heroic character of the Irish survives in tradition as well as in history. I have been reading the life of young Emmet lately. I confess I was practically ignorant of him, and I find that he is alive in the heart of every peasant on the hillside. But how did you come into possession of such a valuable treasure, if "—he added deferentially—" I am not taking an unwarranted liberty in asking such a question? "

" It is a family heirloom; the heroine of the story was a Fitz Martin, one of the families driven west of the Shannon in Cromwell's time."

" That was the way your uncle inherited it then? "

" Not my uncle but my mother, and afterwards myself," Molly answered with a protesting toss of her head, followed by a rippling laugh at Warren's evident discomfiture.

" I'm so sorry," he said, with a look that pleaded for forgiveness. " This is rather a new phase of primogeniture."

" Oh, it was simply a reward for feminine bravery. The girl that risked her own life and achieved an almost superhuman task in recovering the body from the pit became the personal possessor of the harp, and it has since been handed down as an heirloom on the female side."

" If that is made a precedent the future generation of Irish ladies will not lack heirlooms," Warren commented, and soulful admiration sat in his face as he paid the compliment to the girl who was carrying out the spirit of her ancestor.

Molly bowed and said, " I think a Fifth Century ode would be appropriate."

She had a contralto voice, remarkable, not so much for its depth and compass as pureness of tone and mellifluousness. It lent itself to the old-world music of recitative and weirdness.

The composition was in a minor setting but rose into an exulting strain, full of intense fervour. It was the story of the dying chief bequeathing his passion for his country to his successor; the latter is represented as obsessed with the travail of his mission. The climax was reached in the closing words:

> " A spirit within me, mightier than my own
> Although my will moves with it, masters me ;
> And all my past—my greater self—now urges
> To deeds beyond the weakness of the hour.
> Dearer is self-fulfilment to the strong
> Than the entranced oblivion of Love.
> Dearer than hollow sway o'er mighty clans,
> Or fruitless knowledge ; dearer even than life."

Warren felt the ardour of the theme and the dramatic verve of the singer.

" And that is a Fifth Century ode," he said. " Ireland is possessed of a far older literature than England. We have nothing earlier than the tenth century of any note. I wish my education in Irish literature had not been so lamentably neglected."

" England has taken no interest in Gaelic except to repress it," Molly said, a smile counteracting the petulant tone of the remark.

" That is because England didn't know the value of an ancient language, having no literature of her own until a much later date. Let us debit that to ignorance rather than malice," said Warren, lightly.

" Well, that is a charitable construction to put upon it. I'm afraid we regard it as part of the common policy of national extermination. The roots of national life lie in a country's literature. To us its attempted destruction was regarded as a death-blow."

" You know the value of your language more than we of ours," Warren rejoined. " Yours is original, ours a conglomeration. We have no composition that dates two thousand years B.C. No wonder you are ready to fight for its preservation."

" You have been studying the history of Gaelic," Molly said eagerly, as if she had made a new discovery.

" I know enough to wish that I knew more. You mentioned literature as the roots of national life. What else do you consider radical? "

" Oh, love of country more than anything, I think."

" Well, perfidious Albion cannot rob you of that. And your reason? " he asked with a smile, for he liked to hear Molly talk. She was an authority on the subject, and it seemed to him that the beauty of hill and dale and river were woven into the very fibre of her being.

She set the harp down by her side, and turning serious eyes upon Warren asked, " Can one tell why one loves? "

The simple *naïveté* of the question disarmed the very suspicion of any affectation.

" Oh, I think one can."

" But can the complex feeling be analysed so as to be able to say why in so many words? Is it not dissecting the flower to find the secret of its beauty, with the danger of losing it in the quest? "

The words were said without a tremor in the voice or a tinge of deepening colour in her face. It was the first time the tender passion had been touched upon between them. Molly's direct question had given the subject an intimacy that the other had not intended, but he was wholly unprepared for the calm way in which it was discussed. Ninety-nine out of every hundred girls would have shirked, shunting the general question of love of country to the rails of the more delicate personal one. Warren found himself searching her face for an exp'anation, but it had none to give. He had seen her blue eyes grow deeper in intensity of thought, her face pale as the passion of speech held spellbound the disorderly crowd, but here she talked about love without a trace of emotion. He could not play the flirt in the presence of such earnestness. He met her, therefore, on her own ground.

" There is, of course, the mystery that defies analysis, but the love of country—well, I suppose beauty has something to do with it for one thing; the æsthetic makes its bid to the emotior.⁻¹ and captivates it. That much, at all events, is discovered without the use of the dissecting knife. Ireland is beautiful, and beauty always has its votaries. Is it not so? "

Molly listened and nodded her pretty head in acquiescence without attempting to annex any of the compliments for personal use.

" Daniel O'Connell," said she, " was once charged with lacking affection for his country. He didn't wear his heart on his sleeve or attempt to marshal witnesses for the defence. His reply consisted in a graphic description of the beauties of his country until its glories seemed to stand self-revealed; then he changed his tone to one of withering scorn and exclaimed, with outstretched hand, ' And that miserable spalpeen dares to accuse me of want of love to my country.' If," she added, " one can't tell why one loves his country one can show why."

" That illustration is convincing," Warren admitted. " So now we have two things that lie at the roots of national life—literature, love of country," summing up the points in true academic fashion. " Can we find a third? "

" Yes, but only by bringing another charge against your country, I fear," with an apologetic smile.

" Perfidious Albion again—and the third count? "

" Oppression."

" Ah, I was afraid that was coming. You think oppression makes for national consolidation? " Warren asked.

" It is the lesson of history, surely. Adversity knits people more closely than prosperity. The one affects hearts, the other heads. A wrong to fight against makes a stronger bond than a privilege to fight about."

" Miss MacDaire, the bard's harp has been bestowed upon the right person."

" Ah, now, how can I point the moral if you begin to talk like that? Oh, yes, I know you mean it "— this in answer to Warren's deprecatory movement— " but you can only judge by comparison. If you knew what others are willing to do for their country you would confer the harp where it was more deserved. Goldsmith links love of country and oppression as factors in national life," she said, drawing away from the personal equation in the discussion. She lifted the harp, and in a running accompaniment, in the same key as her voice, half-sang, half-recited:

> " Dear is that shed to which his soul conforms,
> And dear that hill which lifts him to the storms ;
> And as a child, when scaring sounds molest,
> Clings close and closer to the mother's breast,
> So the loud torrent and the whirlwind's roar,
> But bind him to his native mountains more."

The manner of rendering the selection from " The

Traveller " seemed to evoke its Celtic spirit. Warren waited in silence, hoping that there was more to follow, but Molly said, " We've had enough of the bards for to-night," placing the harp in a wooden case and locking it. " I should think by this time uncle has had his nap. Oh, I forgot, it was Shaughraun," pulling herself up and laughing merrily. " Excuse me for a moment, will you? Try our piano," pointing to a bijou grand that lay open. " I know you sing and play," and without waiting to give a reason for the faith that was in her tripped from the room.

Warren sat down to the instrument, and with skilful fingers struck a few massive chords, modulating them into relative minors as if more befitting the atmosphere which the talk had engendered. He added tone colours in other combinations, then took a short excursion up the keyboard and gathered into the main current the ripple of fugitive notes that refused to be imprisoned in stereotyped setting, and all in such a way as to prove half Molly's assertion that he could play.

Then he sang a fragment that was nothing more than a thought that flitted in the background of the conversation:

> " We look before and after
> And pine for what is not ;
> Our sincerest laughter
> With some pain is fraught.
> Our sweetest songs are those that tell of saddest thought."

And in such a way as to prove the other part of Molly's assertion that he could sing.

Molly stood in the doorway as the final words died away in half a sigh.

" Now, that is not fair, Mr Warren. My harp has the monopoly of sad songs. If I had left the case open it would have protested in mimicry. You remember the perpetual minor string? Well, let me show you." She unlocked the case and hung the harp on a bracket. " Strike a minor chord in F." Warren did so. " Now a diminished fourth—a diminished seventh." . . . To each of these combinations the harp echoed a weird imitation. " It all comes from this string; that is why I imprison it when the piano is played," she said, replacing the instrument. " Now please sing something else. We live in the present as well as in the past, and although the Irish people have a minor string in their composition we know how to imprison it also," and Molly proceeded to prove it. There was a new animation in her manner; she suddenly became vivacious. There was almost a challenge in her voice as she spoke, and the blue eyes sparkled with merriment. Warren called to mind his first introduction to the laughing, bantering girl on the yacht, and rounded off the memory by recalling the island, the abandonment of his partner in the dance, and the glint of golden hair in the firelight; the very atmosphere seemed to be charged with her buoyancy in the changed mood. Warren caught the inspiration and expressed his obedience by singing " To Anthea—who may command him anything—"

The Squire entered the room in the course of the song and joined his thanks to those of his niece with warmth.

" Now, uncle, your song, please, and then you shall have your game of cards."

" Oh, Molly, Molly, do you mean to shame me in parading my old cracked voice after that brilliant performance? "

" What shall it be, uncle? " entirely ignoring the protest — "'The Cruiskeen Laun' or 'The Vicar of Bray,' or—? "

"Oh, let it be ' The Vicar,'" the Squire said. "I'll go bail you have been dosing Mr Warren so much with the patriotism and the bards that he needs a touch of opportunism as a corrective. A perfect world would be rough on some of us, Mr Warren."

And "The Vicar of Bray" it was, and sung in the most rollicking style. Then followed a game of cards and the visitor took his leave.

It was a beautiful moonlight night when Warren started for the lodge. He swung along with rapid strides, his body vainly trying to keep pace with his mind, which made excursions backwards and forwards, seizing on this point and that. It vaulted over hours at a time, to fasten on some incident of the evening, leaving it as quickly in pursuit of a witticism, an incident, or perhaps only a smile. The bards he cleared in these mental gymnastics would have stocked a gallery, the harps played would have constituted an orchestra, and the precipices into which he peered—in quest of heroic damsels—honeycombed a county.

The short span of road he had traversed led him to the boreen; the track of time that his mind covered filled a century. He was girding himself for another lap in pursuit of a figure that fled before him, staggering beneath a heavy burden. . . . She seemed to be clothed in delicate-tinted garments, flashing gold at every turn. On nearing the figure, the tints became sombre, the sombre black, and the golden hair raven as the wings of a night-bird. Another stride and the pursuer overtook his object, which now stood confronting him, not on the imaginary road of thought but the hard road of traffic, not in mental space but matter-of-fact time, and that ten minutes after he had left Fitz Martin's.

" Good heavens! " Warren exclaimed, as the sudden apparition brought his swaying body to a standstill and his wandering mind to a sense of material actualities, " who are you? "

He might well ask the question, for the figure stood in the middle of the road, and in such a position as to block his way. In the clear moonlight he took in the impression of a woman in a black cloak, with black hair, black eyes surrounded by black rings. Warren's mind, brought back to present time, recalled the woman in black on the stairs on his first visit to Fitz Martin's; the figure he saw at the window, and the scream he heard as he stood with Molly by Poullabeg.

" Who are you? " he repeated, his voice softening at the recollections.

" I am the silent woman." The reply was given in a refined but querulous voice.

Warren recalled Shawn's allusion to this woman.

" Do you wish to speak to me? " he asked.

" I wish to warn you," came the answer. " Go back to England. Leave this place. People are assaulted here, shot here, fall into suspicion and are tracked here. Young men get into bad habits and gamble and drink themselves to death." She paused, as if to gulp down some painful recollection. " You will fall in love here, and love leads to jealousy, and jealousy to crime. She is young and beautiful. So was I once, and could love as she, but now I hate! hate! and I could kill. Don't interrupt," she cried, stretching forth a warning hand as Warren was about to speak. " I saw you at Poullabeg and screamed as she raised the lid. How dare she raise the lid? " . . stamping her foot in passion. " She knows it is seething for me, gaping for me, longing to suck me down and flow up and up and over me. . . . Go away from Poullabeg; leave this place. Flee Ireland. I have warned you . . . go!"

She turned and was about to pass him on the road, but Warren was moved to pity for the poor soul, in whose flaming black eyes he could see the fire of frenzy burning. He put forth his hand to stop her and she paused and looked at him. He raised his hat. "Please, let me see you home," he said gently; "it is late and you can tell me more on the way."

"No! no! no one walks with me, talks to me, loves me. Did I dine with you, sing to you, play cards with you to-night?" she asked bitterly. "There is only one thing I can do—warn you; go!" and without waiting for an answer she fled down the road as though pursued by her own frenzied thoughts, her pace growing swifter every moment, as if to outdistance them. In the stillness of the night the patter of her feet seemed to warn! warn! warn!

Warren watched the black figure until it was out of sight, then resumed his homeward journey, feeling as if a very ugly frame was thrust upon him in which to set the pleasant picture of the evening spent at the Squire's house.

CHAPTER XI

MARY HANNAGHER kept a huckster's shop a little way out of the town of Ballinbeg. Her trade consisted in supplying the neighbours with exceptional articles, of which they had run short, at a halfpenny or a penny more than the usual charge, and regular commodities at current prices. The latter business furnished her with a class of customers who lost nothing economically in paying the same price there as elsewhere, and gained considerably on the ground of convenience. The former branch attracted another clientele, who cheerfully paid the higher price for the articles she supplied under urgent circumstances. The " regular commodities " consisted of bread, butter and eggs, the " exceptional " of porter, spirits and tobacco. Samples of the " regular " were displayed in a window a couple of feet square, the " exceptional " were secreted in a box a couple of yards cubed.

It will be understood from these particulars that the " exceptional " became articles of commerce without making any contribution to the National Treasury; or, in other words, that Mary's shop was a huckster's by profession and a shebeen by trade.

There was a third class of patrons for whom Mary made provision on market and fair days. These consisted chiefly of country farmers and dealers who passed the shop on their way to and from the town. Mary watched them coming in every Thursday, and could tell to a nicety how many she might expect for " tay " on the way home.

One Fair day in September she was engaged in taking stock in this way and communicated her impressions to her daughter, who assisted in these social functions. The latter's name was Mary too, but she was called Warya—an Irish equivalent—by way of distinction.

" The Flynns, the Deignons and the whole faction of the M'Guires are gone to the Fair," the mother remarked. " Will we have enough porther, do ye think, Warya? Sorra much tay the Deignons dhrink, so we can't depend upon it for the entertainment."

" No, nor porther either; it's whisky they have a taste for," the girl replied.

" Is it now? I thought it was the Flynns had a sthrong wakeness that way."

" The Flynns like it in their tay," Warya explained, " the Deignons in its native unadornment."

" We'll open the new keg anyhow; have ye plenty of tebacca? "

" Whips."

" And pipes? They're sure to break a few before the evening's out."

" Lough Melvins."

" Throth, thin, ye must lay in another stock of porther; the thirst comes or them wonderful in the match-making; they floated off Pat Hallern and Biddy Casey on a round dozen at the August Fair."

" I'll tell Micky to put in a few more bottles when he goes for the pigs' grains. But we have enough for a wake as it is, to say nothin' of a match-makin'."

" And, Warya, mind the bad coppers. There was half a dozen July Fair day an' it was only yesterday I passed the last of them. There's no bein' up to their dishonesty."

During this colloquy Mary was busy ironing a muslin cap, which constituted part of her evening dress on these state occasions. It was made of extra fine material, neatly embroidered with sprigs of shamrock and an ornamental front, which was shaping that moment under a hot iron into twenty-six arches, that might have been mistaken for mouse-holes had Mary's head been a cheese instead of a composition of good-humoured, smiling flesh and blood.

Warya was meanwhile engaged in scouring the dresser, which held an imposing array of crockery—dishes and plates at the back, and a regiment of cups swung by the handles on the ledges. There was a large deal table in the centre of the room, which had already undergone the cleansing process and was drying in grey patches. The mud floor was freshly sanded, and on an open hearth a turf fire burned brightly, over which a pot was suspended by a crook from a chain in the chimney.

" There's a load of turf goin' by; call him, Warya."

The girl ran to the door. " Hi, you, how much do you want for the turf? "

The youth, driving a donkey, threw his arm round its neck as if he were about to embrace it, and leaning against its head succeeded in turning the animal round, turf creels and all.

" What do you want for the turf? " Warya repeated.

" Ninepence."

" *Ninepence ?* " emphasizing the word as if it constituted an insulting proposal. " Wouldn't ye take a shillin'? "

" Not from you; it might be a bad one."

" Bring me a couple of sods to look at."

The vender complying brought one in each hand, which were critically examined.

" They're like the potatoes, no doubt, the best on top, the worst underneath. Are they all like them? " she asked.

" They are, only betther."

" Throth, thin, ye have an honest face, an' a handsome one too into the bargain."

" Arrah, whisht now, will ye, don't put the come-hether on me," the youth pleaded.

" Faix, it's sorry meself is that I'm not dressed. Why couldn't ye wait until the evenin' when the scrubbin' is over? Indeed, it's not these rags ye'd be lookin' at thin."

" An' why not indeed? " surveying the girl's figure with an admiring eye.

" Because I'd have me new dress on."

" Stop now, or the picture ye make would rob me of me sinses."

" Throth, thin, I think it's meself can trust ye. Are all the turf like these? "

" Musha, if ye can trust me, why do ye ax questions? It's not meself would be axin' about the owld petticoat that might be beneath yer new dress," with a sly glance in that direction.

" In throth ye got up too early for me, ye divil. Will ye take sixpence? "

" No, ninepence."

" Sevenpence then, an' the sorra halfpenny more if we were to die for the sake of it."

" No, but I'll tell ye what I'll do wid a fine girl like yerself."

" Let me lane against the post before I hear it."

" I'll split the difference."

" Faith, the compliment is worth the extra penny. I'll take it."

Mary Hannagher's patrons began to forgather in the gloaming. The cheery rays of the bright turf fire discovered the crockery on the dresser and made it sparkle, as much as to say, " Eat from us." The gold-rimmed cups arranged on the table glittered and put in their own word:—" Drink from us."

The kettle on the hob was not sure of what it was going to sing and began and stopped several times, as if it had so many tunes that it did not know which to choose, and was simply proffering samples. But the talk of the kitchen seemed to decide it, and it sang to the crockery, " Who washed you? " and to the cups, " Who sparkled you? " and to the legs of the table— that seemed to be showing off—" Who scrubbed you? " and puffed and steamed and rattled its lid until it boiled over, and wiped out the glint of the plates and the cups and the table, and the darkness crawled out of the corners where it was hiding and said, " Sarve ye right."

" Mary, the kettle is boilin'; make the tay fine an' sthrong," said one of the new-comers. " Draw up to the fire, Patsy; bedad, it's cowld for September. We're goin' to have a hard winter av it."

" Throth, if it's as hard as the Fair to-day it will be bad enough," Patsy grumbled.

" Arrah, now, don't be talkin'; sure, I never saw the like of it. Och, the counthry is goin' to the dogs altogether."

" What were ye sellin' anyhow, Patsy? "

" A slip of a pig. Bedam, but if it was a thorough-bred hunter more questions couldn't be asked about it."

" See that now."

" ' How owld is it? ' says the jobber to me.

" ' Owld enough to make busybodies ask questions,' says I, for I saw the fella was coddin' me."

" Oh, bedad, he wouldn't think much of that."

" To be sure he wouldn't."

" ' What do ye feed it on? ' says he, cockin' his head on one side an' lookin' at the pig critically.

" ' Spring water an' slates,' says I.

" ' Well, bedad, it's good clane diet,' says he.

" ' It would do more than the pigs good,' says I, casting me eyes round him.

" ' I'd be the last to dispute the point with so good an authority,' says he. ' I'll give ye three half-crowns for him,' says he. ' I like the shape of his head any-how.'

" ' Faix, there's more sinse in it than in yours,' says I.

" ' Will ye take it? ' says he.

" ' I won't,' says I.

" ' Well, there's no harm done anyway,' says he.

" ' No indeed,' says I. ' If money was as plentiful as talk it would be a great market! ' Just wid that a fella went by carryin' a squealin' bonnuv.* ' There's an infant in arms,' says I, ' it might suit yer purse better than an adult baist.' "

" Faix, ye had the laugh of him there, Patsy, any-how."

By this time fresh arrivals had come and the tea was served round, accompanied by loaves of bread broken across and then cut into four pieces, liberally buttered.

" Here, Mary, put a ' stick ' in this and good luck to ye," said one of the company, giving a knowing wink

* A young pig.

to the widow, and holding out a cup three parts full of tea.

Mary extracted a stone jar of whisky from a cavity behind the dresser and half-filled a brown jug with the contents. The " stick " was added.

" That's great," says the recipient, smacking his lips. " It laves its mark all the way down, like Tim Massey's wooden leg in the bog. Thry a dhrop, Peter, it will make ye forget the low price ye got for the heifer. Bring the cruiskeen laun,* Warya agra; it will take the droop out of Peter's spirits. That's it, me colleen. Faix, it's the bright eyes yerself has; no wonder the whisky is so good, wid such a sparkle playin' on it; bedad, I could be swallowed meself for a glance av them."

" Indeed," said Warya, " if I had another pair of hands they would be of more use to me at the present moment. It's too much trade me eyes are makin'. I can see more than I can wait on. Stop a minuit now, will ye? " she said to an impatient applicant, " ye've had one stick already. I don't sarve bundles. It's sticks with tay in it ye want. We only supply tay with sticks in it; do ye mind the difference? "

The listeners did and applauded it.

" Oh, I've given me word to be married already, so it's no good in threatening to throw yourself away on me, Patsy; it would be waste of good material any-how."

So the feast proceeded, the widow and her daughter serving fresh supplies of tea, adulterated with small quantities of particularly strong poteen. Then the table was cleared, pipes and tobacco were requisitioned, and a row of tumblers took the place of cups and

* A little brown jug.

saucers. The company grew sober-minded at this stage, as if the proceedings were a matter of great moment and not a little gravity.

Mary and Warya, understanding what was due, withdrew, and they were left to themselves. Every man applied renewed energy to his pipe, as if there were something hidden away in its innermost recesses that it was his business to smoke out. The thing was to be done in silence, for it was of such a delicate nature that an unguarded word would spoil everything.

Nobody spoke for some time.

One of the men, thinking the silence had lasted long enough, made some observation about the potato blight, but the subject evoking nothing but a laconic "humph" did not feel encouraged to pursue it. Another thought it would be a hard winter, and ventured to say so; but an allusion to the faith that Providence was good was too self-evident a proposition to provoke discussion, and both speakers pulled harder at their pipes than ever, as if there were something more important in their depths to get at—disparaging remarks notwithstanding.

Some of the men had no more acquaintance with each other than casually meeting in the market from time to time. Although trading in the same town they lived wide enough apart, a mountain or a river perhaps dividing them.

" It's the other side of the Windy Gap yerself belongs to?" one of them observed to a man sitting near him, with an air preliminary to something else. The farmer addressed had been the highest bidder for a couple of sheep his questioner had sold.

" It is indeed, and a good step from here. I must be startin' soon."

" Oh, indeed, the evening is young anyhow, and ye're in good company."

" The best, but I left a couple of slips of girls at home and they're lonesome, the cratures."

The information created a general stir of expectation in the party. Two of the smokers struck the heads of their pipes into their palms with an unnecessary amount of violence to clear out the ashes, another hurried the process of rubbing the twist in preparation for refilling, and a third applied a match to the bowl of his pipe as if the occasion demanded a little more steam to keep pace with the conversation.

" Well, indeed, it's good to have the colleens. It's themselves will have the bit and the sup ready for ye? "

" They will indeed."

" A couple of them too. It isn't everyone is so well off, bedad."

" Throth, then, if one of them was a son it might be betther," the proud owner said. " The holdin' is more than one pair of hands can work, though they're useful at the haymakin' and footin' the turf."

" Well, now, that's mighty quare. I've more sons than I want, and you more daughthers; did ye ever hear the like of it? What sort of a remedy can anyone propose for such a state of things? " and he looked round the company for an answer.

The dead silence that followed showed that the question was no ordinary one, but an out-and-out poser. In the pause that followed, one member of the company seemed to gain light upon the subject, which he ventured with great deference to communicate to the rest. It was conveyed in two words: " Splice them."

The suggestion was hailed with delight for its originality, and everybody seemed relieved that such a simple solution should be discovered of so grave a difficulty. Some of them repeated the words, "Splice them," as if there were a danger of their forgetting, others nodded their heads in a way that showed the matter was not quite as bad as they thought, and everyone looked at the man who made the remark as much as to say, " How is it we haven't heard of you sooner? "

The member of the company, now that he had found the solution, did not seem to know exactly what to do with it, and again appealed to his Windy Gap neighbour to tell him what he thought of that?

The owner of the two daughters thought that worse remedies might be tried.

This was not quite as encouraging as the company had reason to expect, and each one drew harder at his pipe as if the obstacle lay there.

The challenger dealt with the proposed remedy in a hypothetical way.

" I suppose now," he said, " that you might be agreeable to sparin' one of your daughters if a member of the present company was agreeable to sparin' one of his sons? "

There was sufficient point in this statement of the case to cause a sharp rattling of the tumblers on the table.

" Well, if a son could be spared, faith, a daughter ought to be handy."

A louder clatter of tumblers followed.

" An' suppose you were asked to part with one of the colleens, which of them now would it be likely to be? "

" Well, if it ever came to that, sure it might be aither of them." The reply seemed to be addressed to the corner of the ceiling.

" Throth, then, any father wantin' a wife for his son would be asking her age, very likely. He wouldn't choose her too young, nor too owld for that matter."

" Indeed, then, it's meself could tell him. The one is about seventeen years and the other eighteen, and if it's more news he wanted the young one is very fair an' the owld one very black and if he picked aither of them in the dark he woul n't be makin' a bad bargain."

" Well, indeed, it's glad I am meself that it's sons I have an' not daughthers, for the man with daughthers must part with them an' more into the bargain. The boy is a fortune in himself if he's a good one, and indeed it's meself knows a father that has such a son. But the daughther, faix, if I had one I'd be asked what the fortune was, an' if it was in land or in baists, or in sheep or in money. There's no bein' up to some people's curiosity."

" Well, it's meself would be answerin' ten pounds fortune, four head o' cattle, a sheep or two, and maybe a few pigs thrown in."

Here there was a still louder clatter of tumblers, and Mary Hannagher and her daughter exchanged significant glances.

" Indeed, ye might as well be drawin' the corks, Warya; they'll be callin' for the porther immadiately."

" Wait until they spit on the bargain," said Warya. " I've known it to fail after a louder noise than that. It's all very well until it comes to settlin' the fortune; the matter of a sheep often upsets it."

" Throth, I've a good mind to speak for the son that I know," said one of the contracting parties, coming closer to the point.

" Well, if ye do, it's meself won't be behind in answerin' for the daughther," said the other.

Here the interest in the conversation deepened to such an extent that some of the company let their pipes go out.

" We're on a hot sint now," one of them whispered to his neighbour.

" Indeed, a good steady son would be expectin' more than ten pounds fortune. He'll be thinkin' of twelve pounds and a few more baists to stock the farm wid."

" And a good father would not be standin' in his daughter's light for a trifle of that kind."

" Then give me yer fist on it," said the father of sons.

" Here it is," replied the father of daughters.

Then the company broke into a loud cheer and rattled their glasses for the widow's liquor, the corks of which had been silently drawn in the adjoining room. So the health of the plighted youth and maiden was drunk, both of them unaware of the supreme event that was transpiring in their interests; both of them sublimely ignorant of each other's existence. But it was not for them to raise the least objection. It was thus their own parents were disposed of, and what was wrong with their marriages? It speaks well, too, for the Irish peasants that the qualities essential to the welfare of wedded life are always taken for granted, and not without reason. The simple life they live leaves no room for the growth of vices incidental to a more complex state of society. The pure air of heaven breathed amongst their native hills leaves no taint upon body or soul. The pastoral occupations in which both sexes engage, tilling the field, ranging the mountain, tramping the bog, make them sturdy in body and strong in limb. If there were any physical defect the contracting parties at the match-making were in honour bound to declare it and offer a larger fortune in indemnity. Paddy Casey was particular to declare that he got the grey heifer in addition because his wife had a cast in her eye, and proud he was of it, although putting it in such a way that wasn't quite clear whether he meant the eye or the heifer.

Although match-making is always graced by the adjunct of poteen or porter, confirmed drinking amongst the peasants is most rare. There are only three or four Fairs in a year, and a drop too much is limited to such occasions. There is little drinking during intervening periods. It is rarely kept in the homes and only incidental to weddings, christenings or funerals. The best wife for the son is the one that brings the largest fortune; the best husband for the daughter is the youth with the snuggest holding. There is a distinct business edge on the proceedings. But marriages are made in Heaven, and if proof is needed what better can be adduced than that divorce or separation is practically unknown amongst the Irish peasants.

CHAPTER XII

WARREN accepted an invitation to join Squire Fitz Martin in a cross-country ride. He was a good horseman and looked forward with a keen zest to getting astride the pigskin. The fact that the Squire's niece was to accompany them added a rosy tinge to the prospect, and the quicksilver of anticipation registered " set fair " as he left the Lodge. It was a beautiful September day. The bracken was beginning to bronze and skirted in profusion the borders of rocky knolls and climbed up the hillsides until an altitude was reached, where the heather held undisputed monopoly. Hart's-tongue ferns protruded through the loose masonry of grey stone walls, and wild maidenhair clustered in sheltered nooks and crannies.

The Squire greeted his guest cordially on his arrival.

" I am giving you Finn MacCoul for a mount, Mr Warren," he said. " He may be a little fresh at first, but a gallop across the moor will steady him. He has plenty of legs and knows how to stretch them."

They had reached the yard, where Molly stood superintending the saddling of her own horse, which, with well-curved neck, kept looking round and whinnying in recognition of his young mistress.

She was dressed in a dark green riding-habit, the long skirt of which was thrown over the left arm. Masses of golden hair were doing their best to escape from the imprisonment of a dainty hunting-hat; sparkling eyes and a radiant face completed a picture good to look upon.

" Throth, then, miss, it's the stone walls ye'll be clearing to-day, or ye wouldn't be wantin' another hole taken in in the straps," said the coachman.

" And why shouldn't I, Thady, a fine morning like this? "

" You like jumping, Mr Warren, don't you? " extending her hand in a good-morning.

" Not when I'm left on one side of the hedge and the horse on the other," Warren answered with a laugh.

" It is stone walls that must be negotiated in this country," Molly explained.

" I am afraid that doesn't enhance the prospect."

" Oh, you need not fear with Finn," Molly replied, accepting the proffered hand and jumping lightly into the saddle.

They passed through the gate and set off at a canter.

" I wonder the stone walls do not ruin your horses' feet," Warren remarked to his fair companion, who rode between the gentlemen.

" It's all a matter of habit.   They are used to them. That is one reason why Irish horses are such good jumpers.   When quite foals they are left with their dams and soon get into the way of clearing the walls. The fields are small and they pass from one to another, and after a while they never disturb a stone."

Just then Warren's horse began to lengthen his strides and move away from the others, as if the pace were too slow for him.   Efforts to hold him in were resented and he wheeled round, sidling Molly's horse out of the way.

" Let him go a little here," the Squire advised. " We shall soon be off the road and he can have his head."

Finn again drew to the front and Molly was in a

11

position to observe how well Warren sat his horse, and with a quick eye saw in him a rider that would flatter her ambition in a gallop.

The country became more open as the horses rapidly covered the ground, and away to the right the darker markings of the moor came into sight. Finn's companions showed their jealousy and quickened their pace to get into line with the leader. Soon the turf was reached and the sharp ring of the horses' hoofs changed into a dull thud. The moment Warren's horse felt it he gave a plunge forward and shaped for a gallop.

" This way," Molly cried, noticing that Warren responded, and giving her own horse his head, the high-spirited beast straightened himself out with a shiver of excitement. Warren slackened the rein and Finn followed, kicking the turf behind him in large divots in the attempt to get level with the leader. But Molly's horse had been chafing at second place on the high road and was not going to yield on the grass. Forward he bounded, his feet lightly touching the ground, his sensitive nostrils quivering. A long, undulating stretch of land lay before them. The ground was dry and firm and adapted to horse-riding. Both the animals knew it well and took every hollow and ridge with sure-footed certainty.

Warren, skilled in horsemanship from his boyhood, felt the thrill of delight as his knees tightened on the fine Irish horse beneath him. He quickly adapted himself to the long strides, which possessed ease and grace in proportion to rapidity. The noble beast's feet touched the ground so lightly that there was no fear of the rider's teeth being shaken. A fine horse is the real Pegasus. Warren soon felt so much at home that he became sensible of his surroundings. Chief amongst these was his companion, whose horse still led. The ease with which the Irish girl rode was remarkable; only a slightly perceptible rise in the saddle distinguished her as a thing apart from Cuchulain. Erect she sat without a jar or a line of stiffness in her graceful figure. One hand, with the reins, rested lightly on the neck of the horse, the other, holding a whip, hung loosely by her side. A word, an occasional caress was all that the beast—fully sensible of its precious burden —needed. Warren got a side glimpse of the girl's face as his horse gained on the level whilst hers was going uphill. Her cheeks held a deeper tinge of colour and the lips were slightly parted as they drank in full draughts of delight.

On, on the horses sped—the flash of a lake was seen in the hollow, the glow of a whin-patch on the hills. A hare started from its form amongst the heather, a pack of grouse whirred across the hill. On, on, until the moor and heather passed into grazing land. A flock of sheep scurried sideways, long-horned kyloes raised their heads and flicked their tails in startled surprise.

A grey line in the distance cut athwart the open field. It was too far off to distinguish the characteristic Irish wall. Finn MacCoul saw it and raised his silky ears as if in expectation of new excitement. As the horses drew near it seemed to rise from the flat and visibly grew, as if bent on putting a stop to the mad gallop.

Molly stroked the neck of her horse and slightly bent her head to whisper words of encouragement. The wall had grown so high that half the field beyond was cut out of sight. Was she going to face it? Warren wondered; the pace was not lessened, there was no gate or gap for egress. He was not left long in doubt. Only a narrow strip of the divided field was now visible; nearer the riders drew, Molly's hand tightened on the reins, and the horse's head could be seen rising without apparent effort—the forefeet seemed to paw the air— and with a mighty spring the leader was over. Finn MacCoul was almost on his heels, and Warren found himself flying through space and alighting on the other side of the wall with scarcely a jar.

"Phew," he whistled as he wiped his forehead, and the two horses, whinnying, drew together. Molly, radiant with smiles, congratulated him.

"Good heavens!" he exclaimed, "what a ride! and to clear that wall without disturbing a stone. It's splendid. You congratulate me," he added. "I would not have looked at that wall if it had not been for your magnificent and spirited example."

"Oh, these walls are all right when you get used to them. Ah, I know what you want, Finn," as Warren's horse pressed his nose into her hand; she drew out two lumps of sugar and gave one to each of the horses.

"That's how you gain such fine achievements," Warren observed with a laugh.

"It's better than the whip, don't you think so?"

"Undoubtedly, and far more pleasant."

He had been looking eagerly at her, making no attempt to disguise his admiration. The glow from the ride heightened her beauty. Although she discussed the subject with the greatest calmness the gentle rise and fall at her throat bespoke the excitement which thrilled her with pleasurable emotion, as every young life pure in soul and healthy in body feels.

"You have enjoyed the gallop," she said, her own sense of delight dominating her feelings.

"Immensely," Warren answered, and added in all honesty, "I have never enjoyed a ride so much. We have nothing like this in London. I fear it will make me very discontented with Rotten Row."

"Oh, but you have so many other things that we are deprived of. We must make the best of out-of-door life."

"We have society, it's quite true, but it stands in the same relation to your natural enjoyments as Rotten Row does to this moor. It is artificial, necessarily so; we have to create our pleasures. Where the turf does not grow we lay down a substitute for it. We hire professionals to amuse us. Our social functions are not self-supporting and have to be supplemented by all sorts of devices. Artificiality dominates everything, and what ought to be a pleasant evening becomes an insufferable crush."

"Oh, yes. I visited Dublin last year with my uncle and was charmed with its delightful society; but some of the women older than myself seemed to be growing tired of it. But London has its great libraries; how I envy you them. In Dublin I spent several days amongst the Gaelic manuscripts, it gave me such a new interest in Connacht; where Conn of the hundred battles and Cuchulain carried on their exploits—you needn't flip your ears, Cuchulain, it's not you I am referring to," she said, patting her hunter—"I became so saturated with old Gaelic history that I half expected to meet one of the chiefs near the Drimmincill round tower."

"Then they would have run away with you, in keeping with the old-world story."

"Oh, well, that would only have brought another Sir Knight on the scene to rescue me."

Warren thought there would have been no dearth of such heroes, but he contented himself with saying:

" That was the usual cause of bloodshed, it seems. I suppose Erin has its Iliad; let me see, who was it marched across to Sligo and fought a great battle in which three thousand fell? " Warren asked mischievously.

" Ah, that was Columcille, but it wasn't a lady that was at the root of the mischief that time; it was the treachery of Diarmiud to the son of the King of Connacht," and Molly nodded her shapely head triumphantly.

" Oh, well," said Warren, seeing a philosophic side to the topic discussed in so light a vein, " there must be an incentive to heroism; it is the distressful maiden that has created the brave knight. To say women are the root of all mischief is only a bungling way of paying her a compliment. There must be a powerful element in her life or it would not be so. The beauty of Helen of Troy was worth ten years' war or it would not have been waged. These old-world stories, with all their strife and bloodshed, are but the travail of great ideals. Beauty and goodness are always worth fighting for, Miss MacDaire. Oh, look at that! " Warren exclaimed, as suddenly there came into view a magnificent scene. They had been gradually mounting a hill which barred the prospect, and as the horses' feet touched the highest ledge the full effect flashed upon them. A bay, chameleon in its variety of tints, blue and emerald predominating and stretching away into the sombre shadows cast by mountains, gems of islets, " emeralds set in the ring of the sea," some smooth as velvet, begirt with a streak of golden sand, others crowned with the thick, clustering arbutus and laurel bushes. Wave ripples chased one another across the broad expanse, and in their eagerness to overtake each other broke into petulant white crests. A bare rock, wind-beaten and weather-stained, stood out in proud isolation, on which a heron perched—a solitary bird in keeping with its solitary ways.

Below where they stood there was a declivity steeper than the one they had just climbed. The suddenness with which they came upon the scene—under the careful generalship of Molly—the wealth of colour, the shapely islands, the magnificent sea, visibly affected Warren, and after the exclamation of surprise he remained silent. What was the secret of the powerful effect these things had upon him? From the day he sailed down the Western Bay he came beneath their spell. He was by no means ignorant of beautiful and magnificent scenery. The Bay of Naples, the Italian Lakes, the sublimity of the Jungfrau and the Matterhorn were familiar. What affinity had he with these Irish charms, that they made a larger draft on his admiration and thrilled him to the innermost fibre of his being as scenes no less entrancing had failed to do. He, with a Saxon history, never having set foot on Irish soil before; he, with a University training that suppressed enthusiasm and discouraged the expression of feeling as an exhibition of bad taste. What time, in the mystery of nebulous being, had he formed some kinship with it all? He felt, and the feeling had been growing on him with regard to other scenes, that somehow he had been there before, and shadow memories intangible and illusive flitted through his brain.

Molly had been watching the effect; she had brought many of her Dublin friends in the same cunning way, where, unprepared, the scene burst upon them.

But the effect was not always as great a surprise as she intended. It generally was made the basis of comparison with fair scenes in Wicklow and elsewhere, for Ireland is prodigal in her beauty. One lady visitor, on reaching the summit, complained of the strong breeze, and asked her hostess how she managed to keep her hat on so firmly. Not one word of admiration, not a scintillation of emotion stirred her. It seemed in keeping with the fitness of things that she immediately expressed a wish to get down to the low road.

But Warren choked and Molly came to his relief by saying:

" This is one of our Helen's smiles."

" Yes," he stammered, " and, by heavens, it's worth dying for."

They remained on the ledge of the Whinny Hill for some time, Warren drinking in the grandeur of the scene from different standpoints, and his companion, familiar with every aspect of it, finding a new pleasure in the success of her stratagem. Such a sense of vicarious enjoyment was to her, as it is to many, the highest form of delight. To see the beautiful through the eyes of others comprises a new sense of vision.

" The caves in those cliffs yonder are remarkable," Molly said, pointing. " I must row you over some day to see them; we often go for a picnic there. There's uncle on the low road," she added; " he has given up the stone walls lately. We used to jump them regularly together. He talks about getting old, quite a new thing for him."

" But he is not an old man."

" Oh, no, but he is not what he used to be, and I am sometimes anxious about him."

" I am sorry to hear that," Warren said kindly.

" My Cousin Phil gives him a good deal of trouble,"
said Molly, growing confidential. " Uncle does not
say much, but I understand him and know what he
feels. Drink and betting are the two great snares of
young men in the West, and I fear my cousin has
yielded to both."

" That indeed is a misfortune, but I should not have
thought there would have been much scope for gambling
here."

" It is one of the chief elements in sport. Horse-
racing is very popular and everyone goes to see it. It
is considered nothing without a bet. A hare cannot be
coursed without a stake on the hounds, and if two
cocks are seen fighting in the street they are sure to find
backers."

" But the stakes cannot be high where they have so
little to spend," Warren said.

" It isn't that exactly, it is the passion innate in the
Irish blood. Peasants have not much to spend, but the
squireens, better-class farmers and jobbers are very
much given to it. When they win they drink for joy,
and when they lose they drown their sorrow in the same
fashion."

By this time they had gained the low road and rejoined the Squire, who excused himself for not taking
part in the gallop.

" I am not as young as I was, and some of the
luxuries of youth are denied me. A fine view that, sir,
from the Whinny Hill."

" Magnificent, one of the finest I have seen. It's
no wonder you keep so young and fresh with such air
and scenery; it is quite a tonic to breathe on the top
of that hill."

" Begad, sir, it is a good thing, for man and beast

have little besides to thrive on. It's a mystery how some of the peasants manage to keep body and soul together. There have been a good many evictions in this part of the country. There are, perhaps, few places where the extremes are brought into sharper contrast. Natural beauty and human poverty—silk and rags in juxtaposition. Look at that hovel," and the Squire pointed to a hut on the hillside; "Bally-shameon ought to clear all such places and allot habit-able plots on the cattle ranches to the poor wretches."

"But surely something is provided for these people when they are evicted."

"It just depends; if the owner is known to be a hard worker and industrious, or if he can find a pound or two for the rent in advance, he may be reinstated somewhere."

"How can he find money when he is evicted for non-payment of rent?"

"Not always for that," replied the Squire. "He may be suspected of burning the heather. The young growth makes cattle feed, but burning is a crime."

"A crime! Why so?"

"Because it destroys the game cover and the young birds, and shooting pays better than tenant-farming."

"And am I to understand," Warren asked, with growing indignation, "that my shooting has been secured at the cost of evictions?"

"Oh, indeed, you need not be anxious on that score. Ballyshameon has looked after the shooting without injury to anyone. He gets a good rent for it, as you know. The holdings are not very grand, but they are better than those," nodding towards the hillside, "and every farmer gets so much per head for the grouse shot during the season. The keepers make a

careful return, so the better you shoot the more blessings from the tenants and curses from the landlord."

" Then I shall increase my shooting-parties and
double my visits," Warren declared with a laugh.

" You would certainly be within your rights in
doing so, but if you consult prudence you must not
overtask his lordship's trustees. If they are of the
temper of Ballyshameon you need not expect to get the
shooting next year."

" I feel disposed to take the risks, even if I pay
more for it.   I do not expect to exhaust the delights of
the West of Ireland in a season; it is cheaper than the
West of London, and infinitely more pleasant."

" You have very much improved in appearance
since you came," Molly interposed, and saw the *naïveté*
of the remark too late to alter it.   A blush betrayed her
confusion.

Warren noticed it and smiled.   " I am delighted,"
he said, " to hear you say so."

" Ah, now, you have caught me.   Well, never mind,
gentlemen are supposed to think so little of personal
appearance that they are not easily spoiled."

" Well, whether that is correct or not, one's own
opinion does not count, and I shall be delighted to
leave the appraisement in your hands."

" That is risking a monopoly," Molly replied archly.
" I may raise the standard and become exacting."

" I am willing to be bankrupt if you become the
receiver."

" Not for the world; you would not be able to
trade again in your own name, and I might have too
many broken hearts on my hands," and the clear,
bright, musical voice ran out merrily above the clatter
of the horses' hoofs.

MICROCOPY RESOLUTION TEST CHART

(ANSI and ISO TEST CHART No. 2)

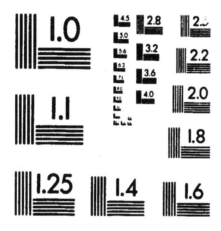

APPLIED IMAGE Inc

1653 East Main Street
Rochester, New York   14609   USA
(716) 482 - 0300 - Phone
(716) 288 - 5989 - Fax

They had been riding side by side, the road being too narrow for three horses abreast, and the Squire had courteously given way. The foothills passed into a low-lying plane, and a glimpse of a winding ribbon of river came in view.

" That is the Goravlaun," Molly informed her companion. " The white trout will be coming up with the next spate. It is very low just now and runs almost dry in summer. You must fish it; it is excellent."

" I should like to do so under efficient supervision. I have only caught white trout lake-trolling. I'm a duffer in the higher branches of the art."

" Oh, it's only a question of *flies*," Molly replied, with a particular emphasis on the word, " and you seem to have a good stock," with a look corresponding.

" I'm afraid they are not attractive enough," he said, laughing.

" Perhaps in the dressing they show too much of the hook," and Molly smiled triumphantly.

They had come within sight of a small bridge where the road crossed the river, and on nearer approach the girl suddenly exclaimed and reined in her horse.

" Look, uncle, look at that smoke coming from under the bridge, what does it mean? " She pointed with her riding-whip and her face showed apprehension.

" It is very odd," the Squire replied, " we must ride on and see."

The bridge had three arches. The centre one was sufficient for the river during low water, the others were needed for the exigencies of high floods. It was from one of the latter that the smoke was proceeding, coming out in blue wreaths on either side of the road.

" Hold my horse, uncle," Molly said, putting the

reins into his hands, and leaping from the saddle. Warren
followed her example and guided his horse to the side
of the parapet, over which the girl was stooping. The
arch had been closed up on one side with loose stones
and partly on the other. The track of the river leading
to it was quite soft from recent rain and showed numerous footprints. Molly, unable to get a view of the
interior from the parapet, gathered up her riding-habit
and jumped into the field below.

"Anyone there?" she cried out on nearer approach. Warren, holding his horse, heard the sound
of a muffled voice in reply beneath him. There was a
grating sound of moving stones and a man's head protruded through the opening.

"Goodness gracious me! What are you doing
there?" Molly ejaculated, recognizing Sweeny, the
evicted tenant.

"Scrra harm, miss, except gettin' a bit av shelter."

"But where are Bridget and the child?"

"Arrah, where would they be, miss, but wid meself?"

"You have not been sleeping here?"

"Indeed, thin, we have, miss."

"I thought Mr Pinkerton was to give you a little
holding in Knappa."

"No indeed, miss, the Deignons stayed on, it seems,
and this place is better than under the sky or the cowld
sod itself; there was nothing else left."

The occupant of this strange domicile approached
the Squire and dutifully touched his hat. The man
was in the prime of life, lank and thin, and presented a
half-starved appearance. There was a frightened
look in his face, which gained intensity from the tufts
of raven-black hair which straggled through the top of a

bowler hat that long since had parted with the crown. The rest of his garments were *en suite*, the old frieze jacket so riddled that it presented the appearance of a cunning device of holes tied together with string.

"Begad, then I wish it was yesterday yer honour came to see me," he said, spreading out his hands and looking down at his torn garments in mute apology, "but Paddy the Pedlar called, as he thought I wouldn't be wantin' so much in these quarters, an' he cleared me out; sorra's cure to him, an' it's angry I am wid meself for partin' wid an illigant coat."

"Oh, don't be talkin' balderdash," the Squire answered irritably. "Why didn't you come to me when Pinkerton failed you?"

"Arrah, why would I be troublin' yer honour? Sure, it's enough I gave yerself an' the neighbours already, an' Mr Doonas gone to gaol on me account. Bad luck to the smoke that betrayed me as it is. I wish I was a badger and could hide in the rocks where no one could find me."

"You deserve to be sent to gaol for risking the life of your poor wife and child. Come here and hold these horses. Give him yours, Warren."

The Squire dismounted and they followed Molly into the arched tenement; the lid of a salmon packing-box was used as an improvised half door.

"Oh, Bridget, Bridget," the old man exclaimed on entering, but in a tone quite different from that used to the husband. "This is bad work. Why didn't you come to me?"

"Well, indeed, yer honour, I wanted to come but the child was so fretful, for the milk failed me, savin' yer presence, and Jimmy himself was losin' heart, an'

I had to keep spakin' the cheery word to him, but I didn't know the place was so bad or I would have come; the wet is terrible, the smell of the damp sickened us, but we're gettin' used to it now."

The smell of the damp!—the air reeked with it, like decaying vegetable matter, and although Sweeny had shovelled away the top layer of mud the moist substratum remained. As Warren's eyes became accustomed to the place he took in the details. The turf fire, which had betrayed the habitation, now burned clear, and he saw the truckle-bed raised slightly from the ground by lumps of bogdeal; rags were stuck between in the hopeless attempt to make the bed level. A pot, plate and one or two other cooking utensils were scattered about. The box belonging to the lid was used as the child's cradle. Molly had taken possession of the baby, lost in the rags in which it was wrapped. Although she spoke calmly to the mother it was evident that she struggled with emotion.

" You needn't be afraid," she said to the woman, resuming the conversation which had been interrupted by her uncle.

" Afraid, miss. Arrah, why should I? Sure, you could take the forty-acre wall with him in yer arms. It's not that, miss, but I don't think he's long for this world what with the damp and the want av the breast. I don't like to part with him."

" Oh, but you must leave this at once, Bridget. Uncle," she said, turning to the Squire, " we can put them up for a day or two until we find a place for Jimmy. I'm going to take the child with me; he is ill and needs a doctor."

" You mustn't stay here an hour longer," the Squire said, without commenting on Molly's proposition.

" I'll see Mr Pinkerton this evening and something must be arranged."

" Well, God bless yr honour, an' it's little delay there will be, with the child leadin' the way in Miss Molly's arms. An' the good God hasn't left the world without angels whilst her likes is here. . . . Heaven's blessin's on yer head, miss. . . ." The voice choked with tears.

The Squire and Warren were imperiously demanded by Molly to wait outside until the baby was wrapped up. The process took considerable time, but at length the mother came out carrying a neatly-arranged bundle, and although a coarse black shawl was on the outside the child was enveloped in a spotless flannel garment of some kind. Where it came from was a mystery. Perhaps it was saved from the raid of Paddy the Pedlar; or does the good God who sends His angels teach them how to turn a feather plucked from their shining wings into a warm robe wherein to fold His shivering little ones entrusted to their care?

Molly sprang into the s   and the mother placed the warm bundle on the rider s knee. There it lay in the embrace of a firm arm, gently swayed by the regular gait of the hunter, that moved as if conscious of his mistress's tender charge. There it slept, with its little head pressed against a beating heart full of kindly intent for it and all God's needy children.

The three horses cantered along the road, their feet at times in unison, at times antiphonal, answering each other in ringing and defiant beats, and at intervals mingling in inextricable confusion. Their riders were silent, but their thoughts were like the clatter of their steeds' hoofs, order and disorder pursuing each other.

Oh, that problem of the poor, how deeply it cuts;

what gashes it leaves in human souls! Oh, that Irish national pride, how it chooses the hut, the cave, the pestilential archway wherein to hide its grief and eat out its heart in lonely detachment! And that deeper and more elusive phase of it all, the irresponsibility of those in high places! What matters it what becomes of the Sweenys and their infants as long as the law has its course and safeguards the interests of property! That fiendish pagan sophistry that a man has a right to do what he will with his own, and claim the strong arm of the State to enforce it! Poor little innocent infant, how nearly wert thou trampled beneath the feet of that hellish monster of iniquity.

On arriving home Molly busied herself with her infant charge, and the Squire and Warren rode over to see Pinkerton. On the way Warren made a proposition. "I should like," he said, "to take that little farm on my shooting and get Sweeny to work it at a nominal rental."

"That is very kind of you, but it would put you in the position of a rack-renter. You wouldn't be able to get a gillie or a beater; in short, you would be boycotted."

"Well, if it were done through Pinkerton, might not that be avoided? The agent could let the holding to Sweeny at a reduced rate and I pay the difference?"

"If Pinkerton would agree it might be worked in that way. He has not a free hand and is not always to blame. He looks after himself, of course."

On passing through the town on their way to the agent's, elements of unusual excitement were apparent. Groups of men and women stood in the street and at the doors, talking eagerly. The hotel porch in par-

12

ticular was crowded and the name of Pinkerton was freely bandied.

"What is up, I wonder?" the Squire said, reining in his horse and beckoning a bystander.

"Mr Pinkerton has been shot at, sir. The bullet passed through his mackintosh."

"Is he hurt?"

"He is not; it missed him by half an inch. He's more frightened than hurt, and looked like a ghost drivin' through the town; a good thing it wasn't worse anyhow."

"Well, that's bad work. I was just going to the office to see him."

"Oh, then it's not second-hand news ye'll be dependin' on, Squire."

"Anyone suspected?" the Squire asked, noticing that his informant had not told him all he knew.

"N-no . . . but there's a report that Mr Pinkerton shot a man . . . that's only talk; very likely ye'll hear the thruth from himself, sir."

"Who tells that story?" the Squire asked.

"Peter MacBride was coming back with an empty cart afther leavin' Mr Mullins in Scragmore; they say he was behind Mr Pinkerton and saw it. But he got drunk since he came home an' the divil a word of sinse can anyone get out of him."

"That's Peter's prescription for silence, I suppose," the Squire commented.

"Ah, maybe they think because he's drunk that he wants to hide something, although the sorra much excuse the same Peter needs to go on the batter."

"Oh, well, I think we'll ride on."

"All right, sir, God keep us all from harm," and the man rejoined the crowd.

They found Pinkerton at home. If the rest of the particulars picked up on the way were as correct as the description of the agent's appearance the Squire's informant was reliable. His face was ghastly and he was labouring under great excitement.

"I was just coming up to see you, Squire," he said. "I've had a narrow squeak of it."

"So I have heard; you are not hurt, I hope."

"No, my body is all right. I wish my mind were," and the agent sighed heavily. "I'll tell you all about it. You know I went down to collect the rents at Rathskeemin? Well, everything passed off all right. There were fewer complaints than usual and less arrears than I have known for some time. I had only to threaten two tenants with evictions. They seem to think that the new lord will do better for them, and they have never been more tractable. I did my best to encourage the opinion, as it wasn't for me to tell them that the heir was travelling and had not been heard of for some time, and that the estate was in the hands of trustees.

"However, I came away yesterday afternoon with a light heart. I travelled all right until I got to the moor, when a mist swept down from the mountains and it began to blow pretty fresh. I slipped on my mackintosh, and just as I was going up the steep hill of Cloonaun a shot rang out and a bullet hit the iron rail of the dickie. I pulled the horse round, scarcely knowing what I was doing, and another shot followed. I heard something rip, but felt nothing. Then I lashed the horse and reached the top of the hill. There I pulled up and jumped off, catching up the little rook rifle I always carry. One of the assailants was running away, but the other stopped and was in the act of raising his rifle when I fired and he fell "—here the agent sighed heavily again. " I stood at bay for some time, thinking someone might be behind a rock, but there was no one. Then I went o·er to where the man lay. . . . I found him dead."

" By George! " the Squire exclaimed.

" I unbuttoned his waistcoat and saw that he was shot through the heart."

" Well, well," the Squire said, " you acted in self-defence. When the cards are on the table play them. As it is it's a marvel that you escaped."

" Here's the mackintosh, with the holes in it," Pinkerton said. " The explanation is simple; it was buttoned across and the wind blew it out and sagged it. That saved me. Another inch and the bullet would have found more solid material."

" Well, an inch of a miss is as good as a mile," said the Squire. " You are to be congratulated. Do you know the man? "

" Never saw him before. I don't think he belongs to this part of the country. I stopped at Cloonaun and reported the affair to the police; the barracks are only about a mile from the place. They have taken charge of the body. I wanted to consult you as to the proper course. I am quite prepared to give myself up."

" Did you give particulars to the police? "

" Nothing incriminating. I thought it best to reserve that."

" They w'll apply to us and we must issue a warrant, but you can be bailed out," the Squire explained. " We came to see you about a small vacant holding on Mr Warren's shoot, but it's not right to trouble you in your present state of mind."

" Oh, it will be a relief to forget the wretched

business. I half wish that it was I who had been shot; it is a terrible thing to feel you have taken human life even in self-defence. . . His lordship's trustees have instructed me not to let any more holdings on the shoot; that's why I had to break faith with Sweeny."

The Squire then told how he had found the evicted family under the bridge.

" You see, I have been away," the agent said, " and this order from London makes it very hard. God knows how I am sick of these evictions."

" What kind of a man is Sweeny? " Warren asked. " Industrious? "

" Well, I can't say he is, and it is difficult to say he is not. Where he lived there was not enough to tax his energies, and if he worked like a slave it would not make much difference; it meant poverty in any case."

" These small holdings seem," Warren said, " to make for indolence, and if the tenants become lazy the system is more at fault than the man."

" You have hit the nail on the head there," the agent agreed, " but they cling to these holdings like grim death. Eviction is resisted as if it meant parting with a stone mansion instead of a mud cabin."

" Yes, but what have they to turn to? What had Sweeny and wife and child but a bridge by the riverside?" the Squire commented.

" That's true indeed. . . . But you will scarcely believe that I have known peasants to refuse to leave a starving holding for a decent one; their plea was, ' Ach, sure, it was father's before us, an' it's where our childer was born. What was good enough for them is good enough . . .'"

" That is the curse of poverty," said Warren.

" Anything about the y ng heir? " the Squire inquired of Pinkerton, givin a new turn to the conversation.

" I have heard nothing except that he is s ll abroad, but who knows what changes he may mak ; absentee sm has many sins to answer for."

" Well, Mr Pinkerton, supposing I take the vacant farm on the shooting and put Sweeny in as a caretaker, would that get over your difficulty? " said Warren, eagerly.

" I think so, sir. My instructions are not to let any more leases. Take it as an annual tenant with power to renew."

" Thank you, that will suit me. I should also like to take the shooting and fishing for another year."

" Come now, Pin rton," th Squire observed good-humouredly, " you see all y tenants are not malcontents."

" Oh, indeed they are n , and if they were all as easily satisfied as Mr Warren it would be far better for me, and I wou t have this weight on my mind," and again the agent sighed deeply.

CHAPTER XIII

THE same afternoon that the Squire and Warren visited the agent a small rowing boat might be seen crossing the beautiful bay which that morning had stirred the Englishman's admiration. Its sole occupant was a man, who had hurriedly pushed the boat afloat and rowed vigorously out to sea. On the lee side of one of the islets he stopped to adjust a small sail that lay in the bottom of the craft. As he leant over the side the reflection of his own face was vividly mirrored. It was pale and drawn, and the effect was ɔ startling that the owner exclaimed, stifling an oath, " Why, I look as if I had committed a murder."

The light mast was fastened in its socket, but before unfurling the sail Gallagher—for it was he—took off his jacket and began laving his face with handfuls of water. A red bandanna handkerchief did duty for a towel, and after a good deal of vigorous rubbing the man surveyed himself again with evident satisfaction, and spread out the improvised towel to dry.

The boat was rowed o t from e shelter of the island, where it caught a slant of wind, and filling the sail the craft soon began to scud before the breeze. Far off on the horizon a bold headland resisted the inrush of the sea; towards this the boat was steered.

" If the wind holds I can have a couple of hours there and get back at nightfall," the man meditated, as he slackened the rope and broadened the angle of the sail. The boat responded by heeling over more and leaving in her wake a well-marked foam line.

But Gallagher's face, like the water he sailed, took its colouring from underlying depths. Thoughts were busy, and for a long time the hard, set mouth and knotted brow showed that the subject was not pleasant.

" Curse him," he murmured. " Next Thursday . . . and it will only add to his popularity. She "—and at the word the furrows straightened out and the mouth relaxed—" she will think all the more of him. If I could only "—and the thoughts in the new channel swept away for a moment the dark obsessions, and a face cheated out of its early prophecy of good looks became handsome; but only for a moment, and the ugly lines crawled back again and snapped into the old places.

The headland grew bigger and more distinct, and with the rapid pace of the small craft it was soon reached. The boat glided round the sheltered coast where Doonas's yacht, three months before, had anchored.

Gallagher ran aground on the Inisheeny beach and took his way towards Ryan's house. As he followed the path that led to it and reached the high level, commanding a view of one side of the island, he caught sight of a figure in the distance. In a moment he recognized the beautiful Rose that he so passionately coveted. It was the thought of her that had stirred into life the better man that evil and intrigue had strangled. The distant glimpse worked a reincarnation and Gallagher was a transformed being. Instead of entering the house he crossed the field and hurried towards her.

Rose was carrying a tin can in one hand for the milk of the cows she was seeking.

Gallagher whistled, and she stopped and looked

round, but the sunny face clouded as the girl's sharp eyes descried the unwelcome suitor.

" Rent - day," she murmured under her breath. " Indeed, I might have known he was coming."

She stopped and waited in response to his beckoning gesture.

" Indeed, I'm very glad to see ye, Rose," he exclaimed. " Shake hands, asthore."

She gave her hand, which he seized feverishly, until a quick movement of the girl compelled him to release it.

" I want that for milking," she said; " it isn't right to hold another person's property too long."

" Then why shouldn't I now? " .

" Why do you come for the rent then the first day it's due? You might have let father hold it for a while longer," and a merry ripple of laughter followed Gallagher's look of discomfiture.

" You're always teasing me, Rose, and I like you the better for it. I'll tell you why I came to-day instead of to-morrow, because my eyes have been hungering for a sight of you."

" Well, it's a pity they're not sore; it might cure them."

" Well, indeed, my heart wants curing if my eyes don't, and you're the girl that has the remedy."

" Thursday is dispensary day; this is Tuesday. You are out both in the choice of the day and the doctor."

" Thursday," Gallagher repeated. " Ah, it's easy to guess why that day is in your mind," and his brow darkened; but recovering himself he added, " well, if you tell me in a word that you've given Martin Doonas your promise I'll go away at once and never cross your path again. I wouldn't do Martin a bad turn."

" I thought you said it was your own heart that wanted curing, Mr Gallagher. Why do you mention him? I don't think there is anything wrong with his, and if so he is not likely to send you for the medicine."

She stood erect as a sapling, her short, simple linsey dress in no way disguising the grace of her figure; a black and white shawl was thrown across her shoulders. Her bare neck disclosed a skin spotless in its purity and smooth as marble, a beautiful mouth with pouting lips, shaping at one moment indignation, at another raillery, and eyes that flashed mischief, not distantly removed from anger.

Gallagher felt the look and quailed. " Well, indeed," he said in a tone of sincerity, " I came on my own cause, but I'd carry a message for my biggest enemy for the pleasure of seeing you."

They moved to the top of the hill, and catching a sight of the cows in a dip of the island, Rose said, " I must hurry on; I'm late as it is."

Love is blind in tact as well as in passion, and Gallagher, knowing the circumstances of the Ryans, endeavoured to exploit them in the interest of his suit, that he felt was making no progress. The season had been bad and the crops meagre. The island produce, at its best, barely enabled them to make ends meet; the potatoes were blighted and the light soil, only suited to oats, had yielded a poor harvest. There were already arrears, which Ryan hoped to meet at Michaelmas term.

The girl's reference to rent-day led Gallagher to infer that his tenant was not ready.

" Look here, Rose," he said, " you taunted me with

coming here to-day for the rent. I told you the reason. Give me a word of hope now and I'll slip off in the boat and your father won't see a sight of my face until Christmas."

She had increased her pace in the hope of getting rid of him. She stopped suddenly. She thought she knew his meanness and despised him for it, but looked in his face now as if she had discovered a depth that was a new revelation.

" This is not market-day any more than dispensary. I am not for sale to so low a bidder."

" Well, some day you may be knocked down to a bid less than I'm prepared to offer. Look here," he said, losing all control of his feelings and pulling out papers, " there's the receipt for the half-year's rent; give me one kiss and it's yours." His eyes gloated, passion choked him, and he threw his arms round the girl.

With a lithe movement she disengaged herself from his embrace, and swinging the can she held in her hand brought it round sharply on the side of his face with a ringing smack.

Gallagher, utterly unprepared for this sort of retaliation, staggered back, smarting beneath the blow, and his eyes blazed to the accompaniment of a loud oath.

He was about to renew the attack but the girl stood her ground, her face aflame with indignation. She held the can in readiness.

" Come a step nearer," she threatened, " and I'll repeat the dose; that's the kind of medicine you want for your heart affection."

Gallagher paused irresolute, but declining a further application of the remedy turned round angrily and walked towards Ryan's house.

The island farmer was repairing a net indoors, and, ignorant of what had transpired, politely bade his visitor good-day.

" It will be a bad day for you," Gallagher said, still smarting with anger, " if you don't pay the arrears of rent."

The rude method of address naturally struck Ryan, but seeing that something had upset the rack-renter, he quietly replied:

" It ill becomes you to use threats."

" Why shouldn't I when the rent is overdue? "

" You made it a loan and got your interest."

" Well, I want the capital now."

" And suppose I say it's not convanient."

" Then it won't be convenient for you to continue as tenant."

" In throth, Mr Gallagher, it's yerself that got out of bed the wrong side this morning," Ryan observed good-humouredly; and after a pause added, " I thought you said you were not going to be an ordinary rack-renter."

" If I was, would you have the farm at such a low rate? "

" It's the same rate that I always paid for it. Th change of landlords was no benefit to me."

" If I were an ordinary rack-renter you know you would pay more."

" And if I were an ordinary tenant you would take less," and Ryan looked at Gallagher significantly. The latter felt the force of the taunt and remained silent.

" I am a quiet man, Mr Gallagher, and don't mix myself up with rack-renting and land-grabbing. Maybe it suits your purpose to charge the same as Lord

Ballyshameon. My tongue is quiet. It costs a good penny to buy up a wagging one."

Gallagher, who had by this time exhausted most of his anger, felt he had erred in making Rose's father the butt of it. He sought to beat a retreat.

"You're right," he said. "I didn't sleep a wink last night and that's worse than the wrong side of the bed; and indeed it was Rose that was in my thoughts all the time, and what do you think, she won't give me a word of encouragement."

This explanation eliciting no reply he continued: "What's wrong with me that she won't give me an answer? I've known her from a slip of a girl, and I'm pining for her. She made me mad to-day, and it's only now I'm coming to my senses."

"Faith, it might have been better for yourself," the father said, looking suspiciously at the mark on the side of Gallagher's face, "if you'd come to yer senses sooner, and bedad, it seems she did answer ye, an' it's red your ear is in trying to take it all in."

"Oh, indeed, she has great spirit, but look here now, put in a word for me and it's not rent and loans we shall be talking about. As sure as you are her father I'll have her and nothing shall stand in my way."

"Your threats don't concern me greatly, Mr Gallagher, but if you think because I'm a poor man that I'm going to sell me girl, well, you're a bigger blackguard than I thought. That's middlin' plain, isn't it? Ye've had me daughter's answer, that's mine. You can take it with the rent," said he, drawing out the money.

"Not a penny will I take to-day; it wasn't for that I came, Ryan. My feelings have overcome me," he said weakly. "I've upset the girl, and you as well.

I'll come another day, please God. There's a month's grace anyhow," and Gallagher turned and abruptly left the house.

" Plaze God," the islander repeated, " as if anything you could do would plaze Him. It's more likely to plaze the divil."

But the subject of the comment was out of hearing, and launching the boat, set sail. His beetling brows drew closer together in the attempt to hatch out some scheme which would make him master of the situation.

It was clear that the girl's affections were preoccupied and that he had a powerful rival in Doonas. The old man's independence—so Gallagher reasoned— might be due to the hope of an alliance with such a popular and well-to-do son-in-law. How to surmount the obstacle was the problem. A direct appeal to the girl had failed, bribery had failed; but the resources of villainy were not exhausted, and with a chagrined mind and a smarting face the rack-renter set himself the task of tapping a fresh one.

CHAPTER XIV

" MY DEAR MAX,—Ride an Irish hunter and die!
I have ridden, but the process of life 'rounding
to a sleep' has not been effected. But ride with a
simple, open-minded, vivacious, humanitarian Irish girl
and live!—that I have managed to pull off, and the
springtide of the vital process has swept a wider area.
Life, my dear boy, is full of anomalies, and Ireland
seems to hold the quintessence of the ingredient. A
magnificent horse, a fine stretch of open country on
which to show a clean pair of heels, a villainous stone
wall that, given a false step, would break like pipe-
shanks the delicate legs that paw the air above it, an
entrancing view—seascape and landscape—with mystic
tinted mountains, islet gems in a sapphire setting, and
tumbled-down hovels, starving men and women,
famishing children; unravel this if you can. The con-
tradiction in such intimate propinquity gives a rude
shock to the Saxon mind—with its innate sense of
decorum and its insistence on keeping things in their
proper places. London has its East end and its West
end, but it takes care to keep them well apart; it doesn't
mix its elements indiscriminately. Silk and fustian
occupy different benches. The site of the cottage is
selected with due regard to its frowziness, the site of the
castle to its winding river and stately park. Piccadilly
does not deface its marble with stucco. Lazarus has
been sent to his proper place; sores and dogs are out of
keeping with purple and fine linen nowadays.

" Here anomaly is the normal state of things. Singular to relate, the Irish soul has a sweep in it that takes in these contradictions. The simple, open-minded, vivacious, humanitarian Irish girl—that was the description I gave—looks out on the landscape with eyes half-blinded with admiration and peers into the depths of your soul for a witness to its potency, and woe betide you if you don't come up to the standard. The same eyes are equally quick to discover the evicted family under the bridge hard by and find a warm garment wherewith to wrap a shivering child and carry it to a place of safety. What a power of soul vision, Max, to see the sublimity of the mount. ins that ' kiss high heaven,' and the depths of human forlornness, and without squinting too l

" And here is another anomaly which does not yield to ordinary philosophic treatment. In our segregation of things, criminals are a class apart. We have no great passion for the man who has done three months hard, and rarely put ourselves out to condone his offence and minister to his martyred feelings. It is true there is a section of the community who raise funds for giving him a breakfast at a cheap restaurant on his release, and an improving tract on the Divine Catholicism, but it does not include the return call on the tract dis-tributer. The fact that he had been. imprisoned carries its own moral. Were he as immaculate as an angel there would of necessity be a stain on the white wings when they were next spread in freedom.

" But in Ireland it is quite different. A man may be plunged into the loathsome prison without any staining, and if he had no reputation on entrance, makes his exit with a considerable one. His case is not despatched with a cheap breakfast; he is fêted.

I have just witnessed a torch-light procession a mile long which illuminated the path of one of these criminals. He informed me that he discovered twenty cousins, of whose existence he was unaware previous to his incarceration. He is very much perplexed in mind in deciding which to accept of the numerous civic offices placed at his disposal.

" Such is the respect shown for law and order in this country, the moral of which is that institutions right in the abstract may be wrong in application. In Ireland, at least, they will not be permitted to besmirch a man's character.

" I was amused at the illustrations of the shooting affray you sent me. The rifle depicted in the *Daily Reflector*—an ancient carbine with shoulder straps and brass mountings—reflects credit on the artist's imagination. As a matter of fact the actual weapon used was a rook-rifle of small calibre, which could be conveniently stored in the barrel of the aforesaid. The encounter with the assailant and the protracted fusillade between the two men is also a piece of interesting fancy painting.

" Amongst anomalies this deserves mention : the man that was shot has not been identified. It is certain he does not belong to the west or adjoining counties, or the police, who are supposed to know everything, would know him. He had £4, 15s. 2d. in his pocket, a sum unusually large for a man who was ragged and without a shirt to his back. To know how he became possessed of that money would be to get on the track of the unfortunate conspiracy of which he was the victim. Pinkerton was acquitted on the ground of self-defence.

" I shall be returning to London in a few weeks, but I have taken the shooting for next season, which is

13

sufficient testimony to the effect of the climate on my health and the enjoyment of my visit."

.   .   .   .

The weeks that intervened before Warren's departure to clubland were crowded. The last day's salmon-fishing came and went. Then there was the big run of white trout, and excursions were made to higher streams, where salmo trutta, in his coat of silver mail, plunged and leaped under the restraint of the quivering rod, to the delight of the angler.

In all these enjoyments Shawn was the faithful gillie, and his skill in the gentle art and familiarity with the haunts of the game fish added considerably to the success of the excursions. His knowledge of folk-lore also proved extremely interesting to Warren, and the tedium of many a weary tramp was relieved by his stories.

On one occasion he became unusually confiding.

"That's where I got the leprechaun's shoes, sir," he said, nodding towards the Black Valley.

They were returning late from a day's shooting in the mountains. The quest of early woodcock had taken them to a distant point on the coast, where the birds first alighted after their migratory flight. The moon was rising, and shadows cast by the irregular contour of adjacent cliffs made fantastic figures in the cutting, giving an added weirdness to a spot reputed for its uncanniness.

It was a lonely valley, where the heron and wild goose heard echoing answers to their call, and flew round and round in vain search for a glimpse of their companions in mir   When the south-west wind swept up the narrow gorge it whistled and shrieked fiendishly.

It was not a difficult task for the imaginative peasants to furnish the valley with befitting occult apparitions. The clouds assumed many a fantastic shape as they flitted across the mountain in the twilight. The rich tints of the setting sun crept up the hillside, making the heather slopes gay as fairy garments. It only needed the poetic temperament to divine in such places a fitting abode for the good people.

Warren, always ready to listen, turned towards the spot indicated and said:

"Just the place I should imagine for a leprechaun," noticing the rock perched high up on the hillside.

"Yes, sir," said Shawn, half deprecatingly, "but they're mighty hard to catch. Ye might come for a month of Sundays an' not clap yer eye on one of them."

Warren saw the working of Shawn's mind and encouraged him.

"How did you manage to see yours?" he asked.

"Well, sir, people say I'm light of foot and can travel fast, but they don't know that I owe it all to the leprechaun, and it's better work I have to do than to go about informin' them, and maybe have them laughin' at me for my pains."

"They haven't your poetic temperament, Shawn," Warren said quite sincerely.

"I was tellin' Miss Molly about it one day," the gillie continued, taking no notice of the compliment. "She's a great listener."

"Yes, indeed she is, Shawn."

"'Ye're the lightest-footed man in Ballinbeg,' she says to me. 'Ye make no more noise than a spark flyin' up the chimney.' I told her it was the shoes the leprechaun made for me."

" ' Oh, indeed,' says she, ' it's no wonder ye're light of foot if ye have a leprechaun for your shoe-maker.'

" Then I told her how I got them," and Shawn paused.

" And how was it? " Warren asked.

" Well, 'twas this way. I was goin' down to the valley, lookin' for a spot where the moonbeams cross. For if ye can find them anywhere it's the place the leprechaun always chooses to make his shoes. He dare not sit down in the daylight, for fear he'd be caught, an' he can only see rightly in the crooked moonbeams.

" When I got into the heart of the Black Valley I saw a lump of a stone on its end, and behind it was Corrigmore, risin' as straight as a gable. An' I thought to myself, ' When the full moon shines to-night it will strike the big rock an' the beams will cross the valley and meet at the stone, an' that's the place I'll find him.'

" So I lay down an' hid, for I knew he'd hear me if I made no more noise than a crunch on a bunch of heather, an' be off before I could fix an eye on him. Then I waited till the sun went down an' the moon caught a skirtful of its light just as it was sinkin'. I watched the two, the light in the west tryin' to cheat the other in the east by runnin' away an' leavin' it in the dark. But the more the sun went down the harder the moon went up. At one time I thought the sun would have the best of it, for it had the hill with it, and the moon had the hill against it. In throth, I was so busy with the two that I nearly forgot me own errand. There were two stars, one near the moon an' the other near the sun, an' they kept runnin' alongside an' cheerin' as they do at a race. I was just goin' to put heart into the moon meself when it came straight over me head an' struck Corrigmore. That instant minuit I heard the sound of a hammer, an' by the same token there was the leprechaun sittin' on the store makin' shoes, an' a purty picture he made with his red cap green coat an' throusers trimmed with shinin' , buttons.

"'Now is yer chance, Shawn O'Grady,' says I to meself, ' an' ye must keep yer eye on that chap as tight as tuppence in a soldier's pocket.' For ye know if ye take the look off him for a second he's as sharp as a snipe with a shot after him. So I jumped up like a jack-in-the-box, an' to show there was no ill-feeling said at wonst, 'God bless the work.'

"Well, the surprise that came upon him was wonderful. He grew as red in the face as his cap, an' one would think that he wasn't over pleased at meself catchin' him unawares. For all that he was wis enough to be civil an' said, 'You too kindly.'

"'It's boots yer makin'?' says I.

"'No, shoes,' says he.

"'Is the thrade good?' says I.

"'Very,' says he. 'We can't keep up with it,' beginnin' to hammer away with all his might.

"'Throth, that's not a common complaint round our way. What makes it so good in your part of the world?' I axed.

"'The dancin' at Court,' says he. 'They're at it every night, an' the boots they wear out is surprisin'.'

"'They must be a great expense to their parents,' says I. 'I wonder they don't have them thicker in the soles.'

"'Thicker; is it the good people with thick soles! They must all be noise-proof,' says he.

" ' Is there many of ye in the thrade? ' I axed.

" ' We're all in it,' says he; ' it's the only thrade except tailorin' an' dressmakin',' he answers me.

" With that he gave his last a great blow an' shouted, ' Mind yer shadow,' flingin' his cap across me head.

" Indeed I nearly turned round at the word, so cunnin' an' startlin' was it, for he wanted to put me off me guard, only I bethought meself in time an' kept one eye on him. But the other eye, bads grant to it, if it wasn't drawn to the red cap. When I looked round, bedad, only half the leprechaun was to be seen; the other half vanished entirely. Another taste would have deprived me of his company altogether.

" ' Give me me cap,' says he.

" ' The sorra give,' says I, not darin' to stir and take me eye off him again. ' Ye have saved half yer skin, but it won't be much good to ye without the other half. I'll stick to that.'

" ' What do you want? ' says he. ' Goold? '

" ' The sorra penny. I've no use for it.'

" ' What is it then? '

" ' The privilege of dancin' with the good people,' says I, as bowld as I could.

" ' It can't be done,' says he.

" ' Very well,' says I, ' I'm in no hurry. I'll keep ye there till the moon goes down an' ye'll be lost entirely.'

" ' How am I to do it? ' says he.

" ' Make me a pair of noise-proof dancin'-shoes; that's the way.'

" ' Ye can only claim half a pair anyhow.'

" ' How's that? ' I axed.

" ' Sure, half of me has escaped ye.'

" ' All right then,' I answered him, ' only half of ye

will go back to the good people, an' a nice figure ye'll cut among them.'

" ' Very well,' says he, comin' round at last, ' I'll make them, but ye'll be only able to see half of them, for half of me is in the shadow an' the work must be the same. It won't matter to the dancin' if ye don't mind the look of them.'

" ' The sorra taste as long as they are fit to dance with the fairies.'

" ' I make no other kind,' says he.

" Well, with that he began to work as busy as a nailer, an' indeed it was a strange sight. I could only see half of everything he did, half of himself, half of the last, the shoe an' the hammer as it swung round his head, an' all because I had taken one eye off him for a second, but in less time than you could say ' thrap-slicks,' the shoes was made.

" ' There they are,' says he, holdin' them up in his hands.

" ' How do I know they're the right kind? ' says I.

" ' Thry them on,' says he.

" ' How can I thry them? ' I says. ' I've only one eye to spare, an' if I take it off ye an' put it on the shoes where would ye be, I'd like to be after axin'.'

" ' Ye're cute,' says he.

" ' Throth, I need to be to be your match,' I told him plainly.

" ' Hold up yer feet an' I'll throw them on,' he says to me.

" ' All right, only no thricks, flingin' them in me face an' blindin' me,' I cautioned him.

" ' I don't tell lies,' says he.

" ' No indeed,' I agreed, ' except where the truth wouldn't answer. Say the word anyway,' for ye know if ye wonst get them to promise they never go back on their word.

" ' I promise,' says he.

" I raised me feet from the ground and the shoes came through the air with a flash, which nearly took me sight away, an' they slipped on me feet as aisy as gloves.

" ' Now dance,' says he, ' on the big flag beside ye.'

" So I did, an' though I jumped high into the air an' came down on me feet with me whole weight there was no more noise than the fallin' of the dew.

" ' Are ye satisfied? ' says he.

" ' I am,' says I, ' an' now I want ye to '—but, bedad, the stone where he sat was empty; for the minuit I said I was satisfied the spell was broken and he was off.

" Oh, an' it's the fine pair of shoes they were, good luck to them, fit to dance with the queen."

CHAPTER XV

THE last of the shooting days had come; the Squire was invited and his niece joined the party.

Warren, in a dull sporting interval, told Molly the story narrated in the previous chapter. The latter commented on the gillie's usual reticence.

" As a rule," said she, " he is suspicious of strangers and will have little to do with them; his openness with you is quite exceptional."

" I take it as a compliment, for he is most interesting, and his folk-lore stories are fascinating."

" No doubt that is part of the secret; he is perfectly happy with a good listener."

" I don't see how one could be anything else. There is an other worldness about him."

" Oh, yes, he is the high priest of the cult; his mother lives in the mountain. You have seen her, I suppose, during your shooting rambles? "

" No, I was not aware he had any relations; he has not even mentioned her, although we have often passed the hut."

" She is demented, poor soul," and Molly's musical voice took the minor key, " and has hallucinations about Shawn being heir to the property. The late Lord Ballyshameon humoured her and let her live rent free in the hut. She must have been very handsome when a girl, and although old now there are traces still left."

" Well, one can easily imagine Shawn coming from a handsome stock," Warren agreed. " Were he properly fed and clothed he would look the part, and had he been educated he would have been a perfect orator."

" The old woman probably accounts for Shawn's knowledge of fairy lore. She is supposed to have second sight. She made a singular prophecy with regard to an Englishman who had the shooting one year, which came quite true."

" What was that? " Warren asked eagerly.

But Molly seemed suddenly confused and evaded the question.

" You quite raise my curiosity," he commented. " We shall be going that way, and if she knows as much of the future as Shawn does of the past their joint mystic knowledge must be encyclopædic."

" There's Ranger drawing on a pack! " Molly cried. " Look at him."

Far up the mountain-side there was a dip in the heather. The dog was seen stiffening, one paw raised, his neck craned forward, and his tail as rigid as a poker. It was too far off to see the tremor of excitement which swept over his body in recurrent waves.

To reach the spot where the grouse crouched entailed fifteen minutes' climb, but the setter stood his ground as if frozen to the spot. Cautiously now and again he turned his head and looked towards the guns, the rufous tint catching the sunlight. The mute appeal, being interpreted, meant, " Hurry up, I can't hold them here all day "; and when at length the spot was reached, and the grouse whirled into the air with a mad flutter of wings, the dog still held his ground. Two or three sharp shots rang out on the air and a small cloud of drifting feathers showed that one had been stopped in its flight. It fell on the brow of the hill, and Ranger was bidden to seek it. Raising his head and sniffing the air the dog zigzagged for a moment, then cautiou ly moved in a direct line and stiffened again. Shawn followed at his heels and picked up the bird.

"That's a great dog, sir," he said, patting Ranger approvingly.

"Excellent, Shawn."

"It's wonderful the knowledge he has." This was said in a tone that invited inquiry.

"Is that so, Shawn?" Warren said, encouraging details.

"Oh, bedad, it is. Now if there was three or four guns out together you'd always find him near the best shot; he's as cute as a fox, and if there is a bad shot he gives him a wide berth."

Warren laughed; the allusion was not quite impersonal.

"Sorra lie in it," Shawn continued. "One year we had two gentlemen from England that had taken the shootin'. The birds were plentiful, and the first day Ranger found pack after pack, but, sure, shot after shot was missed. The dog each time looked up into my face as much as to say, 'Will I seek dead?' but I couldn't give him the word, for I knew it's live enough the birds was. I saw he was losin' heart altogether, an' I tried to encourage him as best I could. At last he couldn't stand it any longer, an' when he saw a grand pack goin' off without one stoppin' behind, bejabers, he turned tail and ran home. I called him and whistled for him but it was no use.

"Well, I made the best excuse I could for him an' said he was sick. That evenin', when I went back to the Lodge, I didn't want the gentleman to think that the dog was disrespectful. So I called him. He came out from under the dresser with his tail between his legs, an' ses I, ' Ranger, I'm ashamed o' ye.' He looked very downcast, as much as to say, ' Indeed, ye have rayson to be.'

" ' Well,' ses I, ' if ye promise never to do it again ye can have yer supper,' putting a plate of mate and pertaters before him. An' bedad, sir, the sorra bit of it he'd touch. He crawled over to the dresser staggering, and lay down agin.

" ' That dog is sick,' ses I. ' No wonder he ran home. I never knew him before to refuse his supper that way.' "

" What was the matter with him? " Warren asked.

" The sorra thing no more than there is now. The minute the gintleman left the room he jumped up an' began fussin' round me, an' I can tell ye that he soon made his supper lave that."

" I'll have to be careful in my shoot ag, Shawn, or I may expect similar treatment," Warren said.

" Ah, he doesn't mind a miss now and then, but I don't know what he'd be doin' if ye let everything go," and there was a merry twinkle in Shawn's eye, for Warren's shooting was not perfect.

Molly smiled significantly, and when the gillie drew off with the dog said to Warren:

" Shawn is a capital novelist, is he not? " .

" Is that one of his romances with a purpose? "

" What do you think yourself? "

" Oh, I know I've been shooting wretchedly. Well, your Irish peasants have a genius to break into poetry like that in order to give a polite hint."

" Oh, Shawn thinks you have improved wonderfully. It's not all romance; the dog left the shooting in apparent disgust undoubtedly, but he has treated the subject with the usual poet's licence."

They skirted the mountain and reached the hut where Shawn's mother lived. Molly, who was on friendly terms with the old woman, leant over the half-door and called her.

"Eh! eh! Who calls me? I only answer to the Wind in the Gap and the Torrent in the Glen."

"It's I, Granny; don't you know my voice?" Molly rejoined.

"Ah, Miss Molly, you're the soft voice in the branches of the rowan tree; it crushed its white blossoms of the spring into your throat and the red berries of the autumn into your cheeks, alannah," the old woman muttered, coming forward.

"Here's a gentleman to see you, Granny."

"Ah, to see the blighted rowan tree with its sap dried up, an' to hear its withered branches moaning in the blast, and to shiver and turn away."

"Ah, no, Granny, no, indeed," Molly exclaimed, opening the half-door and walking in. "You are not the blighted rowan; give me your hand and let me warm it in mine," and she took the wizened fingers and stroked and fondled them, and the weird voice sank into satisfied crooning as one that passes from a sense of pain to ease.

The moment Warren entered the hut the old woman raised her eyes on him and cried:

"Shawn, Shawn, why have ye been so long away? Years, years."

"That's not Shawn, Granny. It's Mr Warren, who has come from London to see you."

The old lady's eyes fastened on the visitor's face.

"Ah, why have ye been so long? Why didn't ye come when the leaves hung in thick clusters an' shut out prying eyes, an' when the whispers of yer heart could only be heard by the fairies? Ah why did the thrush sing in the holly bush, ' He'll bring it, he'll bring it, he'll bring it? ' and the linnet answer from the whins, ' Ah, no! ah, no! ah, no! ' ? "

" Have you been expecting me to call sooner, Mrs O'Grady? " Warren asked, for the sake of saying something and feeling the strangeness of her words.

She looked at him again, a strange light showing in her eyes, flashing and fading alternately, as if the two sides of her mind, light and darkness, were striving for the mastery.

" Sooner," she repeated. " How soon the green bracken turns to rust. Gold? Who says it's gold? I have burned it, burned it, an' raked the ashes, but not enough gold to make a wedding-ring. Rust! Rust! The thrush lied when he said ' He'll bring it,' the red-breasted linnet told the truth, ' Ah, no!' Sooner? Yes, sooner; too late now, the rust has eaten out— where's Shawn? " she suddenly exclaimed. " I thought he was here a moment ago."

Intelligence once more cleared the poor woman's brain as if a curtain were suddenly lifted.

Molly and Warren both welcomed the change of manner and exclaimed, " He's here," and the son, waiting a short distance from the hut, was summoned.

" Here I am, mother," gently putting his arm round her.

" Ah, lookin' afther the property, avic," speaking in a broader and homelier tongue. " Grand shootin' an' fishin; but bad land. Be kind to the poor tenants, Shawn, ye were poor yerself once."

" To be sure, mother. A dance once a week an' a ball every Christmas for all the tenants on the estate."

" A dance an' a ball, Shawn. Ha! ha! that would be grand."

" Dances an' balls and no evictions, mother agra."

" No evictions, Shawn; ha! ha! no evictions, is that what ye say? Ha, ha, ha!"

" The divil a wan. Why should there be? "

" An' all the fairies back in their places again, the old ones of long ago? " she whispered mysteriously.

" Every one of them, mother asthore."

" Every one of the lost fairies that the hard times drove away. They were to dance at the wedding, Shawn, but he didn't bring it, and the gold turned to rust, an' the hard times drove them away. But they are comin' back, avic, the old ones, mind you. Ha, ha, ha! " and she laughed and cried until exhausted, and dropping on to a chair she closed her eyes.

" She'll sleep now," Shawn said, and taking her in his arms as if she were a child, carried her and laid her on the bed.

" It's sorry meself is that ye came to see her now, Miss Molly," he said in an apologetic tone. " She may not be that way again for months. I saw it comin' this mornin' an' kept away."

" I've not known her to be so bad before. I hope our coming has not upset her, Shawn," Molly said.

" Ah, no, miss, it's that way or worse. Sometimes she sits over the fire an' rocks herself for days an' won't take bit or sup until exhaustion comes, an' that's the worst way—for I must watch her night an' day, for fear she'd fall into the fire. She recovers quicker afther the talkin' an' the laughin' fit. But she has the great knowledge of the fairies an' the like when she's well. Ye've heard her yerself, miss. Now, haven't ye? "

" Yes, indeed, Shawn," Molly replied indulgently.

" You must let me know when she's well and I shall come and see her."

" How long have you lived in this hut? " Warren asked.

" As long as I can remember, sir, an' rent free too."

" And a bit of land attached to it, I suppose? " he said.

" Enough to grow a few things an' bother the hunger, sir."

Warren looked round the hut and the picture of its poverty was branded on his mind. He often thought of it afterwards. What a monument to a noble lord's generosity!

" Well, Shawn, you need not come with us now. You would like to stay with your mother? "

" Oh, no, sir, she'll sleep for twelve hours very likely. Besides, I wouldn't like to be inthrudin'," and he walked outside.

" Intruding! What do you mean? "

" Well, ye see, the fairies will be with her, an' they don't like listeners. When she wakes up she'll have the new knowledge, an' if I stayed with her she wouldn't —but there's Dinnis an' the Squire waitin' for us an' beckonin'. I see the dogs drawin' on a pack on Scudmore Bluff," and the gillie stepped out in front.

" Can you see the dogs all that distance? " Warren asked Molly. " When I am with Shawn I feel short-sighted."

" Oh, he can see the grass growing; his ocular powers are not normal; it's difficult to keep pace with the hillside peasants."

" It is these wonderful wild surroundings, I suppose," her companion said, nodding towards the hills, " that quicken their superstition and give them imagination. That poor soul in the solitary hut for years peoples her lonely world with fairies, hears their voices and talks with them."

" You don't believe in the fairies then? " Molly observed with an arch look.

" Oh, don't I, though," answering the look in kind. " One of them has made my lonely life in Ireland so particularly pleasant that if I were the most hardened sceptic the process of conversion would be inevitable."

The reference was so palpable that Molly couldn't get away from it. She looked up and curtsied grace- fully, the pressed berries of the rowan tree deepening in her cheeks.

" Ah, now, you are trying to prove your theory about Granny's fairies," she said.

" Am I really? I wasn't aware of it."

" Well, you see, if you really people your lonely world with one fairy in so short a time, no wonder Granny has such a host round her."

Delighted with this bright flash of his fairy's wing he turned a full-souled look on her.

" That consoles me for my lonely life coming to an end so soon," he said.

" It's my turn to ask for an explanation now."

" Lest I should add to the number of fairies."

" Ah, but think of the one lonely fairy, poor thing, swinging on a bough of heather, or dancing on an island sward and drinking from an acorn cup and all ⌐lone; fairies go in troops and join hands in the dance. Ah, now, a lonely, shivering fairy! And surely it must occur to you, Mr Warren, that that is just the condition of Ireland to-day. Our country depopulated, her best sons and daughters daily sailing from her shores, our brain must create fairies or we would grow melan-

14

choly. Who would come to Ireland for its society? its *camaraderie?* It is the lonely fishing and the lonely shooting that bring visitors like yourself. I daresay in decorous moments you are shocked at our unconventionality."

"Oh, no, don't say that," Warren interposed earnestly. "I have been charmed, delighted at the open, simple ways of the people."

But Molly was determined to complete the thought in her mind.

"Conventionality," she continued, "is an unwritten law of a complex state of life. The West Country will be educated into it one day like the East, and Ballinbeg become as snobbish as Dublin. So you see we must fill in the spaces in our Western life with the fairies for the time being."

"I, at least, am going to show my appreciation of the country by returning next year, and that is part of the work of my good fairy. . . . No, I'll be hanged if I'll have a second, so don't ask me. When you are as sick of conventionality as I am, you will feel like the lady in sultry India who sighed for a 'dear, disconsolate drizzle.' We are to visit the caves, I think," he said, changing the subject.

"My uncle hopes to go in a day or two, if he is well enough. He has been shrinking from hill-climbing to-day, I noticed, and seemed quite tired out at luncheon," and the beautiful blue eyes clouded.

"I am so sorry," Warren said kindly. "I fear I have been taxing his strength too freely."

"Oh, no, it's just what he likes. Your visit to the West has interested him; he often talks about it."

And so, untrammelled by social law, and with spirits free as air, these two young lives tramped the mountain and bog together, until the tired dogs drooped their heads, and the gillies with the game strung across their shoulders turned their footsteps homeward.

As the party wended their way through the valley the light still lingered on the summit of far-off mountain crags, but shadows blurred the rock and heather of mid distances.   Nothing disturbed the silence but the plash of a hill torrent and the call of an old cock grouse in its efforts to rally the scattered brood, and the crunching of the heather beneath their feet.

CHAPTER XVI

DOONAS'S release from prison and the honour paid him by his fellow-townsmen was the subject of discussion round every hearth in Ballinbeg. It followed so soon after the attempted assassination of Pinkerton and the shooting of his assailant that both topics, like contingent streams, flowed side by side, commingling and separating indefinitely.

Bolan's forge, the rendezvous for free expression of opinion, was filled one evening with kindred spirits, who did exhaustive justice to both themes. Gallagher was amongst the number. He rarely said much, but was an excellent listener, and possessed a faculty for diverting into a particular channel the driblets of conversation. The talk had been desultory and was chiefly about a number of people who had been to see Doonas and congratulated him on his release. Dennis Fahy was speaking of his visit.

" Meself and Shawn went shootin' yesterday with Mr Warren and passed Martin's house on the way. He was outside the door, an' of coorse I gripped him by the hand. It was the left one by the same token, an' says he, ' Ye'll excuse me, Dinnis, giving ye the left; me right arm is stiff in its socket with all the wringin' it's had.'

" Well, bad luck to Shawn, if he didn't stand there lookin' up an' down the valley, an' sorra word of welcome fell from his lips. It seems Martin is goin' to enlarge his house an' put a new addition to it."

At this there were exclamations expressive of general

interest, and wagging of heads as if something else lay behind it.

" Oh, begorra," Dennis said, " there's a nice slip of a girl in one of the islands that might have something to do with the new buildin'—" The rest of the sentence was interrupted by Gallagher suddenly jumping from his seat to the floor and knocking down some of the tools. He showed unmistakable signs of agitation.

" I wish you wouldn't leave hot nails on the bench, Jack," he exclaimed. " Bedam, but one of them has burned me," rubbing the affected part.

" Throth, then, it's cold hind quarters ye must have," Jack retorted, " judging by the time it takes the heat to reach them," which raised a loud laugh at Gallagher's expense.

" Go on with the story, Dennis," he said when the laugh had subsided, making a wry face.

" Well, after Shawn had finished looking up an' down an' scratchin' his head, he opened his mouth as if to speak, but closed it again with a snap.

" ' This is bad work, Mr Martin,' says he.

" ' What's the matter? ' says Martin.

" ' The place of your new buildin'.'

" ' It's a breezy place, in throth,' Martin replied, ' but thick walls an' a double coatin' of thatch will be a match for the sou-wester anyhow.'

" ' It's not that I'm thinkin' of,' says Shawn, lookin' very wise. ' Yer going to build in the fairy pass.'

" Martin laughed, but Shawn did not seem at all pleased. And with that he set up the wirr-a-stroo until meself was shakin' in me shoes.

" What do ye think of that now? " Dennis asked, looking round at his audience.

" Well, belief in the fairies is all right in its way,"

Gallagher put in, "but Shawn pretends to too much knowledge altogether. Where does he get it? I'd like to know."

"Well, Shawn is like one of the Good People himself," Dennis answered, "only he can't make himself visible and invisible like them, but, bedad, he can hear them and see them for all that. Faix, I could tell ye a good story if ye are in the mood to hear it."

"And why wouldn't we?" said the smith. "We're tired of murders and inquests and thrials, and the divil knows what."

This sentiment was echoed by several of the others. The theme of Doonas's release from prison was worn threadbare.

Dennis, nothing loath, complied.

"Well, I was crossin' Corrigmore the night of the Fair. It was late when I came to the brow of the hill, and who should I see but Shawn, lookin' down into the Black Valley. So intent was he that he never felt me till I touched him.

"'What are ye lookin' at?' I says, tappin' him on the shoulder.

"'Whisht,' says he, 'or ye'll frighten them.'

"'Frighten what?' says I.

"'The fairies, to be sure; don't ye see them?'

"'Sorra one, or you neither, I'm thinkin,' says I.

"Arrah, with that he turned on me with the anger blazin' in his eyes, for he wasn't the man to be contradicted on a thing like that.

"'Well, show them to me,' says I, 'for me eyes is none o' the best,' just to pacify him.

"'Rub them wid that,' says he, handin' me a copogue * with the dewdrops floatin' in the centre of it.

* Dockleaf.

" Well, to plaze him I did it.

" ' Now look along the edge of the hill,' says he; ' there they are sittin' c : the ground and swingin' in the heather waitin' until the sun sinks behind Corrigmore.'

" ' Why are they waitin' for that? ' I asked.

" ' Then the glen will be in shadow, an' they can join hands and dance. . . . Ah, look at that beautiful crature wid the wild flowers woven in her hair an' the silk bobs danglin' from her girdle, she's the mistress of the revels.'

" Throth, it's meself doesn't know whether it was the dewdrops, but Shawn's fancy got hold of me, and all at wanst there was a strange light in the sky, an' the fleecy clouds that looked like white sails on a becalmed sea were lit up with a goolden tint. Then the hillsides caught the light, and the heather changed into the most beautiful colours. A web fine as gossamer fell across the slope like trailin' robes, climbed up the bare rocks and skirted the wild broom.

" The hillsides began to alter too, as if the sky dropped the material that had been woven in a mystic loom.

" Shawn kept lookin' until the red disc sank behind Corrigmore and the glen was in shadow. Then the excitement came on him. There was a light in his eye and a glow on his cheek, his head began to nod, an' his body to sway to and fro, as if he were keepin' time to music, tho' the sorra sound could I hear.

" ' Oh, look at their beautiful white arms linked together,' he said, nudgin' me, ' an' their feet goin' like the wind.'

" At last the excitement overcame him, an' before I knew where I was he sprang to his feet an' ran from my side, lightly boundin' over heather an' rock. Be-dad, I held my breath, for every moment I thought he'd slip an' be dashed to pieces over Corrigmore, but his sure foot never stumbled. A goat couldn't travel the same ground without disturbin' some of the loose stones, and one the size of an egg makes a noise like a pistol-shot on the rocks below. But the sorra a pebble did Shawn stir.

"In a few bounds he reached the spot we were lookin' at, and the next moment I saw him dancin' round an' round, his arms stretched out an' his long fingers bent as if he held a hand on each side. Maybe it was my fancy, but I thought I could see a circle of light, though indeed it might be only the blossom of the white heather that grows there.

"'Twas with madness Shawn danced and capered such as I never saw the likes of, an' what's more, he kept it up until he fell down in a dead faint forninst me. Well, I ran over to him, an' it was a long time it took me to reach him for I hadn't his sure foot among the loose stones. There he lay just as he fell, his fingers closed as if he still had a hoult of the fairies' hands. . . . It was hard work to get him back to his senses; I called him by name, untwisted his fingers, an' struck him on the palms as hard as I could. At last he opened his eyes, but the same Shawn gave me small thanks for me trouble. Begorra, I thought he'd kill me, an' the strange way he spoke made me think he'd taken lave of his senses. Not a head or a tail could I make out of it at first.

"'It was your rappin' at the door that made them put me out, ye noisy omadhaun,' says he.

"'Arrah, what door are ye talkin' about?' says I, tryin' to quiet him.

" ' The door of the palace,' says he, ' where the fairies took me after the dance, an' where I saw herself, the queen of them all.'

" ' Arrah, how could I knock at it? ' says I. ' Not a noise did I make, except the few slaps I gave ye on your hand.'

" ' Ye did make a noise, bads grant to ye, an' if it wasn't on the door, how could they hear it? Sure, ye have no eyes to tell the differ between a fairy palace an' a barn. It's the quiet an' silence they like, an' it was your shoutin' an' bangin' that made herself put her hands to her ears and rush from the place.'

" Well, when I heard all this, faix it was meself thought of the smart slaps I gave him on the palms. But I saw it was no use crossin' him, an' I wanted to hear about what he saw in the palace.

" ' Then it's meself that's sorry that I didn't know better, Shawn,' says I; ' I wouldn't have disturbed ye for the world. Throth, it's yerself has a right to be angry wid me, none better. Arrah, why didn't ye tell me where ye were goin', an' I wouldn't have made such a blunder.'

" ' Och,' says he, ' I've lost the chance of a life-time.'

" ' See that now,' says I, ' but indeed ye must tell me what happened, so as to put me on me guard, an' if the chance comes yer way again, it's Dinnis Fahy won't be spoilin' it for ye. Tell me, avic,' says I, coaxin' him.

" Well, afther a while he came to himself and began to talk of what happened from the time he left me.

" ' One thing's certain, Dinnis,' says he, ' that it's meself that has danced with the fairies.'

" ' Arrah, now, tell me something I don't know,'

says I; 'I saw ye wid me own eyes, an' by the same token, it's the smart step ye have an' the illigant one. But how did they come to let ye? Sure, no one ever heard the likes o' that before.'

"'It was the shoes that the leprechaun made me,' says he, 'that's the secret. The minuit the sun sank below Corrigmore an' the Good People began to dance, the sorra still me feet would keep with the shoes on them. That's why I raced down an' joined them. Faix, they made a gap in the ring, like the childer playin' "Here we go round the mulberry bush," an' they got bould of me an' welcomed me like one of themselves. An' their hands just felt like a breath of cool air on a warm day. Bedad, there didn't seem to be anything to ketch at all, at all, an' yet there was a grip round me fingers like real flesh an' blod an' the strength of their arms was wonderful; it lifted me from me feet and carried me into the air.

"'Well, we danced round an' round I don't know how long, when all at once the mistress of the revels, the one I showed ye, cried out "All in," an' wid that there was a great race for a door that opened forninst us; faix, I ran with the rest, an' I found meself carried along with the crowd, and before I knew where I was, there I was in the palace. When I looked round an' saw the wonderful sight it nearly took my breath away. It was a big room that looked as if it was made out of an Achill diamond. The walls and ceilings glowed with the brightness—it was like as if a fire burned through them.

"'In the middle of the Court sat the queen on a grand throne. Well, I'd only just time to look about and notice one or two things, when the fairies began to march round Her Majesty. "Plenty of diamonds to-night," says she, lookin' at them, an' it was meself thought the bright spots sparkling in their hair and on their arms were dewdrops, but it's mistaken I was, for a voice cried, " Off with the jewels," an' with that there appeared in the centre of the floor a thing like a big rose leaf with the flowers runnin' over the rim' an' the buds just openin' their eyes a little as if the light was too much for them. Well, each of the fairies in turn jumped over this, an' shook the diamonds into the leaf, an' they fell like the sound of a soft shower of rain, an' so quick did they follow one another that the shower never stopped. Then the light fell on them, and a beautiful rainbow came in the middle, flashin' and dancin', an' it wasn't half a rainbow either, but a whole one as round as the moon herself.

" ' Just at that a voice said in me ear, " What have you to present to Her Majesty? "

" ' " Faix, the best of all presents, meself," says I. Up to that no one took the least notice of me, an' I thought I'd be bold when me turn came.

" ' " Well, come along."

" ' " All right," says I, " with the greatest of plea-sure," but just as I took a step forward the queen put her hands to her eyes an' cried out, " Who brought a shadow from the glen? "

" ' I couldn't make out what she meant, but I saw all the fairies lookin' at their dresses, shakin' out their skirts, an' spyin' into one another's flounces as if a shadow was hid in them somewhere.

" ' " Who brou 't that shadow in? " says she, more sharply than ever; " look at it creepin' all along the floor," an' with that she pointed to where meself stood.

" ' " Cover up the diamonds," she cried; " if that shadow gets in they won't be third water value," an' half a score of leprechauns took up another leaf an' put it over the jewels.

"'Well, she was in a terrible state, when a leprechaun whispered a word in her ear, an' didn't meself know him for the chap I caught in the glen. When he had finished she said "Oh!" in a kind of relief I thought, an' axed him to present me. It was the proud moment of me life when he beckoned me to approach the queen. But just then, bad luck to ye, Dinnis Fahy, if ye didn't spoil everything wid yer loud knockin' on the door. All the fairies began to tremble, an' the queen rushed off to the thunder-proof room, the leprechauns fell on me an' began beatin' me, and drove me from the palace.'"

CHAPTER XVII

IT was Warren's last day in the West. The early morning was spent in preparations for the journey back to London. Fishing-rods and guns stood ready in their cases, and portmanteaux, boxes packed with books and other personal effects presented a melancholy spectacle of labelled readiness in the hall. Their owner surveyed them with feelings akin to those of a schoolboy at the end of a long and delightful holiday.

He passed into the room where the garrulous Biddy had daily regaled him with the small talk of the place, and repeated the latest news circulated by Dorris, the postman, with liberal annotations of her own. An instinct warned him that in twenty-four hours he would be hungering for the repetition of one of these interludes.

On the table in the sitting-room he found a note. He broke the seal and read it. It was from Molly. She had written to say that her uncle was not equal to the proposed picnic and the fuller programme of luncheon on the island would have to be abandoned. But there would be time for a row as far as the caves in the evening, and the boat would be at the slip. The reader's eyes eagerly devoured all the consolation of the amended plan, and Warren placed the note in his breast-pocket. The morning was spent in correspondence; then he swallowed his luncheon, went out and took a cut across the fields seawards. Every rock and whin bush so familiar by this time looked sombre, and even the birds' call seemed to be set in a minor key.

The note said " evening," but there is no afternoon in ordinary Irish parlance, and perhaps an early start was implied. As he crossed the brow of the hill the bay flashed in view. still and smooth beneath a cloudless sky. What a per; ict day for a row! Above the jetty that ran out from the shore he caught sight of a slate-coloured boat. Lengthening his strides Warren quickly reached the spot. It was a small craft, with a light pair of sculls and a rudder lying in the bottom. He took in these details, then looked round eagerly, but no one was in sight. He sat down on the edge of a pit, gathered up a handful of sand and let it trickle through his fingers. It was fine enough for an hour-glass, and as he watched it falling it seemed a fitting symbol of the recent period of his own life which had filtered through.

And what had transpired within that brief period? Things momentous for Charles Warren. A broken constitution rejuvenated, a frame clothed upon with strong muscular fibre, mental flabbiness metamorphosed into tense grip, and the birth of fresh ideals and the subtle quickening of responsibility to a new order of things. Warren had been conscious for some time of the bubbling up of those subtle springs of young manhood, and with them a growing sense of the sweep of life towards a nobler goal. In the background of it all there was a dominating influence. As the breath of the mountain and the ozone of the sea had knit into new strength his physique, so the atmosphere of a noble soul had touched the deep chords of his being and brought them into tune with higher things.

He looked at the small boat and instinct told him that they would be alone. To her influence upon him, at least he would make his sense of acknowledgment;

the girl who had taught him, inspired him, trusted him, should at least know that. His heart had gathered together that bunch of flowers to lay at the shrine. How far it would satisfy her he scarcely dared to think. How far it satisfied him—ah, there were richer flowers blooming in the same soil, but he dare not present them yet.

How little Molly, on her way to the boat, knew of all this. What girl does know of the deep influence she daily engraves on the life with which she is in close social contact?—the artificiality that stains the lad's soul with its pigments, the coquetry that drives the confiding heart to the excesses of despair, the insincerity that slackens the springs of life for wholesome action—this, or the inspirer of the noblest manhood. Coventry Patmore's lines came to him.

> "Ah, wasteful woman, she who may
>   On her sweet self set her own price,
> Knowing he cannot choose but pay,
>   How has she cheapen'd Paradise.
> How given for naught her priceless gift,
>   How spoiled the bread and spill'd the wine
> Which, spent with due respective thrift,
>   Had made brutes men and men divine."

At length the subject of these meditations appeared.

She wore an easy-fitting dark green costume, and a grey turban hat blended softly and harmoniously with her golden shot hair. She took the oars, despite Warren's protest, and motioned him to the tiller.

"There is a good deal of cross-current out here," she said, "but I am accustomed to it. Steer for the Scariff first," pointing to a sharp rocky headland, "to make the caves. I shall have to row chiefly with the left oar. We shall have the flowing tide on our way back, and you can take your turn then."

" Oh, don't talk of coming back," Warren said. " How clear-cut and distinct the islands are. It seems as if we could reach that one in ten minutes "—nodding towards the Scariff.

" If . do it in forty it will be good work; distance is so de . ve on the water," Molly answered.

" I suppose it is because the atmosphere is so wonderfully clear. Every point in that bluff looks as if it were seen in some powerful limelight. Ireland has no need to be ashamed of her effects and mystify them."

" Oh, but she often does," Molly replied, " and only glimpses are obtained."

" Well, that's not characteristic of her; she is generally open and frank, at least in my experience."

" It all depends. We are reserved until we know people, and then—perhaps too confiding. Help me with the rudder a little more here, the current is strong."

" It is perhaps due to our more complex society that the English are so reserved, but I'm going to be an Irishman this afternoon."

" Ah, please, not so hard; the current is slacking," said Molly.

" I'm so sorry; I fear I have not been steering well."

He had never known her more collected and half suspected that she interrupted him at critical moments to show her sang-froid. It was either that or there was a depth in her nature not usually attributed to Celtic emotionalism. Warren had yet to learn that the nature most open is often the most reserved.

" I was thinking as I waited by the slip of what I owe to you for the pleasure and, I might add, the education of my visit. To your uncle I have already expressed my gratitude, now I want to thank you."

The deepening tint of the grey-blue eyes and an answering smile of unaffected pleasure showed Molly's sense of the compliment.

" I came here," he said, " mainly in quest of health; you remember what I was six months ago, perhaps? "

" Oh, indeed I do; you didn't behave yourself at all well during the dance at Inishlyre," and Molly nodded her head deprecatingly.

" Well, I think if I had the chance now I might improve on my conduct."

" Oh, the mountain air and sea breeze work wonders; everyone that comes here says that."

" But my mind was in as flabby a state as my body, and it has been braced up too. I owe that to the stimulus of your clear outlook."

Warren's confession was so transparently genuine that the girl, who was prepared to listen to flattery and meet it on its own ground, did not answer. He continued:

" Social conditions prove anything; as material for debate, they may be used for or against the Irish character. One might fasten on poverty and argue to indolence; hovels, and find a justification for eviction; lawlessness, and deduct—a natural disposition towards crime. You have lifted that mist and showed me what lay beneath. I am not at all sure that you are always right in your judgment of things—that does not sound flattering," he said with a laugh—" but you have taught me the importance of sympathetic treatment. The doctor's visits and talk often do more good than his medicines."

" It's very nice of you to put it in that way; it's a

compliment that I should like to think I deserved, but sympathetic treatment cuts deep and the want of it accounts for outlaw and crime. No doubt economic conditions affect the well-being of the people, so that something more than sympathy is needed. A bundle of dry thorns will boil a pot when honeyed words won't. The tide is not low enough for us to enter the cave," she said, looking round; "we shall have to land and wait here."

The boat was brought round and run up a little cove, where the fierce beating of the waves had ground the pebbles into fine sand. They jumped out and hitched the rope to a ledge of rock. Above them a green sloping sward, backed by a jagged cliff, invited a magnificent view of the bay. Warren looked up at it longingly.

"That is the lowest ledge; there are several higher," Molly said, following his glance. "Are you good for a climb?"

"Oh, certainly, but you must be tired," he said in a deep, low tone.

"I can have a rest on the top; my arms feel it a little, that's all."

"Mine have been grossly indolent," he said; "they are at your service."

But Molly was far more sure-footed than her companion, and her hand was frequently needed to steady him; possibly there was a good deal of unnecessary help on both sides; there usually is in such circumstances.

When they reached the top she sat down on a carpet of grass, velvety in its closeness, and Warren threw himself down at her feet.

"Oh, how magnificent!" he exclaimed, looking out

on the bay westward. A sea of blue swept away to the horizon in an infinite expanse. The islets, multiform in shape and clustering so closely, looked as if it were possible to step from one to the other. A range of mountains flanked the water on one side with heather and bog on the other—such limitations giving definiteness to the setting of the exquisite seascape. A mystic light hung round the mountains and tinted the scene.

" It's no wonder Shawn sees the fairies dancing on these islands," Warren said. " I wish my prosaic mind were capable of the discovery."

He had taken off his cap, and his fine, shapely head, with its wealth of brown hair, reposed on his locked fingers as he lay stretched on the slope.

Molly looked down at him, revelling in his enjoyment, and snatching a draught of pleasure on her own account from the handsome figure lying at her feet. The fine artistic face, the intellectual forehead, the— She gave a start! Where had she seen that physical outline before? It seemed strikingly familiar. The cap had ruffled the hair, naturally disposed to be rebellious, and its *négligé* condition started the likeness, and other parts rapidly pieced themselves in. Was it a proof of metempsychosis? and had some previous age in the distant past found her in the same place and with a similar companion? She listened to the voice; the tone too, she imagined, had the development and music of a rougher organ of her acquaintance.

Warren interrupted the train of thought.

" I wonder how the advent of commercial enterprise would affect all this! "

" It would get rid of that rich colouring on the side of the hills, the patchwork quilt of your first discovery," Molly replied; " æsthetically the outlook would suffer."

" Yes, of course, ' land-making ' would cease as an industry, with the liberation of pasture land. And these mountains," Warren added, " supposing they are full of mineral wealth and were blasted and tunnelled— good heavens! how the poetry of the place would be destroyed. One of the most dismal things I have seen was a Welsh valley in the heart of the coal district— dull, dreary, disfigured beyond recognition, and once it must have been exquisitely beautiful. How would you like that, Miss Molly? "

It was the second time he had addressed her in this half-familiar way. The first was in a less adulterated form, the day when she played the part of the faithful gillie and waded into the river to gaff the salmon. But it was then a familiarity excused by consternation. The effect on the first occasion was negligible; now a pleasant flutter in the girl's breast left her face radiant. He saw it, and a feeling, half joy, half pain, thrilled him.

" I suppose we should lose something," she said, " but not to that extent. The giant's quilt looks picturesque from here, but when one sees the real article that covers the peasants' beds I would not hesitate to part with it."

" Would not commercialism banish the fairies? " Warren asked, raising himself on his elbow and looking at her with intense interest.

" We want more of the real fairies," she replied. " I do not think their advent would dispel our poetic illusions. Their absence has made our country so un- happy," and the beautiful face clouded and the eyes of the speaker dimmed.

Warren's pent-up passion struggled to break loose, and the love-flowers seemed to burst into sudden bloom. He drank in their fragrance. He could have stretched forth his hand and gathered them in clusters and heaped them on the altar that was ready—ah, he knew it—to receive them. But all along he had steeled himself against such a declaration. What did she know of him? Nothing of his history of the past that might have blasted him and branded him in her eyes. For the time being he was committed to silence. Just then the surging tide threatened to sweep everything before it, scruples and all. His eyes devoured love, and love responded, and now he thirsted to drink from its deep spring. Was hers great enough to forgive him afterwards when she knew all? The passion within him answered yes. Why should he not gather her to his breast and confess everything? How his heart bounded at the very thought, the impulse had half taken shape, and in another moment would have swung into action.

But Molly's words checked it.

" We've had plenty of bad fairies like Ballyshameon," she continued. " What we want is good ones to come and live amongst us. . . ."

The spell was broken. Warren heaved a deep sigh.

" Ballyshameon is dead; how do you know that his successor may not be different?" he asked, almost petulantly.

Molly noticed the changed tone and looked inquiringly.

" I mean," he said, " it is scarcely right to prejudge the son's case before anything is known of him."

" I was thinking of the inevitable practice of absenteeism—the son following in the father's footsteps," Molly replied. " The old lord never brought his children over here, so that they know nothing of the place or whose money, after all, has clothed and educated them, and enabled them to be globe-trotters."

" That can scarcely be counted to them for unrighteousness," Warren replied.

" No, but it accounts for prejudice towards Ireland."

" Good heavens! how, Miss MacDaire? They can scarcely be prejudiced against a condition of affairs of which they are practically ignorant."

" You forget," Molly answered astutely, " that the time would come when the father would have to explain to the children why he lived in England instead of Ireland, and seek to justify it. The young heir, whoever he may be, is not likely to take risks which his father declined, and will probably content himself with drawing his rents and travelling where there is no risk of getting a bullet through his mackintosh like his agent."

" Yes, but the fact that the attempted assassin was not a tenant and unknown ought to spike that gun. Besides, it is said that the son turned radical on his father's hands. That, at least, shows independent judgment, which might be taken to stand sponsor for a different policy."

" I wish I could think so," Molly sighed. " When I see the conditions on which that man is battening I hate the name of Ballyshameon. When you go back to London, if you ever meet him, tell him so from me," and the speaker's beautiful face glowed with anger.

" Come now, Miss Molly, that's not like Irish good-nature to hate a man you have never seen."

" I did not say the man," she corrected, " I said the name."

" Oh, well, if I ever meet the man I'll tell him so, and then when I've told him what I know about you "—

and Warren looked smilingly at the face, grown serious with passionate indignation, as a lover might do who pleads for forgiveness—" if he's the man I think him to be, he'll change his name."

Molly could not help smiling at Warren's method of defence, nor fail to feel pleased with it.

He followed it up by adding, " Don't be prejudiced against a name because a previous owner besmirched it.   I think I heard your uncle say that Ballyshameon's grandfather was a fine specimen of an old Irish family, honoured and respected by the tenantry.   History may repeat itself and the stain be erased from the escutcheon."

" That's a hopeful view of it, but a dream.   Come," she said; " the tide has fallen, we can row into the cave now."

Warren jumped to his feet and offered his hand. Molly placed hers in it, and the man's fingers closed with a firm pressure.

" You have made one adherent to your cause, Miss Molly; let me pledge myself your devoted servant," and he bowed like a courtier and reverently kissed the hand in his keeping.   " I have been defending the new heir because I confess I know him."

Molly started.

" We were at Cambridge at the same time, and it is quite true that he holds views very different from those of his late father.   He has his limitations and failings, but I think an open mind.   He is pretty certain to pay you a visit."

Molly felt the tell-tale sense of embarrassment rising in her face and immediately combated it.

" Oh," said she, " ancient history may repeat itself in that case.   It was supposed to be in this cave "—

tossing her head in the direction—"that the Mysterious Lady dwelt who kept the gleaming pearl boat in which she spirited away Connlan to the land where the sun never sets. The new heir would not care to run risks like that, although the Irish prince was supposed to be translated to a place where death was unknown and from which sin and strife were banished."

Warren laughed and looked his thoughts on that subject; put into words they would have been, " Ah, Molly, if you adopt the rôle of the Fairy Lady it will be impossible for Ballyshameon to resist your ' comhethei ' "

They descended the hill and re-embarked. The tide had fallen and the wide mouth yawned in the side of the cliff. Molly knew the ways of the tide and skilfully managed the boat. A cold chill fell on them as they passed from the sunshine into the cavern, which rose above them in an arch of solid natural masonry. What countless ages it must have taken aggressive Neptune to pierce with his soft drill that rigid rock!

Everywhere there was evidence of great seas periodically hurled against it, of fierce storms that clamoured for admission, shrieking and howling like countless fiends mocked by its spacious emptiness.

Warren looked round, his mind absorbed in its wonders.

" Marvellous," he said to his companion, scarcely above a whisper, but the word was caught up and the voice multiplied an hundredfold, as if he had shouted.

" It would not do to talk secrets here," said Molly, in a megaphone voice, every word thrown back with " house-top " publicity.

" If the other powers of the Mysterious Lady were

in proportion to her voice, she would be irresistible,"
said Warren.

"Oh, but you haven't heard her full-toned witchery
yet; wait a moment," and Molly pushed the boat
further into the depths of the cavern and sang:

> "There are at the Western door,
>   In the place where the sun goes down,
> A stud of steeds of the best of breeds
>   Of the grey and the golden brown.
>
> There grow by the Eastern door
>   Three crystal crimson trees
> Where the soft-toned bird all day is heard
>   On the wings of the perfumed breeze.
>
> And before the Central door
>   Is another of gifts unto'd,
> All silvern bright in the warm sunlight
>   Its branches gleam like gold."

The changed position relieved the exaggeration of
the words and had a softening effect. Molly's voice
invested them with an exquisite charm.

Warren's impulse to declare his love half strangled
him. Just as the last words died away in a passionate
whisper on the girl's lips, a strange thing happened.
Far back in the dark recesses of the cave there came a
plash and tumult like the soughing of a great wave on
a pebbly beach. It was so out of keeping with the
stillness of the cave that it broke on Warren's hearing
with startling effect. It seemed to him like the
materializing of his own passion that expressed itself
in a long-drawn sob of pain.

"What is that?" he exclaimed in surprise.

"It is the launching of the Mysterious Lady's boat,"
Molly replied, enjoying his sense of mystification.
"I think we had better be going."

"Oh, but I'm not a prince," Warren answered, recovering himself.

"No, but perhaps you might be mistaken for one and the result would be the same."

"Ah, that would only prove the lady's perspicacity inferior to her witchery, but I'm afraid you are right about the advisability of tearing ourselves away from these mysterious charms. As soon as you have piloted the boat out I shall relieve you of the oars. Look at those rocks, how jagged and dangerous they are; a careless stroke and they would pierce the bottom of the boat like a lance. Why do such sinister dangers always wait on things beautiful?" he said, looking round the cavern.

"Oh, I suppose on the principle of the flaming s word at the gate of Paradise, to keep mischief-makers at arm's-length."

Warren pondered the answer as if it solved larger problems.

"You have got hold of the true philosophy of things, Miss Molly; life would be tragedy if it were not for its guardian angels."

Outside the cave he took the oars with a firm grasp, as if his own feelings were surging tides through which he must perforce cut a passage.

"I shall depend upon you to steer me," he said, his thoughts still intent on the subjective tumult. "You really did so on the way out, although I was supposed to have the helm."

She sat opposite to him and gave inspiration to every stroke of the oars. His long, muscular arms reached forward as if they would fain draw her into a close embrace. The western sun had lit up the heavens with brilliant tints, and the rich light falling on the girl's face gave intensity to its fine moulding and its calm strength. He thought he read in it a subdued sadness, as if she too had had her struggle. . . . How bravely she had tried to hide it he little guessed. Mentally he compared their cases. It was an accidental circumstance that kept him silent, and in his heart he cursed it. It was an eternal decree, the inexorable logic of decorum, that sealed her lips. One word from the girl would have sent him from the Irish shores a happy man, but that word could not be spoken. Truly, the " superior vessel " has to pay for its privileges.

Shawn was waiting on the shore to take round the boat, and Warren and Molly walked across the fields. The conversation flagged as they drew near the house.

The Squire was still confined to his room, and Warren spent some time with him pleasantly chatting before saying good-bye. He excused himself from staying to dinner on the ground of travelling preparations. Half an hour later he was out beneath the shining stars, his lips still bearing the impress of the soft hand that had been firmly pressed against them in a final adieu. He hurried along the road, grown so familiar to him— every stone and gap associated with memories that leaped into life with an intensity bordering on pain. He reached the boreen that led up to the lodge. That too had its recollections. It was there he had been startled with an apparition of— He pulled up sharp, there was something more than the unlocking of memory; there stood the reality again—the silent woman a second time blocked his way.

" Oh," he exclaimed, " Mrs Fitz Martin."

" Yes, Mrs Fitz Martin, the wife of drunken Peter Fitz Marti , the black sheep of the family."

" What is troubling you? " he said. " Tell me how I can help you."

" Everything is troubling me. My thoughts are as restless as Poullamore when the merrows are disturbed. Ah, Poullamore," she repeated in an awe-struck tone, shivering and drawing the black shawl closer round her shoulders. " It will have me yet if he does not mend his ways."

" You are referring to your son Philip, I suppose. I thought he was doing better," Warren said sympathetically.

" Ah, she told you that, did she—she that has fanned the spark into a flame. She has driven him to it; how can you help me? Well, you are going away; don't come back again, she won't listen to his love by the side of yours."

" I have never spoken a word of love to Miss MacDaire," Warren said earnestly.

" Spoken! " she exclaimed. " Has she spoken a word about hers? "

" No, not a syllable."

" And do you think because of that she doesn't love you? Ah, well, you know she does. ' Not spoken a word!'—ah, that's it. Fine sport for the English gentleman. If you had spoken it would have been better for my Phil. He might have got over it and settled down. He is right after all; she has been spoiled for him. And you have spent the day with her and left her to-night without speaking a word."

The taunt stung Warren to the quick. What explanation could he give to this raving woman. Here was a double wrong which his fate had inflicted on him. On the surface it looked as if the charge were just. . . . Would she take that view of it too, that Charles Warren came to Ireland for sport and included her amongst the quarry? The thought was maddening. . . . And yet he could not say, " I am going away, the field is clear for your son; let him try his luck." He could not make Molly a prize to scramble for. To say, " I have not been amusing myself at Miss MacDaire's expense; to-day I had to struggle to prevent a declaration of my love," would be leaving himself open to still graver misconstructions.

These thoughts rapidly coursed through his mind. He parried the thrust by replying to Mrs Fitz Martin. " I am extremely sorry for you, but is it right for your son to pay his addresses to any lady whilst he spends his time as he does? I do not feel called upon to defend myself against the charge you have urged. Your concern for your son is natural and leads you to say extreme things."

" It is necessary to go to extremes to prevent extremities," she replied bitterly. " I warned you before about crime in Ireland. I repeat the warning now. I may be a Cassandra to you, but the ugliness of the prophecy is no disproof of it."

" Ah, well, prophecy is not a thing to argue about; one can only accept or reject it," he answered. " I should gladly accede to any reasonable wish of yours, but I think you must see that you are hinting at conditions which it is impossible for me to discuss. Once before you asked me to go away, now you warn me not to return, and hint at possible dangers. I am not in a position to commit myself to a particular course of action, and as for personal risk, I hope I am not a coward."

" Oh, you are steady and strong; if your father had been a drunkard you might be as weak as Phil is. It was bred in his blood, poor boy. . . . Molly might save him, I cannot," and the woman buried her face in her hands and shook with poignant grief.

"Let me walk back with you," said Warren, taking her arm as the unhappy woman turned to go. "Perhaps I can serve you and your son. You see he has avoided me. If you would send him over to England it is quite possible I might be able to assist him in making a career. He must break with his gambling and drinking companions, and there is only one way—leave the country. I have friends who could help him; tell him this. I'll go as far as to promise him an appointment on an English estate if he turns over a new leaf. Pinkerton knows my London address. Tell your son to write to me."

"Oh, I knew you were kind and good," she said, grief setting her voice in soft, subdued tones. "I wish there were any hope of my son acting on your advice. God bless you for it, and save you from harm. . . . Now leave me. I must return alone." And the poor crushed woman broke away from Warren's side, ran down the road and was lost in the darkness.

That night two souls beneath the same roof struggled with heartache—the mother for her son, bemoaning his wild ways; the fever of drink and gambling set aflame afresh with the fuel of unrequited passion. She rocked herself from side to side in the room where she daily spent long hours of loneliness. The sight of Warren's handsome person—his manliness, his gallantry—sent her back along the winding way of bygone years and recalled a face and figure of no less strength and charm—the early days of her wedded life, buoyant with hope, prophetic of soulful happiness. She recalled the rides together on the springy turf. Ah, how the sight of

Warren and her niece going forth on horseback a few
days before smote her.   Then came the last ride, and
the last bold leap . . . and the months of sweet ex-
pectancy.   But alas, the black clouds that began to
drift on the horizon!   She could see them now and the
arms folded across her breast tightened, and the finger-
nails dug deep into the flesh—the betting and gambling,
that twofold brood of hell which first inflames the
soul then drags it in the foul mire of dishonour.   The
nightly drunken home-coming, with fits of violent
madness or maudlin imbecility, the agony of it even
in retrospect. . . .   Then the premature birth, the
brain fever, and the blasting of a young life that began
fair as a May morning. . . .   Her red, tearless eyes
stared into the darkness, and heart-strings once attuned
to music, touched by these brooding thoughts trembled
into pain.

And in another chamber the strong light of newly-
awakened love beat on a young soul unused to its fierce-
ness and frightened it.   Flowers, rich-tinted, which
had sprung up in the crevices of bare rocks, lay bruised
as if by some ruthless heel, yet in the bruising yielding
sweet fragrance. . . .   Would they ever raise their
heads again, these fair, unsought, unexpected blooms?
And in thought lips ripe in all womanly loveliness were
pressed against   And the lu ea that brought
the fairy pri   d . . . with
silent lips   he harp
island that   music   se to song
the lapping of   rock-bound shore . . .
ah, the mag   a   pulsion of a strong
arm that knew not how it   amed a wild island bird
and circumscribed its flight. Oh sweet, sweet sea
that gave so much . . . oh, cru l sea that would bear

it away again. . . . The perfume of the flowers still lingered, the music of the sea rose and fell, and the heather struck from its tiny bells a peal of love chimes. Fair, shapely arms gathered all in a close embrace against a fluttering breast that sighed itself into dreamless repose.

CHAPTER XVIII

ON his return to the Lodge Warren found Biddy in a state of consternation in regard to his luggage. During his stay the number of books that had arrived from London, and other personal effects, were so numerous that Paudeen declared that they would want another car to hold them.

" Arrah, howld yer whisht, Paudeen; sure it's neither a wedding nor a funeral that two cars would be needed. The one that brought them hasn't grown any smaller than it was, an' himself hasn't grown so much bigger that it can't take him as it brought him."

" 'Tisn't himself I'm talkin' about," Paudeen answered, " but his things; it's them that's grown bigger."

" Oh, bedad, it's great the air is, that things thrive that way," Biddy replied, believing that her son was at fault and not the accommodation. " Is the well full? "

" Packed to the mouth; it wouldn't take another— hairpin," Paudeen suggested in his hurry for a small object. " Come an' see for yourself."

" Oh, the Lord save us! " Biddy exclaimed, looking at the pile of unpacked things and the car already loaded. " This is a nice time to be tellin' me; why didn't ye say so sooner? "

" Arrah now, how could I know until I found out, an' if I came to ye any sooner ye'd be askin' me how I could tell before I had tried; sure, there's no plazin' ye."

" But how can we get a car this time of night, an' himself not in either? "

" Ah, I can go in the mornin' an' bring one for the luggage; he'll want the other for himself."

On his return Biddy explained the difficulty to Warren. He smiled at her embarrassment, but willingly acquiesced in the suggestion that Paudeen should fetch another vehicle.

" What kind would ye like him to bring, sir? Is it an outside car or an inside car ye'll have? "

" What is the difference, Biddy? " Warren asked, puzzled by the nice distinction.

" Sure, sir, an outside car is a car that has the wheels inside, and an inside car is a car that has the wheels outside."

Warren recognized in this definition of the outside car the Irish jaunting patent, and replied: " Well, Biddy, we'll patronize native industry and have the one with the wheels inside."

If Biddy's prayers and blessings at parting could have been realized, Warren's fitness for a better world would have been more than assured. The good offices of all the saints were invoked and long life on a scale which would have made a youngster of Methuselah.

" It's the longin' will be on us all until we see ye back again, and a ' cead mile failte ' to greet ye," and Biddy's apron found its way to her eyes a good many times before the final farewell.

At the quay, with her white sails unfurled, rode the *Witch of the Wave*, the yacht that brought Warren to the hospitable shores he was now leaving. It was manned by Dennis Fahy, Shawn O'Grady and Shamus, the cabin-boy. No warrant prevented the captain, Martin Doonas, from taking command that morning. Every gamekeeper and poacher that had tramped the bog and mountain with " his honour," and every tenant of the little holdings on the mountain-side were at the quay, jostling each other in their efforts to get near and shake the hand of the gentleman that had been so " lauhy."

Warren was deeply touched by this display of feeling. It puzzled him, as it puzzles every visitor who does not understand that the temperament of the Irish race is the most kindly of any under God's sky; once disarmed of suspicion, the people throw open a nature in which are stored up all the urbanity and grace of true gentle-folk.

There was a smart breeze, and the deep blue of the sea crested into brilliants where long, sweeping waves broke. The yacht, rocking at anchor like an impatient bird chafing to spread its wings, was released and went off at a rapid pace. It headed for Inishlyre, which lay in the direct route for the destined harbour. The boat struck across the bay to keep clear of the rocks and shallows, and was soon abreast of the parting head-land which lowered above the coast-line.

Warren was watching a gannet or solan-goose, which poised in mid-air and cunningly balanced itself before its wings suddenly collapsed, and it plunged into the foam after the sprats that broke the water.

Scalloped Shawn in the bows was looking towards the headland, and his sharp eyes made an important discovery.

" Look, look! " he exclaimed, pointing to the crag, " by the virtue of me oath, there's the colleen herself."

Warren and Dennis turned round. High up on a narrow ledge of rock an object could be seen, apparently no larger than the gannet, the Englishman had been watching.

" My God! " said Dennis, " she's climbed **Mauhereen** Joul, think of that now; there's not half a dozen men in the county could do it."

" Arrah be dhu hist," * Shawn interrupted, noticing Warren's startled look, " it's **meself has** shown her the path. Didn't she take an eaglet out of the nest from the same place when she was only a slip of a girl? There, she's waving her handkerchief now," said he, suddenly breaking off.

Warren jumped to his feet and waved back ardently. As his eyes got more accustomed to the view, and Dennis brought the boat a little closer, the figure became more distinct, and intrepid Molly, in a white serge dress, stood revealed on the towering cliff.

" Ah, my sweet bird, that I could fly to you! Farewell, my beautiful, farewell! " That was what Warren sought to wave back as he stood there, his eyes glowing with love's passion.

Molly's heart answered, could her lover but have heard it, in the words of an ancient Irish heroic:

> "Oh, youth, whose hope is high,
>   Who dost to truth aspire,
> Whether thou live or die,
>   Oh, look not back nor tire.
>
> Thou that art bold to fly
>   Through tempest, flood and fire,
> Nor dost not shrink to try
>   Thy heart in torment's dire.
>
> If thou canst Death defy,
>   If thy faith is entire,
> Press onward, for thine eye
>   Shall see thy heart's desire."

There were words, too, of tenderness that never reached the ears of the listening youth, for they were

* Hold your tongue.

only given to the zephyr that played in and out among the sheltered cliffs.

They watched the slim figure on the cliff which momentarily grew smaller and fainter until it looked scarcely larger than a guillemot in a niche of the rock, then faded out of sight.

The final surprise came to Warren as he was settling down in the railway carriage a few minutes before the train started and Shawn stood before the door. He had said farewell to the boatman at the quay and had ridden on a car with Doonas to the station. But Shawn was there as soon as they. When discovered he blushed like a girl.

" I thought I'd have a run across the fields, sir," he said in half apology for his presence. " I was stiff after sittin' so long in the boat." The two-mile run had no effect on the mountain-climber.

" You mustn't be surprised, Mr Warren," Doonas said, " if Shawn meets you at the Broadstone; he'd outstrip the train as well as the car."

" Ah, well," said the faithful gillie, " if I don't meet you in Dublin, sir, I hope we'll meet again on the mountain."

" I hope so indeed, Shawn," came Warren's hearty response.

" Throth, the grouse will be as plentiful as bilberries next year."

" That will be capital; but what makes you think so? "

" Because, sir, the divil a farmer on the estate will burn the heather afther the way you've treated them. The hens' nests may be robbed and Farmer Mahoney's goats milked on the sly, but the sorra grouse's egg will be touched, I'll go bail."

" You see, sir," said Doonas, smiling, " what a good influence you have had on the tenants to be able to cure them of that weakness."

" Well, the malady could not have been bad if it lent itself to such simple treatment," Warren replied, looking amused, and not without feelings of pleasure.

" Ah, kindness is a great medicine in this country; it's a pity it is not dispensed more." This from Doonas, who turned to the gillie and asked:

" How are the salmon likely to be, Shawn? " winking slyly at Warren.

" It's goin' to be a great year for grilse, bedad; they'll be so plentiful that the river will be stiff with them."

" Oh, come now, Shawn," Warren laughingly said, " we can't bribe salmon like the tenants, you know."

" It's not that I'm dependin' on," the gillie replied, " but the spawnin' season two years ago was great, and the fish will come up next year in such numbers that ye'll be able to walk across the ash-tree cast on their backs without wettin' yer feet."

There was appreciative laughter and then a silence fell on them during the awkward moment which immediately precedes the departure of a train. Doonas had touched upon every subject of interest, exhausted it, and had grown silent.

Shawn had said the last great word on the salmon and stood back from the carriage door, with his large eyes devouring the man who had so fully won his affections. Just as the train began to move he rushed forward and thrust his arm through the window for another farewell clasp.

" God speed ye—" he gasped in a broken voice, the words trembled on his lips, his eyes clouded, and

as Warren responded and the train drew away from the
station the faithful gillie's cheeks were wet, the pent-up
storm of feeling broke, and Shawn O'Grady wept like a
child.

" Come along, Shawn," Doonas said kindly; " he'll
be back again next year."

" Back! " Shawn repeated; " he will never leave
me night nor day. He's been like a brother to me.
We once met in another world—whisper," he said,
leaning towards Doonas's ear. . . . " Whisht, that's
why we'll never part." Shawn's eyes flashed with
frenzy, his face twitched in the intensity of emotion.
Doonas became concerned. " One of his mad fits,"
he thought. " I must get him away at once."

" I can't recollect myself where it was . . . she
knows, but she won't tell me—whisht! " concluded the
mysterious whisper.

Doonas was glad to get back to the yacht, where
they slept that night. A heavy gloom fell on Shawn,
who crept into the darkest corner of the boat and remained there in dogged silence.

The yacht reached Inishlyre the next afternoon and
Doonas landed. It was only a fortnight before, that a
suitor bent on a similar errand received his *congé* from
the beautiful girl that was the genius of the island.
Gallagher found the Wild Rose beyond his reach and
his rough clambering only resulted in pricking his
fingers.

It was the same path which Doonas took that afternoon. The girl had gone down to the point of the
island, and seated amongst the luxuriant bracken that
concealed her from view looked out upon the sea,
dreamed her dreams and abandoned herself to the sense
of its mystery. She watched the rolling tide sweep

up the rocky shore, finding voice amongst the grey stones which it had polished with infinite patience. Its high-water flow was marked with a line of withered seaweed that each tide essayed to push further up the bank and peg out larger territory. Rose found an interest in watching the breakers, until the force was exhausted and a thin wash spread out and sank among the interstices of the loose stones. A pair of oyster-catchers, driven by the tide from the point of an adjacent islet, flew towards her, their shrill piping call resounding far over the silent water, which they hugged in their flight. They lit close enough for her to see their long orange beaks scouring amongst the treasure-trove of crustaceans brought by the incoming tide. "One for sorrow, two for joy," Rose counted.

These sea-magpies, as they are called, like their land congeners, are not without omens to the peasants, and the lustrous black eyes looked out again in quest of the white sail of the yacht which had signalled to her as it passed the island on the previous day.

A bunch of dandelions was within reach of her hand. She plucked a stalk, and putting it close to her lips blew the delicate white-winged seeds, repeating the words: "He will . . . he won't . . . he will . . . he won't . . . he will." The last breath sent the remaining seeds into the air, and a blush overspread the girl's cheeks at this second favourable omen.

When would he come? She had been looking towards the Frenchman's Rock for more than an hour, but there was no sign of the *Witch of the Wave*. Her hand went out towards another seed stalk. "(Blow) one o'clock, (blow) two o'clock, (blow) three o'clock, (blow) four o'clock, (blow) five o'clock."

She looked towards the sun. "Why, it is that

now," she said. The sea-magpies, which had been forgotten, rose with a startled cry. Rose knew that something must have alarmed them, and looked round for the cause. . . .

" Martin!" she exclaimed, for her lover stood within a few paces of the spot.

" Rose!"

He doffed his cap, and holding out his hand drew her near him. But Irish freedom is safeguarded by Irish bashfulness. With a swift movement she evaded the attempted embrace.

" How have you got here?" she inquired. " I didn't remark the boat coming in."

" It was high tide, and we got across the bar and took the short cut north of the Frenchman's Rock. It's long enough it has been keeping me from you, aroon. Rose, I have been starving for a sight of you," and the still-imprisoned hand was warmly clasped and another attempt made to draw the treasure within his arms.

" Ah, now, Martin, you mustn't. You can see me very well from where I stand; you are not short-sighted. Tell me about Mr Warren; you have been taking him to the train?"

" Well, and what can I say but that he has gone away again."

" He's a lovely dancer, Martin. Do you mind the night he came to the island?"

" Of course I do."

" It was a schottische we danced together."

" Was it? I don't remember."

" He is taller than you, Martin."

" You seem to have a great memory for all his good points."

" Oh, that's only two; he has lovely hands and he

can squeeze without hurting you—a-ah1 not like some people."

" Did he squeeze yours, Rose? " Doonas asked, half in alarm.

" He'd be a muff if he didn't."

" Why do you say that now? "

" Because a muff is something that holds a lady's har_ɹ without squeezing it."

" Ah, now, Rose, you are bent on teasing me; let us sit down here, agra; I've something to say to you."

" You're taller standing, like the dog sitting."

" Ah, now do, acushla."

" Well, let go my hand then, and you'll promise to behave."

" To be sure I will.   The new wing of the house will be soon finished, Rose."

" Will it indeed? " plucking the grass with one hand and turning over the blades in a thoughtful mood.

" I'll be wanting you then, Rose acushla."

" Mother and I will come to see it when it's finished. When is the house-warming?   You're great at the reel, but you must practise the schottische more, Martin."

" Ah, teasing me again!   I want you there alto-gether, agra," and Martin captured the hand with the grass in it.   " The day is long and the night black without you.   I see my Rose's eyes in every twinkling star, and at daybreak the thrush in the fuchsia hedge wakes me with a song of her, and every day I sing my own:

> " ' But soon my love shall be my bride,
> And happy by my own fireside,
> My veins shall feel the rosy tide
> That lingering hope denies.
>   Shule, shule, shule agra.'

Oh, 'tis longing I am for my jewel.   Rose, to me you

are like a gem in deep water that my arm is not long enough to reach. But when I ruffle the deep, trying to grasp it, the gem sparkles all the more. Come to me, my treasure," and the lover's arms were thrown open.

She hung her head for a moment, then with a passionate gasp threw herself into the strong arms that encircled her and the full perfume of the island rose yielded itself to his embrace. Then, tearing herself free, she bounded off like a deer, alarmed at her own temerity, and sped to the house at the other end of the island.

CHAPTER XIX

THREE months had elapsed since the events re-
corded in the previous chapter took place. The
little western town pursued the even tenor of its way
uninterrupted by undue excitement.

Soon after Warren's departure, Phil Fitz Martin
renewed his matrimonial addresses. The Squire was
showing signs of breaking up and his nephew pleaded
with Molly to give him the right of being her companion and protector.

"It's no use, Phil," she answered. "I told you
before that I cannot marry you, and I have not changed
my mind. Your wild ways are quite enough to prevent any decent girl from looking at you, but if you
were all I could wish in that respect, my answer would
be the same."

"Of course it would, as long as the London swell
was eligible, but now that he is gone I thought you
might look at it differently. Who is to manage the
farm and the tenants if anything happens to uncle?
I—"

"I have as little desire for your management as for
your gibes. I wish this subject closed, and never re-
opened," said Molly, rising indignantly from her chair.

"Then by God it will be opened in a way that you
little think," and with that Phil flung himself out of
the room.

One day the Squire was superintending the erection
of a fence round Poullamore. Shawn O'Grady ap-

proached him, and after watching the operation for some time in silence said:

"Ye have lost one baist, Squire, but I'm thinkin' it's nothin' ye'll save by the fince."

"It's only a few palings and wood is cheap," said the Squire, who was always civil to Shawn

"Throth, it's not the wood I'd be sparin but the cattle," said Shawn. "Sorra a palin' ye'll sink that won't cost ye a baist."

The Squire's nephew was standing by and was for ordering Shawn off, but his uncle would not allow him.

Shawn left the place muttering to himself and no one thought of his remarks until next morning, when Kitty, the kitchenmaid, came running in from the yard and exclaimed:

"Arrah, the lid of the well is off, and the water is risin' up an' down in a way terrible to see."

A couple of hours afterwards a heifer was found strangled in the palings. The next morning the fence was gone; it had vanished in the night like magic.

The old Squire did not attempt to replace it, and it would not have been easy to get workmen to go near the pool. Molly was riding the next day, and taking the walls as easily as she did the heather, when she met Shawn. She always liked to listen to his stories and his prognostications in regard to Poullamore had made her curious.

"You are quite right about the pool, Shawn," she said, pulling up the horse. "Uncle told me what you said."

"It's not hard to know, miss, for the likes of those that want knowledge. It was wrong to touch Poullamore."

"But why should it be wrong to protect the poor cattle from being drowned?"

"Because, miss, Poullamore belongs to the Good People. An' it's not right to interfere with them. It's few cattle they ever axed, an' in throth there was good reason for the one they took. But it's slow some people are to take warnin', an' it's meself must go about givin' them the friendly word, an' more often than not gettin' the hard word back."

Molly held out her hand and touched him on the shoulder. "Now, Shawn," she said, "you know neither uncle nor I ever say a harsh word to you."

"Ah, no! acushla, it wouldn't be you I'd be meanin', ye're ten thousand miles from such a thought, but indeed there's sorra in store for ye, mavourneen, though it's meself wouldn't be wishin' to bring ye the bad news. When one stone of the buildin' is rotten others fall with it. The goold in Poullamore has caused one death, and it won't be left at rest until the last drop of bad blood in the Fitz Martin family is purged out, and it's yerself must take a share in the purgin'."

He leant forward and whispered: "Someone is listenin'."

Molly raised her eyes towards the rocks, but nothing was in sight. Aloud Shawn said:

"May your joy be as deep as the sea an' yer sorrows as light as its foam."

Then he turned and fled up the hillside, and in a few moments was out of sight.

The sorrow in store for the colleen came swift enough. The old Squire took to his bed. His devoted niece was constantly by his side, nursing him with the tenderest affection and so soothing the hours of pain and depression with cheerful companionship. He

could not bear her out of his sight and the shortest
absence from his room caused fretful inquiries. The
end came peaceably and Bryan Fitz Martin was gathered
to his fathers.

There were two more people in the Big House
affected by his death—his sister-in-law and her son.
The widow had offered to take her turn in the nursing,
but the old man's preference for his niece asserted itself,
and only on rare occasions did he become her charge.

The morning succeeding his death Poullabeg under-
went one of its periodical disturbances. The lid was
thrown off and cracked in two, and the water tossed
and foamed as it had not done since the bullock was
drowned in Poullamore.

The reason for all this was generally attributed to
the demise of the head of the ancient family, but
Shawn O'Grady, who was usually in the minority of
one, asked:

" When was Poullabeg disturbed except by Poullamore? "

After the funeral the family met to hear the reading
of the will, but the chest where it had been deposited,
on being opened, was found empty. The lawyer who
had drawn the will up and was present declared that he
had placed it there and locked the strong box with his
own hands. Then, after a good deal of talk Phil asked
who were the witnesses.

" Kitty, the maid, and Tim, the coachman," the
lawyer answered. " They were the only persons on
the spot when the Squire signed it. Perhaps," he said,
" I'd better put that right by calling them."

Tim took off his old cawbeen on entering the room,
tucked it under his arm and marched to the table as if
he were going to be tried for his life. He saw how the

well had been disturbed and was greatly alarmed at it.

"Do you remember witnessing the Squire's will, Tim?" said the lawyer,

"I do not," Tim responded bluntly.

"What!" said the lawyer, almost jumping out of his chair, "what do you say, you spalpeen?"

"I do not mind witnessin' any will."

There was a movement of surprise in the family party and Phil smiled cynically.

"What!" said the lawyer, louder than before, "you witnessed no document?"

"Ye didn't ax me about a document, ye axed me about a will," said Tim, who strongly objected to making admissions.

"Oh, indeed."

"How could I tell it was a will; I didn't read it."

"Oh, that's it, is it? It's smart you're growing for your mother's son. We'll all live to be proud of you. You remember witnessing the Squire signing a document?"

"I do, to be sure."

"See that now? Stand down."

"Now, Kitty, it's to yerself I'll be putting the same question. Do you remember witnessing the Squire's will last Tuesday?"

"The sorra lie I'll tell ye, sir," said Kitty, "nor demane meself by going round Ballybrig to reach Ballycush "—casting a side glance at Tim—" I do."

"Indeed, you have a clear head, Kitty. Now I want to ask you jointly, and severally, if you left the room before I locked the will in the strong box—the document I'll say, for the sake of Tim's conscience, which is tender as his head was when he fell from the loft after drinking the poteen in mistake for water."

" I did," said Tim.

" Of course you did; we all know that."

" That's not me manin'."

" What is it then? "

" I did leave the room an' left yerself in it."

" True for ye, Tim, and I ˜emember now how I missed your company. You didn't see me put the will— document, saving your presence—in the strong box? "

" I did not."

" Stand down."

" I suppose your answer will be the same, Kitty? "

" Faix, then, it isn't meself that saw you, sir, for I left the room immediately after signin' me name. But there was one thing I did notice, if I might be bowld enough to mention it without taking a liberty."

" What was that? "

" I noticed the strong box in the corner was opened as it is now, for the goatskin that used to cover it when it was closed was lyin' on the floor an' I nearly tripped over the same skin as I was hurryin' from the room to stop the milk from bilin' over that I left on the fire."

" See that now, did you notice anything else, Kitty? " Mr Wheedle asked encouragingly.

" No, sir, but there was one thing I didn't notice."

" That's not evidence in the ordinary course, but as the inquiry is informal we'll hear what it was, Kitty."

" I didn't notice the goatskin next mornin' when I came to sweep the room, nor indeed for that matter have I set eyes on it since."

The lawyer gave a start, but immediately pulled himself up.

" Ah, well, Kitty," he said, " the old goatskin is not of much value, it's the loss of the will that's bothering us."

Nothing could be done under the circumstances, and a provisional arrangement was agreed upon in regard to the management of the estate. The nephew went the pace. There is wild youth that has good in it, but there was little of the ingredient in Philip Fitz Martin. Every bit of money he could lay his hands on melted like salt in water. There was not a race within forty miles that he did not attend, and he became the talk of the country for betting and gambling. Every fair saw the Squire's fine head of cattle sold for far less than their value. He became the prey of unscrupulous jobbers, who pocketed two pounds for every one that came to the estate. He proposed new schemes of improvement for which mortgages were required, and consulted Mr Wheedle, but the lawyer gave him no encouragement. The latter was watching every move of Phil's as a fox watches a hen's roost. He had taken the disappearance of the will greatly to heart.

And how about Molly all this time? The Squire had been a father to her, and his death left a deep wound. Although of gentle blood her father died poor, and her mother had little to leave her. But the fortune she had in her face and her tall, graceful figure, straight as a sprig of mountain ash, many a squire would have laid down all he had for.

But not one of them would she listen to. Her eyes clouded, and if the beauty of all the rosebuds in the garden was woven into a pair of lips, they could not be sweeter than those which refused many a would-be wooer.

And worst of all, her cousin plagued her with his

offers, and his mother pressed her too, more for the son's sake than any great love she had for the colleen.

After repeated refusals Phil grew wilder than ever in his attempts to raise money. Debts hung round his neck like a millstone. Then he disappeared for a week and returned with Gallagher. They were first noticed prowling round Poullamore and dropping lines with lead weights into the water. Shawn came on them and asked: " What are ye doin' to the pool? "

" It's a purse I dropped in the pond by accident," Phil said with a poor attempt at humour.

" And is it an eel it is turned into that you're fishing for it with a hand-line? " Shawn asked.

" You've guessed it now exactly."

" Faix, then it's plenty the money must be wid yerself to handle it so loosely. Are ye sure it isn't somebody else's money ye have dropped? Listen to me now," said Shawn, "for the last time, the sorra a ha'p'orth of it ye'll ever handle," and with that he turned on his heel and left them.

That night Phil's mother had a dream. She thought she stood on the cliffs at Corrigmore and was looking across the sea. There was a bitter wind blowing that cut into her flesh and made her tremble. . . . Someone came beside her and took her hand. He wore a long cloak and the face was familiar. When she shivered he put the cloak round her and she grew warmer. The bitter wind lost its harshness, the rough sea grew smooth, the islets in the bay smiled and the water sparkled with light.

Then far away to the west a mist commenced to gather, and as she watched it it shaped itself into a cloud, which grew bigger and bigger. The light of the sun struck it, and along the edges it grew golden, the colour quickly spreading until it glowed in the centre as with a hidden fire. Then the cloud began to drift. At first it seemed to be coming her way, but altered its course and floated towards another part of the cliff. As she looked she saw the figure of a woman there—a familiar figure too—and a man by her side like him who put the cloak around herself. With that she stretched forth her hand to beckon the cloud towards her, but it drifted away. . . . She ran to where the woman stood and with all her might pushed her over the cliff into the depths of the sea. With the splash the cloud burst and a hail of sovereigns began to pelt her on the arms until she cried out with pain. Then a host of little men gathered on the cliff with hammers and anvils. One of them had a goatskin in his hand, and quick as lightning he cut it into strips. Others caught the sovereigns as they fell and punched holes in them. More of them began to tie the coins together with strips of skin until they formed a net which they threw over her. They flew through the air as on winged feet until they came to Poullamore. There they plunged her into the water, then dragged her to land as a meshed salmon. When she felt the water choking her she woke with a start.

She sent for her son. He saw how ill she was, and although she complained of cold her body burned like a fire.

" What are you doing at Poullamore? " she asked. " Is it not enough harm you have brought without causing more? I have been dragged through the pool and the cold has frozen my blood."

" If I don't get money I shall be ruined," Phil answered madly. " There is plenty in the pool—you have told me so yourself, and Shawn knows of it. I'd be a fool if I let pishrogues* stand in my way."

The woman's eyes blazed, and she exclaimed, " Stop that, I tell you. It's a curse will be on you if you drag Poullamore."

These words made Phil all the more eager, and whilst he pretended to obey her he made up his mind that he would procure the nets and fishermen that Gallagher had recommended.

She remained quieter during the day, but at night the fever returned, the restlessness was renewed, and she began to wander in her mind.

" Ah, they are at Poullabeg, the water is rising, it is over my feet."

" We'll stop it then," said the nurse, putting an extra fold of blanket over her.

Before long she cried out again: " It's up to my knees, send for . . ."

" The water is within a few inches of my heart," she was saying, as a closely muffled figure entered the room. " Tell Phil to stop dragging Poullamore, or it will be the death of me. Send to him at once."

" There is more than the fear of the water on your mind," came the answer in a stern voice. " You must make a clean breast of it."

.   .   .   .

" I tell you she has just sent out to say that if you don't stop it, it will kill her. Arrah, put it off for a day or two; sure, ye wouldn't like to have your mother's death on your mind."

Tim, the coachman, was the speaker, but Phil took little notice of him.

* Fairy spells.

"Take a cast lower down, the last one was too high up," said Phil, resuming the superintendence of the netting.

"The sorra use in it," a voice answered from the bank; "we couldn't get a foothold for the net there. Bedad, someone has dug the bottom out of the pool."

The moon, rising high in the heavens, was deeply mirrored in Poullamore. The ruffled water made it tremble like a polished shield, over which shadows flitted in rapid succession. With every throw of the net it broke into silver bars, which darted through the meshes as if mocking them.

The net was cast lower down and the men, one on each bank, began to haul in the moment it was well sunk. . . .

"It's a bit heavier this time, and bedad it's a live thing we've got hold of and not a dead one," cried one of the men.

As the net drew nearer there was a flash in the meshes like silver.

"It's the moon we have in this draw and no mistake; look how it glistens," came the comment.

Phil started.

"Be careful now and keep the sole lines well down and close together," said he, his voice trembling with excitement, for something had at last been achieved.

When the net came to the bank and the meshes were untwined there was a leap on the grass so unexpected that Phil, about to grasp the prize, started back and it splashed into the pool and disappeared.

"Och, tare and ages!" cried one of the men, "'twas a big pike covered with diamonds." This was his explanation of the glistening phosphorus.

"The sorra pike it was at all, but a merrow," interrupted the other, nudging his companion. "Didn't ye see his green hair and pig's eyes as he jumped? Bu' what's this in the bottom of the net?" stooping and pulling out a dripping bundle.

"That's mine," said Phil, clutching at it.

"Not so quick," said Gallagher, "it was to be share and share alike; there's something hard and bulky in it anyhow," pressing the dripping bundle and making it squelch.

Phil's temper rose and his excitement overmastered him. As Gallagher was stooping he lifted the heavy stick in his hand and swept it round his shoulders. In a moment it would have fallen on his accomplice's head, who was too busy to notice the treachery, had not a hand caught the uplifted arm. Phil turned round but failed to recognize the man who had come from his mother's bedside.

"Would you add murder to your other crimes, you villain?" he said, tightening his grip like a vice and swinging him back. "Do you know your mother is dying?"

"Let me see what's in that bundle," Phil replied sulkily, "and then I'll go to her. Bring it here, Gallagher." The group of men walked towards a lighted lantern on the bank, and the dripping bag was examined. In the light the bundle looked as if it were covered with slime. It was a skin tied at the neck by a strip of leather. Whilst clutching it with his left hand Gallagher pulled out a clasp-knife, drew the back of the blade across his mouth and wrenched it open with his teeth. Every head was bent whilst the point of the blade severed the fastening.

In a pause of breathless interest the puckered neck

fell open and the contents were disclosed. A coarse yellow substance clinging to red hair which lined the inside of the bundle lay before them.

" Goold! " gasped a voice.

" Well, if it's goold it's changed to gravel," was the comment that followed closer inspection, " or has it changed to leaves? " drawing a parchment document from the yellow heap.

" Let me see that," said Phil, reaching out his arm.

The hand that still held the open clasp-knife was raised in a significant way. Phil's treachery had forfeited confidence.

" Let this man see it then," said Phil.

No one taking objection, the closely muffled figure advanced.

" There is something familiar about this," said the man, examining it. " It's a goatskin, what do you think of that now? And indeed," said he, on unfolding the document, " it has kept this in a fair state of preservation. . . . Ah, what have we here?—the last will and testament of Bryan Fitz Martin of—"

There was a choking exclamation from the organizer of that night of strange adventure. The man who had just spoken took up the lantern, and holding it close to his own face threw off his disguise and cried:

" Do you know me now, Philip Fitz Martin? "

The full blaze of light showed the exultant face of Wheedle the lawyer.

There was silence by Poullamore. No one said a word or moved, and for a moment Wheedle did not lower the lantern.

A breath of wind, cold as a blast from the grave,

suddenly ruffled the water and blew out the light. When it was relit, one of the actors in the singular drama was missing from the group.

" Half-past twelve," said the lawyer, looking at his watch.

At the same hour that night Philip Fitz Martin's mother died.

MICROCOPY RESOLUTION TEST CHART

(ANSI and ISO TEST CHART No. 2)

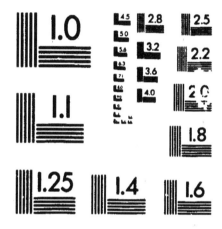

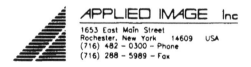

APPLIED IMAGE Inc

1653 East Main Street
Rochester, New York   14609   USA
(716) 482 – 0300 – Phone
(716) 288 – 5989 – Fax

" COME in, Miss Molly, come in, mavourneen, it's a cure for sore eyes to see ye, and even the aigle himself would have his sight strengthened by a glance at your sweet face."

So Molly was welcomed by Biddy when she called at the Lodge one summer's day. Eight months had elapsed since the Squire died, and Molly often looked in on Mrs Maloney despite the demurs of the latter to the rarity of her visits. She was very lonely now, deprived of the companionship of her uncle. Either riding or walking there was no direction she could take that did not stir memories of him, which robbed them of their pleasure, and frequently blinded her eyes with tears. Her cousin, too, upon whom suspicion had fallen for foul play in regard to the will, pestered her with his attentions. He proved, however, to be a beneficiary to a degree he had not anticipated. This was made the excuse for urging his suit afresh.

" It is a blessing to escape from myself a little while," Molly said in reply to Biddy's greeting. " If other people liked my company as little as I do myself, your welcome would be different. But how smart you are making things, Biddy," looking round the Lodge, which was in the hands of workmen.

" Well, indeed, it wasn't before it was wanted. It's meself that used to be ashamed when Mr Warren was here to see the paper droppin' off the walls and the ceilin' as black as a crow, and as for the outside, the pebble dash had fallen off in such patches that it looked as if the same place was recovering from a fit of the mazles."

" Well, the new tenant won't have much reason to complain. What with the game protection and the extra water-bailiffs, Lord Ballyshameon ought not to have any trouble in letting the shooting," said Molly.

" I suppose it's the young heir that's makin' the changes. A new broom sweeps clean, as the sayin' is. The next thing we'll be hearin' is that he's comin' over to see the property. It's an unnatural man that doesn't care to have a look at his own childer."

" Nobody seems to know who the new heir is or whether he is living even," Molly said as if thinking aloud.

" Oh, faix, there's one person anyway that knows something about him."

" You mean Mr Warren, Biddy. They were at college together, I know."

" Well, if he gets a howlt of his lordship's ear, it isn't long he'll be keepin' away. It's wonderful how Mr Warren took to this part of the country," and Biddy smoothed out her apron with great care and looked at her visitor slily.

" He did seem to enjoy himself."

" Throth, he went away wounded."

" You mean he came wounded; he got over that, I thought, while he was here."

" He got rid of one pain only to ketch another. Some people are always in the wars," and Biddy continued the hand-ironing of her apron.

Molly could not pretend any longer to be ignorant of Biddy's drift. " Oh, you dear old mystery-monger," she said, " how you do draw on your imagination."

" Throth, if my imagination was as deep as someone's sighs I could write a great book. If these walls could spake, an' didn't know how to howld their tongues, some people would have reason to blush in earnest."

" Ah, don't, Biddy dear, you only hurt me," and Molly put her arms about her old nurse lovingly.

" An' why shouldn't ye be hurt? Sure, ye couldn't expect the poor boy to feel all the pain. Indeed I begin to believe that the little boy's darts are sharpened at both ends, alannah, an' there's only one cure for that ailment, a bit of the hair of the dog that bit ye. An' why wouldn't he be comin' agen? London, big as it is, an' wise as it is, hasn't the medecine that can cure his wound. But me own beautiful flower, with the breath of the mountain air and the pureness of the sea, has the cure in it." And the beautiful flower was pressed close in Biddy's strong arms.

" Your old nurse's eyes haven't grown so dull as not to be able to guess eggs where they see shells. Sure, didn't he nearly snap off Shawn's head when he wanted to send away the first salmon he caught. ' Not that one,' says he, ' I'll kape that fish. . . . It's Miss Molly's salmon,' he said to me afterwards. . . . ' Pick out the youngest and fattest of them grouse, Shawn . . . they're for Miss Molly,' he said to me carelessly morroyeh! an' indeed I could see that the words were like a spoonful of honey in his mouth. An' indeed, it's great trouble some people take to hide their feelin's . . . he'd run up the stairs in three bounds, an' get in the words ' An' then transported I should be ' as if I didn't know it was ' Molly Bawn ' he was singin . . . .'

" Arrah, whisht now, isn't me jewel worth a place in a prince's crown! And for that it's the proud man he ought to be, to be allowed to look the side o' the road

ye're walkin'. . . . The sorra more news I'll give ye
at all, at all, if ye keep stoppin' me mouth with yer hand
in that way. . . . Oh, indeed, I thought ye'd want to
hear the news. Well, I've just one month to get everything ready before he . . . why don't ye give me
another opportunity of kissin' yer hand now? . . . an'
with so little time to spare, here I am wastin' the blessed
mornin' talkin' nonsense. . . . Not a word more, 'to
be continued in our next,' as the story says, just where
the woman was going to push the man into the well, ye'll
have to guess the rest. Maybe ye might send me a few
flowers for the table for the fifteenth of next month
anyway.''

As Molly left the Lodge what an interest seemed to
centre in everything. Biddy, waving her adieux from
the door and filling up the entire space with her ample
person, had all the charm of an idyll that might have
inspired a Shelley or a Keats. Had the gap in the
broken-down stone wall been fitted with gates of wrought
gold it could not have appeared more alluring. How
everything takes the colour of the soul through which it
is contemplated. Milton understood it and gave the
true explanation. " The mind . . . in itself, can
make a heaven of hell—a hell of heaven." Oh, the
wonderful ether of romance, eyes bathed in it see love's
Paradise! Molly tried to banish details, even as she
sought to silence Biddy's lips, but the atmosphere was
there, she yielded herself to that, and it permeated
every interstice of her being. The hurt of her heart
was soothed and lonely tracts in her life filled with
sweet companionship. All Biddy's imagination perhaps,
and yet what delight to dwell on these unsubstantial
things. Like forbidden mysteries lying behind thick
curtains, what rapture to pull aside the folds and have

a peep—if only to drop them again half-guiltily frightened.

On her return home Molly found Shawn waiting for her. His head was buried in his hands, and his shoulders rose and fell in deep sighs. It was evident that he was in trouble.

" What's the matter, Shawn? " Molly asked in the soft, sympathetic tone that made her such a welcome visitor amongst rich and poor.

" She's very bad, miss, an' she's been callin' for ye all night. She never recovered rightly from the last attack, an' she told me this mornin' that she would soon be seein' themselves."

" What do you mean, Shawn—the Good People? "

" Oh, indeed, the same, miss."

Molly sent a note to Dr Mahan, asking him to call on Mrs O'Grady, and packed a small basket with invalid necessaries.

" I'll ride over," she said, " Cull has not had a stretch for days. You will come after me, Shawn."

" I will, miss, but I won't hurry. I think she wants to talk to yerself. I'll carry that," he said, taking the basket.

Molly soon reached the cottage and tied up the horse. A rough partition divided the room into compartments, and on a bed in the corner of the inner chamber the woman lay.

" Ah, colleen, it's you at last. I was afraid you would be too late."

" I've only just heard of your illness, Granny, and I have come without delay."

" Ah, acushla, it's never late ye are where there's sorrow and trouble, and so much of it in your own life too. Your uncle is gone . . . they used to ride and shoot together, but he never came back again, though he said he would. Ah, that's the great sorrow, that breaks the heart and deranges the brain. It's worse than death, may ye never know anything like it. But ye won't, colleen, he'll come back to ye, though he didn't to me."

" Hush, Granny, and don't excite yourself. Let me make you comfortable, the bed is all tossed," and in a few moments Molly showed her efficiency as a nurse.

" When I first him I thought it was himself that was in it," she went on, taking no notice of the girl's domestic attentions, and falling into the Irishism in regard to the chief person, " just about his age and build, an' the same handsome face."

Molly started. " Who are you speaking of, Granny —Mr Warren? "

" Mr *Warren*, indeed. Who's Mr Warren? I know who he is, every line is too deeply cut on me heart not to know."

Molly's own heart throbbed violently. What, could it be possible that this was—

" But how could ye, colleen? Ye never saw himself, but I won't tell Shawn, he's so fond of him. Himself is dead now, an' I will soon be too and the secret buried with me. I carried it in my heart above the sod an' I'll carry it in my heart under it."

The build, the likeness between Shawn and Warren, the similarity of movements all came back to Molly. Given this key, what did it mean? Why had he disguised himself and come and gone wrapping himself round her heart? Was he afraid of making himself known? Her hero a craven coward? All these thoughts flashed through Molly's active brain; the sick woman watched her face and divined them.

" No, no," she cried, " he made no promises; he'll come back. He has not robbed the treasure and left the empty casket. Who cares to gather the heather when the bloom is scattered, except to stop a gap or make beddin' for the cattle? "

She sat up, and placing her arms on the shoulders of. the girl drew her closer. The piercing black eyes looked into the depths of unsullied blue as if to read their secret.

" Ah, you love him, he'll come back."

Molly again appealed to her that she was exciting herself, and gently constrained her to lie down. She smoothed the flushed face and spoke soothing words. The effect of this treatment became apparent; the wild look in the eyes gave place to one of calm restfulness, the hot cheeks scarred with the ⸳⸳⸳ ʼava that welled up from deep mines of memory ⸳⸳⸳ ₋own to grey ashes.

The doctor came whilst ⸳⸳⸳ sitting by her side. He felt the woman's pulse, ₋₋₋₋d at the poor starved body and shook his head.

" She is worn out," he said. " The fire has been burning too fiercely to last any longer. It has burned itself out. She has been subject to intermittent fever, and a high one for the last two days. We cannot do much for her, Miss MacDaire."

But Molly stayed by her bedside, holding one lean hand, and Shawn, reverently kneeling, bent over and caressed the other until the last wave of ebbing life flowed up and divided between the two hand-clasps in a final flutter. Then all was still.

Warren was later in returning to Ballinbeg than he proposed. A great deal of critical business called for attention, and a pile of documents that affected his interests had to be perused. When he had got rid of the lawyers it was well into the autumn, and Biddy had more time to prepare for her visitor.

When Molly and he met, the shadow of a great grief still rested upon her, and although she had come to her own, and was heiress to the bulk of her uncle's estate, the road by which she reached it had been a rough one, and left its mark upon her spirits. She seemed restrained and lacking in the easy grace of friendliness that Warren was accustomed to. He attributed her changed manner to the death of her uncle and the worry and anxiety that the responsibility of the new position imposed.

His time was spent ˙ long walks, excursions to distant parts of the distric , and prolonged interviews with farmers on the Ballyshameon estate. These were frequently combined with shooting and fishing excursions in the company of Shawn, and at times with a staff of beaters. Warren paid his attendants liberally and treated them well. His sporting tastes, with rod and gun, and general urbanity won for him increasing popularity.

But there was a hunger which not one of these recreations satisfied, although they helped Warren to forget it. When he returned to the Lodge in the evening, and sat down to his solitary meal, the sunburnt brow would knit, and the handsome face become overclouded, as if there were a tangled thought there, the unravelling of which baffled him. He unlocked a portfolio, and taking out a document began to peruse it. He read quickly, turning over the pages with a gesture of impatience in keeping with his thoughts. He enclosed it again in the long blue envelope and locked it away. . . . " What a poor reparation," he murmured. He

18

pictured the mother, the simple, innocent, trustful girl betrayed, forsaken, ashamed to lift up her head in a country where such sins were rare and not readily forgiven. Then consigned to the lonely hut, seeking communion with the solitary hillside. It was infamous. His blood seethed in indignation. And Shawn—the one that was left! . . . What could be done for him? Content in poverty, happy in his Bohemianism. The restoration of his moral rights would probably be a new injustice. He thought of the Irish bull. Shawn would never be happy unless he was miserable. He had been cheated of his birthright, and had not even received the mess of pottage in exchange. . . . His loyalty to himself, too, no brother could exceed it in affection, no slave in devotion. Warren stood up and paced the room. . . . Well, he she 'd know all—the r ent the accursed ban was lifted . . . how it stood, to etween him and the woman that he cared for most in the world. . . . What would she say when she knew all? How could he justify the part he had been playing? Supposing she discovered it before his own hand took off the mask. . . . She was with her when she died. . . . Molly was restrained, almost cold in her bearing towards him now. Was that the explanation? Did she know all? And did he appear to her as—merciful heavens!— How he cursed the pledge that sealed his lips.

CHAPTER XXI

HALLOW-E'EN, the annual festival of imps and fairies, is an honoured institution in Ireland. Its ancient mystic significance is probably unknown to many peasants who keep it with great fervour. The name Hallow-e'en would probably sound unintelligible to most of them, whilst the corruption, "Holleve night," would convey a meaning understood and honoured by every gossoon in Connacht. To him it would appear as the occasion for cramming his pockets with nuts and apples to be consumed at leisure, and indulgence in a kind of mischievous sport at the expense of his neighbours.

Paudeen Maloney, still in the hobbledehoy stage of growth, was engaged in solemn conclave with a few congenial spirits over whom he exercised a more or less despotic dictatorship, by right of twelve to eighteen months' seniority. This distinction was not wholly determined by the birth register or by outward appearance. A more sporting method was adopted by the juvenile community. It was called "Proving the best Man," and was carried out in a form eminently popular amongst the fraternity. Paudeen had successfully boxed each of his companions in turn and so won the championship of Rex or leader amongst them. And none of your 2-oz. gloves or such devices. Gloves indeed! probably they had never been seen in Connacht— the entire financial resources of the youthful community would not have run to the purchase of a second-hand pair. No, the good old-fashioned bare fists, Nature's natural endowment of weapons, antecedent to gloves, pistol or rapier, were the means employed to secure Paudeen's mastership in the ring. Handicap in regard to size and weight was fixed on the same principle of rough-and-ready expediency. All boys younger and smaller were fought with one hand by Paudeen, the other being tied behind the back throughout the encounter.

The council of war was held on Hollcye afternoon as to the best methods of attack on the evening in question. The rendezvous was the Lodge hayloft. There the chief and his subordinates were engaged some hours beforehand in active preparation. A number of large cabbage-stumps were strewn about the place, some bored through, others undergoing the process of having the pith removed. A second heap that caught the eye on entering the improvised arsenal consisted of tow, some of it the raw material used by the rope-makers. The funds, however, being at a low ebb—the normal state being no funds at all—several pieces of rope-end were being teased out, which gave a decided marine back-street odour to the hayloft.

In addition to the cabbage stalks the arsenal also contained several balls of string of a very knotty character and varying in thickness. The number of joins showed that the collection of odds and ends must have extended over a considerable time and entailed no small amount of labour.

" We'll take Staball first and then Altamont Street, and begin with the knockers," Paudeen said, pitching a ball of string to each of his companions. " We'll all meet at the corner of the Fair Green after the first bout."

" We'll have to pass the hearse-house that way," Ned Collins demurred.

" You're afeared, Ned," Sam Dougherty commented.

" Ye're a liar, I'm not."

" I'll bet ye two throu..ers buttons that ye won't pass the hearse-house alone," Sam challenged.

" I can't part with any more buttons or I would. I lost a couple in a bet with Jimmy Quigley yesterday, an' me galloses are comin' down as it is," and Ned displayed a detached suspender. " Arrah, why would I be afraid? Sure, the hearse hasn't been out since Micky Fadden's funeral, an' he had a wooden leg; it isn't his ghost I'd let overtake me."

" Stop talkin' about ghosts," Paudeen remonstrated. " Mockin' is ketchin', an' we might be comin' home late. Here's a piece of tow for each of ye," dividing u he ammunition. " I'll whistle t'.e curlew call three ... es before we begin to pull."

" Give us time to fasten the twine on the knockers, Paudeen," said one of the accomplices. " Last Holleve nigh: you were too soon. Ned began rappin' before I got away from Mary Hannagher's door and Warya threw a can of water over me from the window."

" Divil's-cure-to-ye, Jimmy. Here, put this in yer pocket," and Paudeen threw him a scooped-out cabbage stalk.

" Sorra one I have to spare this minute, they're full of nuts. I'll carry it under me oxter," and Jimmy tucked the weapon beneath his arm.

Thus equipped the boys went forth. The ght aided th n in their purpose. No oil-lamp or othe illuminant lit the streets, and save for an occasional glimmer that came from a cottage window, or an open door, the place was in darkness.

The strings were soon dexterously attached to the knockers, the each boy, stooping behind any obstacle or lying flat in the road, pulled the string until it became taut. When the curlew notes were whistled, the cord was suddenly released, and the knocker fell with a loud rap.

The inhabitants of Staball had been spared for a year or two from this particular trick, although some of them had reason to remember how their rooms were mysteriously filled with smoke. A single knock therefore brought several of them to the door on a fool's errand. Some were expecting visitors on the festive occasion, and finding no one at the door closed it again and returned to the hearth. One old man who did so had scarcely seated himself when a second and louder rap came. He hobbled out again and opened the door.

" A runaway," he grumbled, " musha, bad cess to the gossoons." He had only just taken a step back when rap! rap! went the knocker again.

" Oh, it's just outside ye are? " he said, speaking to himself. " Faith, then, I'll be a match for ye," and he filled a tin pail with water, quietly undid the bolt and waited.

In a moment or two he heard a footstep and a hand groping for the knocker. Rap it went, and the old man, awaiting this psychological moment, suddenly flung open the door with one hand, and with the other emptied the contents of the pail in the breast of an innocent neighbour.

" Ow! Ow! damn your— Is it mad you are, Andy Kane, pitchin' water about in that way? "

Andy's surprise at the success of the stratagem was quite as great as the victim's. He stood staring at the dripping figure before him.

" It's drunk ye are, begad," the victim exclaimed, " or I'd flatten yer nose for ye, ye disrespectful baist; it's early in the night that the whisky is on ye."

" Musha, is it yerself that's in it," Andy said, when he had found his tongue. " I ax yer pardon, sure the blackguards of boys—"

But the youth to whom the description applied with some justice had witnessed this unrehearsed part of the programme and could control himself no longer. The coat sleeve, which he had jammed into his mouth, failed to keep back the stifled laughter.

" There he is, the divil," says Andy, rushing out, but a snap broke the knocker string and a sharp patter of feet up the road signalized the escape of the youthful misdemeanants.

The boys met to recount their experience in turn. Paudeen had mystified Sally Gay.

" She came out," he began, " an' looked up an' down the road, sayin' nothin'. Then I tapped a second time, an' she came out again.

" ' Lord save us,' said she, ' but that's quare; it couldn't be a runaway.'

" Then, man, after I brought her back again, an' she put up her hand to the knocker, I tightened the string, an' she shouted, ' Och, mercy preserve us, but the knocker is risin' an' rappin' itself. It's the fairies that's amusin' themselves, the poor cratures.' But when she heard me titterin' she nearly went mad with the anger, an' rushed into the road, so that I'd hardly time to get out of the way."

The boys worked in couples. One took charge of the string whilst the other fastened it to the knocker. Ned Collins and Sam Dougherty were in partnership. After a time Ned joined the others at the corner of the Fair Green, but his companion was absent.

" Where's Sam? " Paudeen inquired.

" He's taken," Ned answered with a gravity be-fitting the occasion.

" Taken? " They all echoed the word.

" Lame Tony Cochlane caught him, just as he was fastenin' the twine; he carried him into the house under his oxter. I saw him kickin', but he never spoke a word."

" An' what did you do? "

" Do? Arrah, what could I do? Tony bolted the door after him. When ye gave the signal I began to knock."

" An' bad luck to ye for doin' that same," said Sam, suddenly appearing on the scene. " It's meself that's suffered for yer amusement. Och, wirra! is there a hair on me head at all? " he said, pulling off his cap and looking round for sympathy.

" Did Tony scalp ye with his sword? " Paudeen asked, scenting tragedy.

Cochlane was a pensioned-off soldier, and in view of that distinction was regarded by the boys as possessing rights to do anything in that way with impunity.

" Worse than that, he pulled the hair out in hand-fuls," and Sam rubbed the affected part tenderly.

" Tell us what happened," eager voices pleaded, and a ring was formed round the delinquent, who suddenly blossomed into a hero.

Sam was by no means averse to playing the part.

" Well, just as I fastened the twine on the knocker an' turned to go, who should I meet but Tony. I dodged him, but bad luck to him if he didn't put his crutch between me legs, and I fell. Throth I didn't know where I was till I found meself in his arms. He put his hand on me mouth, all as one as if I was a Red Injun."

Tony was supposed to have gained his medals and pension by distinguished active service against savage tribes, the current opinion amongst the boys being that " Red Injuns " cut off his leg and roasted it and ate it in his presence.   Tony made himself responsible for this explanation of the missing member, and used to wind up the story of the roasting by adding that the " Injuns hadn't the good manners even to offer a bit of it to its rightful owner," an' him as hungry as a wolf all the time.

" When he got me inside," Sam continued, " he held me between his knees, an' the first thing me eyes fell on was the sword hung up over the fireplace, so that I felt sure he put me there just that I might see it.   Oh, it's the great sword it is too, with brass mountin's and spots on it near the handle made with the blood of the Injuns he killed for cuttin' off his leg.

" ' Arrah now, let me go, Tony,' says I, ' I didn't mane any harm; it's Holleve night, we're only havin' a bit o' fun.'

" ' It's meself knows that well,' says he in friendly way, so that I thought I was all right.   ' I'm goin' to join in the fun if ye haven't any objection.'

" ' Arrah, why would I? ' says I.   ' Come an' join us.'

" ' Arrah, sure, I can't run as fast as I could with the one leg,' says he, ' an' I'd get ketched.'

" ' I might help ye,' says I.

" ' Oh, well, ye can help me here,' says he, ' when the knockin' begins.'

" ' How can I do that? ' says I.

" ' By answerin' the knocks,' says he.

" ' Oh, sure, it's glad I'll be to oblige ye,' says I, an' me heart gave a bound, for I thought how aisy it would be to open the door an' bolt.

"'Let me go out an' see if the signal is given anyway,' says I. Arrah, man, ye ought to hear him laughing
when I says that.

"'We'll have to do without the signal,' says he.
'I'm not goin' to lose me fun for a thrifle of that kind.'

"Just with that the first knock came.

"'There it is,' says I, 'let me down, an' I'll answer it.'

"Arrah, man, with that I thought it was the roof
pulled off me head, he gave me hair such a drag.'

"'Och,' says I, 'how can I answer it if ye do that.'

"'That's the way ye'll answer it,' says he.

"Then he caught me just down here on the scruff of
the neck, an' with every pull ye gave, Ned, bads grant
to ye, he gave another, until I thought he wouldn't
lave a hair on me at all, at all.

"'Orah! stop, Tony,' says I.

"'No,' says he, 'I must answer every one of them,
that's politeness, an' sure you said you'd do it for me.
... That's a good one, a threble, an' here's a threble
answer.'

"Well, man, that went on until I didn't know
whether I was on me head or me heels.

"'It's not cryin' ye are,' says he, 'ye seem to like
answerin' them knocks.'

"'Well, whether or not,' says I, 'the sorra tear I'll
shed over them,' an' with that the knockin' stopped.

"'It's over now,' says he, lettin' me go, 'an' bedad
it's a nice agreeable way to spend Holleve night. I hope
ye've enjoyed it as much as me,' says he.

"'Arrah, sure, we've Altamont Street to do yet,'
says I, 'an' we've great fun before us.'

"'Well,' says he, 'if ye do as much runnin' back-
ward and forward as ye've done for me it's tired ye'll
be, I'm thinkin'. But as ye don't seem to enjoy me

company as much as I've enjoyed yours, I suppose I mustn't keep ye. But here's a few apples for ye to rub on the sore spot,' and with that he filled me pockets with croftons.

" ' Well,' says I, ' if there's any virtue in them I'll thry them,' an' with that I bolted off as hard as I could.''

Paudeen and his companion listened to this story, ejaculating and commenting as the narrator proceeded. Some of them were disposed to treat it as apocryphal, but the evidence of the apples and the red spots on the boy's neck were proof positive of its authenticity. One sceptic thought that pulling the hair could not hurt so much as the sufferer pretended. But Sam's finger and thumb closed on the short hair of the unbeliever's neck, and the cry that followed had the salutary effect of checking the spread of scepticism amongst the others. Some of the boys proposed to return and smoke out Tony, but Sam demurred to this on the ground that it was the fortune of war to meet reverses, and that having accepted compensation from the enemy, in the shape of apples, it would be a breach of good faith to renew hostilities.

" It's getting late, boys," Paudeen said, " we must be off to Altamont Street. Who e the first to reach the corner? " and they set off at a The object of this improvised competition was to get by the hearse-house as soon as possible. The spot was particularly dreaded by all the youngsters in the town. The coach which stood behind the large wooden doors was a spectacle so gruesome that it was not surprising that it struck terror to the mind of the rising generation. Its black glossless body caricatured the grief it simulated. The sombre, nodding, lugubrious plumes when the hearse was in motion seemed to be in a chronic state of intoxication. Paudeen had the impression that these symbols which rose from the four corners and swayed to and from each other in such helpless imbecility were daylight ghosts that came to full life in the darkness, and stepped down from the hearse to enjoy themselves at the expense of mortals.

The boys flew by with incredible speed and pulled up at the light from the first habitation. Then, puffing and panting, they grouped round their leader and took their orders for the smoking trick. Paudeen rehearsed the proceedings. " Don't put the tow in too tight. Don't light a match in front of the window, don't draw yer breath in when it's alight, or ye'll cough and get kotched. Put the tube to the keyhole if there isn't a key in it; if there is, kneel down and blow the smoke under the door."

The boys were to choose the most convenient houses for their purpose, the leader selecting Mary Hannagher's for himself. There was always the chance of finding a few convivial spirits in the shebeen, and as these usually belonged to outlying districts they were less likely to be familiar with the boys' pranks. Seeing no sign of life in the front he jumped a wall and approached the back of the premises. There a well-lit apartment attracted attention. From this a jingling of glasses and a buzz of conversation proceeded. As Paudeen was making his way toward it he had to pass a window dimly lighted. A broken pane of glass offered a tempting passage for the smoke. He stooped beneath the sill to prepare, when he heard a conversation carried on in voices which he recognized. One of them was Gallagher's, the other Phil Fitz Martin's. One word overheard was sufficient in itself to arrest attention. It was " Warren." The fire had burned low and there was neither candle nor lamp in the room.

Paudeen, now fully on the *qui vive*, listened.

" You talk of money as if it didn't matter whether I get it or not.   I tell you straight, Mr Philip, that it does matter, and I'm not going to wait much longer; that's why I asked you into this room where we could be alone."

" Yes, and if you don't speak quieter, everyone in the house will hear you, which might be as inconvenient for you as for me."

" Fiddlesticks ! " said Gallagher, " that lot's too busy drinking poteen to hear anyone but themselves. Besides, if you don't settle up with me, more than Mary Hannagher's customers will know of it."

" Oh, well, as for that, other people will have to face the music, and one man that I know won't care to dance to the tune."

The turf fire stirred and a flare of light disclosed the lowering anger in Gallagher's face.

" What have I to fear from you? " he asked.

" Well, there might be another trial about "— and Phil jerked his head in a particular direction—" and fresh witnesses called.   I know someone that could throw light on Pinkerton's assailant."

" Pshaw, don't think you're going to get over me with your pretences.   Speak out what you know."

" I'd rather not, Gallagher; we might be overheard."

" I tell you they can't hear next door, and there's nothing but the pigs in the backyard to listen."

" Well, it isn't fit for anyone else to hear but the pigs; all the same I'd rather whisper it."

" Very well, whisper it then."

Paudeen carefully raised his eyes and saw Phil leaning forward. . . .   What was said was too low to be heard, but the effect on the listener was remarkable. He jumped to his feet with an oath and his hand dived into his breast-pocket. "The man that betrays me . . ."

" Don't do that! " Phil exclaimed, arresting his arm. " A shot would be heard next door and a knife would leave a stain. Mary Hannagher showed two of us in; it would be inconvenient if only one came out. . . . That's right . . . I thought you said you wanted to talk the matter over quietly. I'd advise sticking to your original plan."

" Very well," the other replied sulkily, " but you must be smart about it."

" You want the money you won from me in bets and cards—that's the size of it."

" Exactly, and what you borrowed too, bear in mind."

" Well, you can't expect me to lay my hands on it at five minutes' notice."

" Five minutes," the other sneered, " you've had five months."

" Oh, well, I have to carry out my own plans; you haven't been able to mature all yours in five months."

Paudeen noticed that Gallagher turned sharply round at this observation.

" What's your new plan? Anything like the dragging of Poullamore? That was brilliant, and damned fools we looked in pulling out an old pike and a sheepskin, with a fine fortune wrapped up in it for you." The comment ended in a forced guffaw.

" Oh, well, the money's there right enough, as you'll see. I'll pump it dry some day. It wasn't as great a failure as your own, Gallagher, and no lives were lost over it."

" Drop that talk now, I tell you."

" I won't drop it unless you help me in my plans;

it's a trump card, and by heavens, I'll play it for all it's worth."

Paudeen noticed that Gallagher stood up, and the firelight showed an ugly scowl on his face. He sat down again and the other continued:

" My only chance of getting money to meet my needs is to secure my cousin's hand in marriage. The obstacle is that damned Warren. I want to frighten him out of the country. You are the man to do it."

" Whew! Indeed . . . and how . . . I'd like to know? "

The answer was given deliberately:

" How did you manage to make it too hot for Pinkerton to keep on the agency? "

The boy noticed that Gallagher winced and again faced his companion in anger.

" Now look here, Gallagher," Phil continued, " I know all about it; you can serve my purpose or leave it. If you serve it, you serve your own; if not, well—you can whistle for your money. That's plain, isn't it? "

" Quite. Make equally plain this new proposal of yours."

" Frighten Warren out of the country."

" Oh, that's what you're going to do, is it? "

" No, but you're going to do it for us."

" Us? " said Gallagher.

" Yes, us; he might be a rival for the agency, and I think I know a local man who would like the job," and Phil nodded significantly at his companion.

" Well, I think I could manage it a damned sight better than Pinkerton, but the man I'd like to see appointed is Doonas."

" Whew! " It was Phil's turn to whistle. The act was followed by the laconic comment: " You devil! "

Gallagher's look was a black note of interrogation.

" You want to put him on that list, do you? " said Phil.

An ugly laugh followed. " Oh, make it Warren, if you like. He's on it already for land-grabbing; he's the middleman for Jimmy Sweeny's place."

" Oh, then it's on the cards that a bullet might be put through the flap of his mackintosh. Now listen, Gallagher, I'll have no murder on my hands. Get him out of the country, that's all I want."

The other felt he had said too much and sought to beat a retreat.

" All I know is that someone was practising the golden plover call to bring the swell near enough to the Black Valley for a shot."

Phil started. " Why the golden plover call? " he asked.

" Warren is said to be fond of these birds and likes shooting them," Gallagher answered.

" Ah, the sneak! My cousin once 'old him she liked the birds and he's always sending them to her. Well, anyone can have his chance to-morrow. Warren is shooting in the island to-day and returns to-morrow. He generally comes home by the Black Valley unless he goes round by Tubberscrag. There's high tide before dark; he would be returning about that time."

Gallagher said nothing for a moment. It was evident he was rapidly considering the suggestion in all its bearings. He welcomed it on the ground that Phil Fitz Martin was making a proposal which implicated himself. He was seriously alarmed on discovering that his companion knew more about his affairs than was desirable, and would not hesitate if driven to it to use his knowledge in inconvenient ways. He was willing to buy silence by abandoning all financial claims.   But Gallagher was not at all sure that it would be secured that way.   Nothing worse was known against Fitz Martin than drink and gambling.   If Warren were to be hurt, well, that would compromise Phil and he would no longer hold the only trump card.

Paudeen first knelt on one knee until it grew tired, then changed to the other until it became stiff, finally knelt on both until he forgot that he had such things as legs or arms, so eagerly did he listen to the conversation in the dimly-lit huckster's room.   His mischief-making tube, charged with the lump of tow, was not brought into use, but absolutely forgotten in the excitement of the colloquy he overheard.   At first he was interested as one in quest of adventure, and began to conjure up a graphic description for his companions. But as the plot developed he became seriously alarmed, and his knees trembled beneath him.   Apprehension for himself seized him, and to get away from the place as quietly as possible became his first care.   He felt certain that if he were discovered the villains who were plotting against the life of such a man as Mr Warren would give him short shrift, and he imagined himself being carried home in his gore, his companions following silent and affrighted.

When breathlessly he reached the rendezvous it was easy to see from his white face that he had a tale of adventure to tell.

" Arrah, man, were you kotched? " they asked. " S   . ve all been back this half-hour."

" Whisht ! " said Paudeen, looking nervously behind him.   " Not a word, I tell ye."

" Orah, what's the matter?   You're as white as a corpse."

19

" So would you be, Sam, if ye heard—saw—what I saw."

" What did ye see now? " came from half a dozen voices.

" Two ghosts."

" Two? "

" There was two, quarrellin' an' fightin' and stickin' each other with sharp knives that length," and Paudeen indicated a liberal distance on his arm.

" Orah! orah! "

" And neither of them cried or bled."

" Where wor they? " one boy asked, after the paralysing effect began to relax.

" Arrah, don't spake about it here," came the demur. " We have to go home by the hearse-house again. Paudeen can tell us about it in the loft to-morrow by daylight."

The hero seized on this proposition as an easy way out of the difficulty of having to invent then and there the details of the ghosts he had suddenly launched on his companions. Fright made short work of an amendment for an immediate rehearsal by one of the braver spirits. As it was, most of the boys that night put their heads under the blankets lest Paudeen's ghosts fighting their bloodless battles should suddenly appear.

But Paudeen's eyes did not close for hours after the usual time. He saw Mr Warren shot a score of times in imagination, his mackintosh riddled like a sieve. When at length the boy fell asleep he seemed to be crushed beneath the weight of a corpse which two men insisted on strapping to his back, and whilst he laboured to carry his gruesome load the air was filled with the call of golden plover.

CHAPTER XXII

PAUDEEN went about next day with a hea , load on his mind. His first thought was to tell his mother what he had overheard, but the words, " The man that betrays me," and the hand thrust into the breast-pocket where the " long knife " was secreted, convinced him that his mother as well as himself would assuredly meet with a terrible death if they betrayed Gallagher. He thought of Mr Warren and all his kindness to himself and his mother, and he could hear the golden plover's treacherous no' that would beguile him near enough to the Black Valley to drop dead at the ring of the rifle-shot. . . .

Would he perhaps, like Mr Pinkerton, only have his coat pierced, and would he shoot someone as Mr Pinkerton had done? . . . The boy was restless and uneasy as he turned the problem over in his mind.

Meanwhile, the subject of Paudeen's anxiety, un-conscious of any malicious intentions, was enjoying himself amongst the islands. One of the largest, with a border of marshland, harboured wild duck and snipe, and Warren shot over it until the afternoon, when he started for the mainland. Shawn rowed. The appearance of the gillie on that day presented a striking contrast with the figure he cut eighteen months before, when the sobriquet of Scalloped Shawn applied to him. Warren's clothes fitted him so well that there was no need to let down the hems, with the result that he developed from a primitive type of savagery to one of well-conditioned civilization. In this rapid evolution points emerged hitherto unsuspected, which proved that if the clothes do not make the gentleman, they at least supply a setting in which the article previously latent stands revealed. Shawn's knickerbocker suit, tweed hat to match, and smart leather gaiters, had revolutionary effects on the wearer. A corresponding metamorphosis seemed to be wrought in his personal appearance.

As Warren sat and watched him rowing the boat he noticed the improvement and prided himself on being instrumental in effecting it. When he took out a game licence for him and invited Shawn to take his share in the shooting instead of playing the part of hired henchman, he knew that he had won the man's affection, and everything that the gillie had to bestow, and at whatever sacrifice, was at his service. As far as faithfulness in a servant was concerned, Warren lost nothing by such condescension. O'Grady continued his loyalty and devotion, and the work that his employer wished him to remit to others Shawn insisted on carrying out himself. In this matter he proved obdurate; in all others Warren's word was law. His build was so like his master's that when he appeared in his new sporting outfit the resemblance was emphasized. On one occasion a car-driver touched his hat to Shawn and addressed him as Mr Warren. Shawn's bony fingers closed like a snap-trap on the driver's neck. When he threw him from him he simply remarked, " That will teach ye to know yer betters next time ye meet them." It soon became obvious that it was not wise to take any notice of Shawn's altered appearance.

He mentioned the matter to Warren next day.

" Well, I hope you're not ashamed of being taken for me, eh, Shawn? "

" No, sir, but I know me place, an' I think there's one man in Ballinbeg this mornin' who knows it better than he did yesterday."

It was quite evident to Warren that summary jurisdiction was not confined to the Bench.

The boat headed for the creek. The tide was not high enough to run up it, and Shawn suggested landing Warren on the point where he could get across country without delay. The dog jumped out, glad to stretch himself after the cramped position in the boat, then started off, intent on any game that might be scented on the way home. . . . The boat lightened, Shawn was able to row up a good part of the creek and got away after his master sooner than he had expected.

Warren's route lay for half a mile through a dip between the hills, then a gradual ascent led to a table-land of broad expanse, difficult to travel, owing to the tangle of heather. This in turn sloped down towards the Black Valley, which was a long natural cutting. By keeping to the left and following this course a round of over a mile was cut off, the valley to the right reached the high road by a more circuitous route.

Despite the activity in the islands, Warren was still fresh, and covered the ground at a good pace. His gun rested across his arm, ready for a grouse or hare that he might find in the heather. The dog kept well in front, ranging from right to left and taking short excursions windward, his head raised high in quest of the quarry. As Warren descended into the glen he felt the loneliness and desolation of the spot. He raised his eyes. In the distance there was the rock which Shawn pointed out as the spot where the leprechaun was surprised at full moon. It was indeed in keeping with the story, detached, weird, and yet beautiful in the conformation of hills that lay behind it.

His thoughts dwelt on the gillie. Ah, what a change had taken place in O'Grady. His smart clothes, his regenerate appearance. What a metamorphosis a tailor can effect in a mortal. Would the civilizing process expurgate the romance and banish the fairies? Warren wondered. He stopped suddenly. "I thought I heard the golden plover call," he said, thinking aloud. There it was undoubtedly.

He called the dog. "Don't you hear that, you rascal?—golden plover," but the dog took no notice.

"What! superior to everything but game of the first degree. These are not ware birds, you scamp. Go along."

The direction of the plover led him to the right and away from the short cut homewards. He looked at his watch; there was time. He hurried down the valley for a hundred yards, then stopped and listened. Again the note sounded in the same direction. Another short walk brought him to a place where he could get a view of the higher ground. He cautiously climbed the bank and peeped over — there was nothing in sight. In such a position he would be able to ascertain the whereabouts of the birds. The tableland which he scanned sloped down like the others towards the level was ground. Again the call came, and soon afterwards repeated. He summoned the dog to heel and followed. From the brow of the hill he might get near enough to flush the birds without being seen. There was a hillock at the bottom, and like a careful stalker Warren put it between himself and the plover. When he reached it he lay down, Ranger crouching at his feet as if the proceedings were unworthy of the true sportsman and he was not going to take any further interest. . . .

If there were birds about, so reasoned the dog, why wasn't he sent forward to find them? He was not going to " run in " and flush them before his master came up. Ranger was disgusted with the entire performance.

From the vantage afforded by the hillock a grass field could be seen with clumps of whins scattered over it, just the spot likely to be chosen by plover. Warren closely scanned the open spaces between the bushes, but no birds were to be seen. One large patch cut off a portion of the field from view. A lapwing, which rose from the bottom somewhere, was flying towards it. Warren crouched lower so as not to be seen by the arch alarmist, but when it came over the whins it uttered a wild cat-like call, wheeled round and flew off in the zigzag fashion that showed it had been surprised.

" It must have seen me," Warren thought. " Hang the bird, it will put the others to flight."

But the peewit had seen something else of which the sportsman was unaware. . . . Clear and quite close the golden plover call sounded. Warren started, it was so near.

Ranger heard it, raised his head, and sniffed the air. The wind was blowing from the spot. The dog sprang to his feet, and to his master's annoyance ran towards the furze.

" Here, Ranger, down, sir, down! " but the dog drew on the clump rapidly.

" Oh, you wretch! what abominable disobedience! "

Warren exclaimed, finding Ranger indifferent to the call. There was nothing for it but to follow, and, jumping to his feet, he stealthily ran after him. But just as he came in full view of the whins, every moment expecting to see the birds rise into the air—probably out of range through the dog's wildness—he heard a whining, yelping noise from the setter now half buried beneath the whin bushes, his tail wagging in evident excitement.

Warren hastened to the spot and pulled the dog aside. . . . "Why, Paudeen!" he exclaimed. . . . Then, realizing that he was the golden plover, the human will-o'-the-wisp, that with his clever call had allured him out of his way, a wave of anger followed on surprise.

"Come out, sir! ' Warren cried sternly.

Paudeen obeyed.

"How dare you trick me in this way? What—? " But a glance at the face before him, blanched and stained, checked Warren. The boy's eyes were bloodshot.

"What's the matter? " Warren asked in a more subdued voice. "You seem scared to death."

For answer, two large tears rolled down the frightened face; Ranger was affectionately licking the hand thrown over his neck.

"What's wrong, Paddy? "

"I wanted to stop ye goin' back by the short cut, sir. . . . I thought if I got ye this far ye'd go home by the road. I wouldn't have whistled again, but Ranger smelt me."

"What's the matter, my lad? "   ...en was now alive to the fact that there was meaning in the trick.

Paudeen hesitated, memories of the words, "The man that betrays me," was the explanation. Warren's appearance, his broad shoulders and tall figure—the gun across his arm—all impressed the boy and revived his courage. With such an ally he need not fear Gallagher. He told everything he heard in the shebeen.

" They were to use the plover call," he explained, " when ye got into the valley an' took the short course behind the rocks. So I hid at the entrance, an' when I saw ye I imitated the bird meself, an' so I kept bidin' and drawin' ye on."

" And so, my lad, you have done this to save me from a bullet. . . . Good God! " he suddenly exclaimed, " Shawn will go home that way; in this light they will mistake him for me. Run, Paddy, run," and Warren turned to the hill.

All Warren's concern for himself was now changed into anxiety for his gillie.

" This way, sir, it's quicker," and Paudeen set off towards the Black Valley. Warren followed, barely ble to keep up with the swift youth. The light was ll good enough to distinguish the gillie from the master, but Shawn's build and the new clothes might easily lead to mistaken identity.

Whilst the chances of danger and the hope of escape were turned over, a sharp shot rang in the distance.

Warren pulled up. " The devils! " he exclaimed. Paudeen heard it too, and quickened his pace. The report only too plainly indicated a rifle barrel. A terrible misgiving seized Warren. He tried to believe that it might be a stray shot at wildfowl and that the distance affected the detonation. Shawn himself might have fired it. Could he have got there within the time? Warren looked at his watch; it was nearly an hour since he had left the boat. Paudeen's ruse had taken about twenty minutes. . . . Ah, God! he would have time. . . . Had the bullet missed its mark? . . . Was he wounded? . . . dead? Oh, these terrible obsessions! how they crowded in, piercing the very quick of deepest sensitiveness, one giving place to another of blacker hue. He looked across the heath—what secret did it hold? What writhing, moaning body lay amongst its bloom? What ghastly patch stained the purple crimson? The sky beyond it so peaceful compared with the storm of apprehension that brooded within his breast. Did no eyes look down to mark the villain that levelled the deadly weapon? Would some herald from the blue proclaim: " The voice of thy brother's blood crieth to me from the ground "?

Paudeen led the way, the dog drawing the heath in front. The lad, fully alive to the situation, used his wits in the service.

" If we go this way, sir," he suggested, pointing, " Ranger will get a slant of the wind, an' he'd find him anywhere."

It was evident to Warren that the boy shared his own apprehensions as to Shawn's fate.

" All right, Paddy."

A whistle brought the dog to heel, and they took the direction suggested. It was a considerable detour, but the moment the dog began to work on the windward side, Paudeen, quite unconscious of the ominous nature of the words, cried, " Seek dead, Ranger."

The dog began to zigzag in obedience.

Warren winced, but the wisdom of using the setter's power of scent soon became apparent. The heather was so thick and there were so many pits and hollows that hours of searching might have proved fruitless. Night, too, was closing in, and would soon be upon them.

" If he finds nothing before we reach the head of the Black Valley, Shawn will be home, sir. The shot came from that spot," said Paudeen, pointing to the rocks on the hill overlooking the valley.

" Why, that's near the leprechaun's stone, isn't it? " Warren asked.

" It is, sir."

" Then the shot might have been fired by Shawn, who would pass that way? "

" Ah, no, sir."'

" Why not, Paddy? "

" He wouldn't fire a shot there, sir, on account of the leprechauns. . . . There's Ranger drawin' on somethin'; look at him now, he's off."

The dog's behaviour was very similar to his way of discovering Paudeen. He didn't stiffen his tail and point in the manner that the presence of game inspired. He simply ran on as if in response to a call from his master, raising his nose now and again to keep the scent. Warren and the boy started off in pursuit.

Ranger soon began to alter his course, stopped dead, wagged his tail, and went off again at a canter. A pang shot through Warren when he saw him going in the direction Shawn would undoubtedly have taken when coming from the boat. . . .

The dog passed into a hollow and was lost to sight.

Long before they reached the spot they heard a loud bark, and when they came up with Ranger he was sitting with his head erect, filling the air with plaintive baying. Close to him, lying on his side, was his master, one arm limp and extended, the other folded across his breast.

The heather had a crimson stain on it.

CHAPTER XXIII

" THERE is a chance of saving him, but to be frank, Mr Warren, it is one to a hundred."

Dr Mahan, the local practitioner, was the speaker. He had been called in when Shawn was carried to Molly MacDaire's house.

" He is still unconscious, you say? "

" I don't think much of that; it is from the loss of blood. I can't understand how it was he had not bled to death by the time you reached him. You say it was about a quarter of an hour after you heard the shot—the damned villains—you found him? How was he lying? "

" On his side, his hand across his breast."

" And unconscious? "

" Quite."

" That's the explanation. He dropped on his side in that position, the clothes pressed on the severed artery. Then of course the fainting lowered the heart's action and the flow of blood. But, Lord! what a good thing you came on the spot. Half an hour later ' all the King's horses and all the King's men '—that was a grand tourniquet you put on. If Shawn recovers, he'll be the proud man to know that the butt end of a cartridge saved him. He was a grand poacher; many a fine hare of his I've tasted. Well, we've done all we can for him, except get out the bullet—swipe it, that's the rub."

" Is it in a dangerous place? " Warren asked in a tone of deep anxiety.

" Difficult and dangerous. Its extraction would take the skill of the best surgeon in Dublin. We haven't the appliances down here for anything but minor operations."

" Who is the best man in Dublin? "

" Tim M'Linton and no other."

" Telegraph for him at once."

" What, for Tim? He'd charge a hundred guineas, the divil."

" I shall be responsible," Warren answered.

The doctor looked him up and down. . . . " That's damned noble, Mr Warren, but it's one chance in a hundred, mind ye."

" One in a thousand, we must take it."

" I'll examine him again before he comes round; just hold him for me in this position, Miss Molly. It's a bad case when the smile is out of your face "—looking at the white countenance of the girl, who had been devouring the doctor's remarks. He probed the wound.

" It's the off-chance, the running is strongly against Shawn;" then turning to Molly he said, " you hear what Mr Warren proposes? What do you say, Miss MacDaire? "

" I quite agree, Dr Mahan; we ought to have the surgeon."

" I suppose he was brought here because it was handy? " the doctor said. " It will be awkward to move him "—looking at her tentatively and seeing a fresh difficulty.

" Move him? He must not be moved. Besides," Molly added, " he'll want nursing. I'll do anything in that way under your instructions."

" Well, it's not often one finds two such bricks in a day's walk," the doctor commented. " Begad, we're getting back to the good old times when the streets were paved with twopenny loaves and the houses thatched with pancakes. Why, there isn't a better nurse in the Rotunda than yourself, Miss Molly. With someone to take a hand with the night work, and Tim M'Linton's skill, Shawn will have good backing, anyhow. I'll wire at once."

The doctor left, and an hour later the assistant nurse arrived. She took charge of the patient whilst Molly left the room. On the way downstairs she met the maid, who told her that her Cousin Philip was in the anteroom and wanted to see her. When she entered it she found him leaning on the table with his head buried in his hands. As he raised his face the ghastly look of terror startled her.

" What's the matter, Phil? " she asked apprehensively.

" Is he dead? " he blurted out, giving no heed to the question.

" He's unconscious still; Dr Mahan has little hope of his recovery."

" Any suspicion of who mur—shot him? "

" None of the man whose finger pulled the trigger, but it's known who put the rifle into his hand."

" Good God! Who? "

" Tim Gallagher was one. I have not heard the name of the other. They were overheard making their plans in Mary Hannagher's shebeen."

Her cousin sprang to his feet and staggered towards the door like a drunken man. The perspiration stood in large beads on his forehead.

" What's the meaning of this? Where are you going? " the girl asked.

" Gallagher will have to swing for it. I know something. I am going to lodge information," and like a madman Phil rushed from the room and escaped by the back door.

He took a short cut towards the town, crossing the fields in the direction of Poullamore. As he was skirting the pond a crouching figure sprang from the shelter of the old castle wall and faced him.

" What luck? . . . oh, curse you, it's you, is it? " Fitz Martin recognized Gallagher.

" Who were you expecting? " Phil asked, startled and thrown off his guard—" the murderer of Shawn O'Grady? Fine work that, but I wash my hands of it," and he attempted to push by Gallagher, who barred his path.

"Where are you going?" the other asked fiercely, suspicion of Fitz Martin's intentions flashing on his mind.

" That's my business; let me pass."

" You'd blab to save your own neck, would you? By God—" and Gallagher threw himself on his confederate fiercely, knitting his arms like steel bands round his body. Fitz Martin utterly taken by surprise, struggled to free himself. Once out of his clutches he could run and out-distance him, being the lighter and swifter man. But Gallagher had stooped in taking his grip and Phil found himself lifted off his feet. The next moment he was carried a step nearer to the pond, and an intuition of the intention of his assailant warned him. His arms were pinioned, and no defence was possible from his hands. Gallagher was now on the edge, determined to drop his victim in the pool. But Fitz Martin's legs were free if his hands were not, and swinging them behind, he brought them down in a rapid stroke. One of his heels caught the ligaments in the hollow of the thigh, and the limb, tense and fixed with the weight it held, suddenly relaxed and his assailant lost his balance; the natural result was to let the burden go. Fitz Martin jerked backwards, his freed hands clutched and gripped Gallagher's neck, precipitating his fall. Two screams rent the air, and with a loud plash, locked together, both combatants fell into the water. . . .

The curtains of Poullamore rolled aside in black crinkled folds, then maliciously closed, heaving and throbbing like a breast convulsed with fiendish laughter. A gurgling sound followed, then a succession of bubbles ascended from the depths and broke at intervals on the surface of the water.

 .   .   .   .

" Let me go, will ye, let me go. . . . I tell ye something has fallen into Poullamore . . . look how Poullabeg is disturbed . . . the merrows will be mad with me if I stay away."

" All right, Shawn, we'll send someone to see about it. You can go yourself in the morning; it's late now, you will disturb the house."

" Arrah, who would I be disturbin'? Sure, she's dead and gone and there's no one in the hut but meself. . . . Who are you? " and the eyes were turned on the watcher.

" I am Warren, Shawn. Don't you know me? "

A smile lit up the drawn face.

" To be sure I do, sir. Have I been dramin'? What's the matter with me? Oh, I've such a stitch in me left side."

" Don't stir, my poor boy; you've met with an accident."

This was Shawn's return to consciousness. Warren came back from the Lodge late that evening, and the nurse assisting Molly was in charge. He was just in time to use his persuasions with the patient, and calm him in the height of his delirium.

" Where am I, sir? " he asked, turning his head and looking round the room half affrighted.

" You are in Miss Molly's house."

" Miss Molly's? " he said in alarm. " Arrah, how did I get here, at all, at all? "

" Some of the boys and myself brought you, but you mustn't talk now. You are very weak. Here's Miss Molly; it was she told us to bring you."

" It's meself is sorry for intrudin', miss, in this way," Shawn managed to get out as Molly approached.

" Oh, Shawn, I'm so glad to see you have come round. Not a word, now, about intruding. You are heartily welcome; you know that. We are going to look after you and get you well."

" But how can I be stoppin' here? Sure, this is no fit place for me. Can't I go back to the hut? We could draw the side of Tubberscrag, sir, on our way there. I saw a pack of nine there last Tuesday," turning to Warren.

" Hush, Shawn, if you don't want to hurt my feelings; you are not well enough to be moved," Molly said. " You must stop a while in my care, so the quieter you are the sooner you will be able to leave me, if that's what you want."

The large, full eyes of the gillie turned on his benefactress and answered in mute affection.

" Ah, I thought you didn't want to leave me, Shawn. How often have you taken care of me when I was a child, carried me when I was tired and watched me when I slept in the heather and helped me to climb the eagle rock? There now, that will do; another word about intruding will hurt me."

20

" The hurt word will never be spoken to ye by me, me colleen," Shawn said in his pure, soft voice, tremulous from weakness and falling into the familiar way of early guardian days.

" I know that well, Shawn; now, here's your medicine. Dr Mahan will be blaming us if you're not better when he calls again."

She slipped her arm under the pillow, gently raised the large head as if it were that of a little child that had been coaxed into docility.

Shawn drank, his eyes looking with reverent wonder into the face of the queen girl that leant over him.

When Molly left the room she found Kitty, the maid, in a state of excitement.

" Oh, miss, Poullabeg is ragin' an' dashin' the wather all over the yard the way it did the night Mr Phil's mother died."

" Ah, now, Kitty, don't bother me with your pishrogues; I've enough to trouble me. Dr Mahan doesn't seem to think poor Shawn will recover. There's my cousin, too, gone off like a crazy madman." The thought of Phil and the disturbed pool made her pause and think.

" Perhaps there's a strong wind on Poullamore," she said, as if her mind were in quest of some explanation of the commotion.

" No, indeed, miss, there isn't a puff of wind to-night."

" Well, some of the cattle have fallen in, but we cannot do anything now. Dennis Fahy is sure to be up early in the morning. Ask him to go round and see what's wrong."

" Listen to it, miss," Kitty cried, throwing open the back door. The sound of surging water beating against the wooden cover of the well could be distinctly heard. It sounded like the valves of a great throbbing heart contracting and expanding and beating its life-blood against some barrier that choked its arteries and prevented them from carrying the flow on its destined course.

Molly shuddered as if a blast of cold air smote her, and left the kitchen without a word.

The patient spent a restless night, the fever at times reaching such a high degree that delirium followed and the nurse had difficulty in keeping Shawn in bed. The frequent repetition of sedatives told, and towards morning he slept. The doctor called early and informed them that the Dublin surgeon had accepted the engagement and would reach them that evening.

" All we can do now," he said, " is to get the patient as fit for the operation as we can—keep him quiet and maintain his strength."

Warren had a private interview with the local doctor. " I am very anxious to know," he said, " if you will be in a position after the operation to say what the chances of recovery are likely to be? "

The doctor was about to reply, but Warren interrupted him. " I know what is due to professional reticence. Perhaps I had better give my reasons for asking you to relax your usual rules. The fact is I have much more than an ordinary interest in this man. I want to say something to him of great importance, whether he lives or not. If you think he will recover, naturally I will postpone the communication lest it might excite him. But if we are going to lose him he must be told."

" Professional reticence, Mr Warren, is another name for professional ignorance. A doctor may be sure, but he can't be cocksure. M'Linton himself can't say offhand. He has a cubic inch too much of common-sense in his cerebrum for such an indiscretion. As I told you, the case is very critical."

" I understand that," Warren said. " The surgeon cannot answer then positively, one way or the other?"

" That is so, before the operation. If the bullet has reached a vital spot, a fatal prognosis is a matter of child's play."

" In that case, would it be too late to make the communication? " Warren asked.

" I do not think so. M'Linton may, of course, find it impossible to complete the operation. Then the way would be clear."

Warren bowed silently and the doc 't.

The day was a busy one at Th. . House. A stream of inquirers called to know the latest news. Shawn's popularity and the tragic nature of his illness deeply touched the whole community. Feelings of indignation ran high at the dastardly outrage, and were the perpetrator known, it would have gone hard with him. Warren had to make a statement, and the officers of the law were busy in search of Gallagher and " another." But no trace could be found of either.

That night the merits of the high priest of the fairy cult and the celebrated poacher were discussed in many a cottage and cabin, and the subject suffered nothing at the hands of generous-minded people.

Dr M'Linton brought all his skill to bear on the case, and in due course the bullet lay amongst a number of surgical instruments on the table. After a short interview with Warren the distinguished surgeon left for the Irish metropolis. All that remained to be done for the patient could be carried out by Dr Mahan and

the nurses. But the eyes of one nurse were red with
watching and tears. Shawn lay white and limp, far
removed from all sense of the interest and anxiety he
was creating.

Warren watched by the bedside, eagerly awaiting
the return of consciousness. When it came, a smile
lit up the pale face as the patient saw the eager brown
eyes of his master fixed upon him. A few moments
afterwards he was pressing the hand that held his.

" Leave it until later," the doctor replied to Warren's
questioning look. " He is too weak to understand
anything now. We must take our chance."

At night Molly relieved the nurse, and Warren and
she were in charge. There was a strange light in
Shawn's eyes. He looked from one to the other and
said:

" I've seen her; hush, don't speak loud or they'll
turn me out again."

" Who have you seen, Shawn? " Warren asked.

" Herself. She has a grand palace and all the
fairies dance attendance on her. She wants me to
come and help her, but I told her Miss Molly would be
angry if I left her without lave."

" Do you mean your mother, Shawn? "

" Hush, now, they'll hear ye an' get frightened.
What she wouldn't tell me in the hut, she'll tell me in
the palace, she says. I must go soon, if Miss Molly
will let me. She said how grand I was dressed, an'
I was more than ever like him now, but she wouldn't
tell me who she was spakin' about."

" She meant me, Shawn. I'm your brother. Don't
leave me now that I have found you. I—"

" Hush, too loud . . . . Bads grant to ye, Dinnis
Fahy, for rousin' the whole palace with yer knockin."

Molly raised his head and he sipped a stimulant.

" Do you know me now, Shawn? " Warren asked eagerly, noticing a calmer look in his eyes.

" Of course I do; ye're Misther Warren, me master."

" I'm your brother, Shawn."

" Ah, whisht now; I have no brother—never had one.   Who would be ownin' me for a brother—Scalloped Shawn, the poacher!   Cracked Shawn O'Grady! "

" But would you not like to have a brother, Shawn? "

" A brother!   Sure, I'd have known him if I had. He'd have come to me long ago.   I never had a new suit until Mr Warren gave me this one," and Shawn stroked the bedclothes and there was a proud look in the lank, pale face.

" Well, your brother has come to you now, Shawn, and you will never want for anything."

" Come! where is he?   I don't want for anything now; Mr Warren has provided me new clothes, a gun, shootin' an' fishin' galore.   Why didn't me brother come when I had to poach the mountain an' the river to keep the hunger from her, when she was left broken-hearted? . . ."

" Well, I have come to you now, Shawn.   I am your brother," and Warren placed his hand in the sick man's. Shawn's closed on it.

" Ah, no! no! you're Misther Warren, me master; ye did what my brother never did for me.   Tell him it's too late to come now.   She's beckonin' me; I must go. . . .   Comin', mother.   Keep the gate open for me. . . .   The dazzlin' brightness is blindin' me eyes. . . .   Oh, there they are, the beautiful cratures, with wings like mayflies flashin' in the sunbeams. . . . Who is that in the middle of them . . . herself?   She used to look old with the grief lines in her face. Now she is young and fair like one of themselves grown up, and wid shinin' garments. . . . It is herself; she's beckonin' me; sure, I know her hand. Let me go, Miss Molly. . . . Comin', comin' . . . it's me brother is keepin' me . . . call him too . . ."

A shudder shook the lank frame, the fingers on his master's hand relaxed and Shawn O'Grady came into his estate.

CHAPTER XXIV

IT was a lovely day in the young year. The mild winter had come and gone and the footsteps of spring could be traced in unfolding bud and early blossom. A light emerald tint dominated the variegated carpet of grass spread within the confines of rough stone walls. The whins were already growing golden, and light breezes stole rich perfume from the close-set bloom and wafted it down the hillside. The cotton grass proudly waved its white plumes on the margin of the bog, and milky blossoms were sprinkled amongst the branches of the blackthorn.

The throb of young life was in the air, the hum of bees and the ardent call of wild-fowl amongst the islets. On one of these the throb was felt in two human hearts and marked time to deep, passionate feeling.

" I have not been here since the eve of my departure for London; how fresh everything looks! "

" The springtime is beautiful," Molly answered shyly, as if she half distrusted herself.

" Shall we climb to the old spot? " he suggested.

Molly accepted the proffered hand.

Scarcely a word was spoken during the scramble, outside the perfunctory directions of a self-constituted mountain-guide, whose instructions, generally speaking, made for sudden death and destruction. These were prudently ignored by the really skilled climber. What a merciful provision that the wave of deep passion is not permitted to invade the strip of common-sense territory on which life's practicalities depend.

But feeling had its way all the same, and the two clasped hands became a medium through which love impetuous, unbalanced, tyrannical in its ardour, swept and met an answering wave that wrapt in a blinding mist the souls that felt the tumult.

They reached the highest ledge and sat side by side on the velvety grass carpet. " It was here," he said, " that you gave me a message for Lord Ballyshameon. Do you remember what it was? "

" Perfectly."

" I gave it, and I have brought his answer."

She looked into the face that bent over her. Was this more acting? she wondered. The answering look said " No." " It would not be difficult to guess it," she said—" that I was very rude, of course, in saying that I hated the name. '

" No, but that you could not hate it more than he did."

There was silence, whilst Molly put her thoughts into a question.

" Is that why he dropped it and came here under an assumed one? "

" Not exactly."

Again his face was searched. Ardent passion was in every line of it. Something in the girl's breast fluttered back in response. Oh, why had not the conquest been won openly, fairly? Her heart capitulated. Call himself by what name he would, and act what part, those strong arms had only to open and she would have responded to them.

But Molly's head was still bent on battle, though her heart had gone over to the enemy. His next words gave it its chance.

"Lord Ballyshameon sends you a message in return."

" Indeed? " Molly interrogated.

" He asks if you will help him to redeem the name? "

" I do not think he has established the right to make such a request. I have not the honour of Lord Ballyshameon's acquaintance."

" I deserve that," came the answer of the other, now throwing off the mask. " I know; I seem to have been acting a part. Let love claim the privilege to which Ballyshameon is not entitled, and confess and plead at the same time."

A little catch in the girl's breath betrayed her emotion.

" Some years ago I had a difference with my father in regard to the management of his estate. I had studied the Irish question for the purpose of a debate in which I was taking part at Cambridge. *Leckie's History* was the text-book. It seemed to me that if Leckie was right, my father was wrong. He was annoyed at the speech I made, and said that such views were unworkable, and as I was to succeed him, the sooner I abandoned them the better. He was suffering from angina pectoris at the time, and I refrained from argument.

" It seemed expedient to me that I should visit Ireland and study the question on the spot. His answer to the proposal was that they would either shoot me or flatter me, and that neither method was likely to prove enlightening.

" The upshot of it was that I undertook to come here and hide my identity under an assumed name for eighteen months, engaging to return to England and think out my plans before proposing any alterations. I gave my father my word of honour on that point, and we agreed that if I could not carry out the duties of my inheritance to my own satisfaction I would abandon all claim to the estate. Meanwhile I purchased a commission in the Guards and was called away to active service.

"That is why my lips were sealed when we sat together in this spot on the eve of my departure. Oh, how I yearned to gather to my heart my beautiful one, the fairy that had brushed my eyes with her gossamer wings and cleared them to see things in right proportion."

He folded her hand between both his, and felt it flutter, then nestle like a tired bird after a long flight.

"During my first visit here I suspected that Shawn was related to me. It was due partly to instinct, partly to a family likeness, but particularly to idiosyncrasies which I had noted that reminded me of my father. On returning to London the old family solicitor informed me of the truth of the surmise. I could not make immediate reparation without breaking my promise. By a strange fatality, when I was free to tell Shawn, he had fallen by that fatal bullet which was intended for me."

The deep blue waves broke below them, the expanse of sea stretched to the distant horizon. One long, long look, in which both souls read and understood each other, and his strong arms gathered her to his heart. The golden hair glistened on his shoulders, the eyes with the sea-depth in them looked into his.

"My darling," came in broken speech.

Molly's lips answered for her. All the virgin wealth of that sweet mouth yielded itself in an impassioned kiss.

CHAPTER XXV

IT was summer redundant, and the sun was sinking in the deep blue sea. Its trailing garments, rich in crimson and saffron, scintillated on the waves that a brisk breeze gathered into folds.

From the number of people already on the quay it was evident that something of unusual interest had stirred the calm of Ballinbeg. The peasantry were dressed in their best, and jests followed by merry peals of laughter indicated that the event was not of the depressing nature that too often occasioned the massing of the people.

" Here comes *Inishfesh*," exclaimed a bystander, pointing towards a four-oared boat in the distance, " and *Loon Island* is not going to be behind in its honours. The women are more than the men, too, judged by the number of head shawls on the hooker."

" That's right," exclaimed a third; " if you want a thing done well, the women are the men to do it."

" They will have a grand breeze anyhow, and with a spring tide they ought to make the harbour by dusk."

" Indeed, then, we don't mind if it is dark, for it won't be the sunlight they'll be dependin' on for the brightness of the welcome."

" That's true; sure, Dr Mahan, the chairman of committee, has collected every tar barrel in the county, and as for turf and bogdale, they've stripped Longford parish."

" The divil a penny that will cost, either; sure, they had to stop the people from bringin' it, and there were so many ass loads even then that they had to draw lots to see which was to be kept, and indeed Michael Molloy was the disappointed man when the lot went against him. I met him meself outside the town where he was emptying the creels on the roadside. ' Why are ye doin' that? ' I asked. ' Arrah, because,' says he, ' it's ashamed I'd be to be seen takin' it home agen. Didn't himself come into the cabin the very first day he was here and talked to me and Sally as if we were his equals, an' didn't I crack jokes with him, not knowin' who it was, at all, at all. Sure, when I found out that it was himself, I was quakin' in me shoes an' dreaded a notice of eviction. Instead of that, isn't it the fine farm he gave me and the new house. It's a hard case indeed that I cannot give a few sods of turf for the bonfire.' "

" But how are they to know the time to light the bonfires? " came the question from another part of the crowd.

" Oh, that's aisy enough; Mr Martin Doonas is to let off a rocket before the yacht comes round the headland. By the time she's at the quay they'll all be in full blast. Sure, every house is to be illuminated too. As I was comin' down they were fightin' outside Mary Hannagher's for candles. The divil a one can be had now for love or money and they're offering Mary twopence apiece for dips three a penny."

" There's Jimmy Sweeny an' Bridget an' the child Miss Molly swam into the river after and rescued from drownin'. Throth, it's fat an' well Jimmy looks compared with the lantern-jaw he had when he was evicted. Wasn't it himself was payin' the rint for him all the time and Gallagher sayin' he was a middleman and a rack-renter? "

" What became of Gallagher? " was the question that followed.

" No one knows rightly, arrah; he was a bad feller, but he knew more about the man that shot at Mr Pinkerton than he let on. Sure, someone saw him one night carrying Mr Philip Fitz Martin in his arms an' taking him off in a boat to America, but the boat san. an' no wonder, with a murderer on board. They say Gallagher's body was never found, but Mr Phil's was, forty miles down the coast, and Miss Molly buried him at her own expense, although when he was alive he didn't deserve it."

" There's Biddy Maloney," interrupted this spinner of fiction founded on fact. " She's housekeeper now that the old house is turned into a new castle, and it is the proud woman she is. Sure, she was housekeeper for his lordship at the Lodge before anyone knew who he was, and isn't he sendin' Paudeen to the best school in Dublin? He took a great fancy to him and he's on the yacht now with an elegant suit of new clothes. There's the boys he is the ringlader of; look at them, with the bogdale torches in their hands. They're innocent enough when they are not up to mischief. I hear they were greatly disappointed yesterday. Ye see, they think a great deal of Paudeen now that he's goin' to Dublin, and they planned a little surprise for him on their own account. Paudeen is great at bird-calls, an' didn't he teach them all how to whistle them. Well, they wanted to go along the cliff, and just as the yacht came in sight light their torches an' set up the golden plover call. They had rehearsed it when Dr Mahan heard of it and stopped it. He told them that his lordship was once very fond of shootin' golden plover, an' one day he heard the call, an' lookin' up saw a flock flyin' over his head.   He raised his arm to fire, but stumbled, an' the gun kicked him in the chest an' gave him a pain in his heart that he wouldn't get over for many a long day.   Paudeen was with him at the time an' his lordship had to lean on him or he'd never have got home alone, and from that day to this his lordship couldn't bear the call of golden plover. . . . So the doctor told them to bring their torches an' join the procession instead, and he'd get Paudeen to head it himself and—there's the rocket! "

With that a loud shot rang out from the hillside. " That's Jack Bolan's old anvil; he loaded it with blasting powder.   Oh, do ye hear the echo in the hills? "

A few minutes afterwards the blue smoke of the bonfires began to show itself at several points along the coast and lights twinkled in every cottage window. Soon the smoke was streaked with red tongues of flame, and when the yacht reached the quay a score of glowing beacons flashed their welcome across the water.   The landing-place was thronged with eager, human faces smiling in the ruddy light, and as the young lord and his Irish bride stepped into the carriage that awaited them the horses were unyoked and the vehicle drawn by willing hands to the loud cry of " cead mile failte! " " cead mile failte! " until voices grew silent with exhaustion.

Dennis Fahy, who had been left in charge of the yacht and joined in the vociferous cheers, had no breath left for speaking, but he had time for reflection to the effect that the new lord, who was also the new magistrate, would have a great many cases in court next week, for which in a way he would be personally responsible.

Meanwhile the carriage was drawn along the road,

lit at every turning with some new symbol of ardent Irish affection. Fresh relays of hands gripped the carriage shafts at each stoppage, and when a stretch of steep hill had to be climbed, stalwart fellows vied with each other in drafting the heavier load. They tried to march in time, but found it impossible. Then they broke into snatches of song, " Come back to Erin, Mavourneen," " The Minstrel Boy," and " There came to the Beach a poor Exile of Erin," with delightful obliquity to relevance and absolute indifference to incongruity. Feeling was let loose like a flood, and refusing to run between defined banks overflowed where it would and as it listed.

At length the enlarged building came into sight. The fresh masonry could be picked out in the light of an enormous bonfire in the grounds. They dipped again into the valley and a sobering effect fell on the people as they passed a little cemetery on the roadside. A white marble cross reared itself clear above the low holly hedge. It gleamed in the light of the boys' torches and the inscription to Shawn's memory could be seen.

The new heir took off his hat, and in a moment every head was bared. Thus in the glad home-coming and the new order of things the man who could take no part in the rejoicings was reverently called to mind; and if for a moment the young lord's brow was clouded, and tears stood in Molly's eyes, these feelings did them honour and proved anew their fitness for the great trust they were elected to fulfil.

COLSTONS LIMITED, PRINTERS, EDINBURGH

Lightning Source UK Ltd.
Milton Keynes UK
UKHW021631021218
333216UK00011B/1245/P